# The Coming of Schades
## Heroes of the Line: Nick of Time

By: J. A. Carlton

The end of the line... the first time.

Sedona Arizona, Boynton Canyon.

"I'm beggin' ya man, whatever you're plannin' don't do it! The world needs what you can do!" Harry Armstrong; Nick and up until recently Frankie's best friend pleaded as he looked the young man up and down with a deepening frown. "What the fuck happened t'you man, you look like month old shit."

The corner of Nick's lip flicked upward, he was gonna miss Harry. "It's been a little rougher than I thought."

"Dude, you been here 3 days, what the hell kinda shit did you manage to get yourself in while you were waitin' for me?" Harry shook his head and pulled a flask from his back pocket, handing it to his best friend before nipping from it himself. "tell me you didn't pick up some road truck tacos or something on the way in...," he muttered trying to remember if Nick had been wearing the same clothes when he left. It smelled like he was. "Speaking of which, when's the last time you got some sleep? Or food? Or a shower?"

A strange kind of chuckle huffed out of Nick, "It's been a while."

For eighteen years they'd been through thick and thin, fighting to keep their little corner of the world safe from impossible beings that didn't belong here and left nothing but destruction in their wake.

They met as teenagers, Harry'd been seventeen, Nick either fifteen or sixteen, Frankie, nine or ten. He was already used up by the same sick son of a bitch that used Nick as his own plaything, until he got too old that is, that's when he went after the little guy.

Harry asked him once why he didn't just take Frank and run but all he said was, "I didn't know I could."

But last week everything changed.

Harry didn't know how Nick could do what he could, it was the coolest damned thing he ever saw, but it didn't last long and Nick never said much about it. Sometimes Harry just couldn't figure him out, unless it had something to do with Frankie. Other than that, when it came to talking about his power, there was almost nothing he could or would say. He didn't know where it came from, didn't know why it was him, didn't have a clue even how long he could get to.

Still, a lot of shit could be done in 3 minutes, and 3 minutes head start running from a child molesting scumbag could've got them both free a lot sooner.

Harry's finger caressed the long, wide, strip of scar tissue down his breastbone and he nodded. After all, everyone has their own baggage and it wasn't his business to question how anyone handled what they were dealt.

Nick finished tracing a circle in the canyon floor and wiped his hands on his jeans, "get my bag willya?" he motioned to a dusty, beat up backpack leaning up against a boulder, it was so dirty it was hard to make out the silly grinning face of Frank's favorite cartoon Great Dane. It really didn't surprise Harry that Nick would bring Scooby with, but somehow it really did.

"Jesus what the hell's in here?" he asked watching Nick break out his lock back knife and drag it across his palm. Even after so many years he still hated seeing that.

"Really oughtta just put some in a jar man... or one of those plastic bags from the blood drive truck."

Harry opened the backpack and frowned at the half dozen, five subject notebooks in there, "what's all this?" he asked as Nick finished the spell and joined him on the boulder.

"Notes," Nick sighed, his face looking even more gaunt and haggard than he had just moments ago. His eyes were deeply bloodshot with cavernous half circles under them.

"What spells 'n shit?" Harry asked then shook his head and thrust the bag at the younger man, "you know I'm no good at that stuff... whatever it takes to make magic happen Nicky, you know I ain't got it."

"You will." Nick looked into the distance, the sun just about to set behind the canyon ridge. Once it was gone this little area was going to become a very dangerous place, but he knew Harry could handle himself if any of *them* got through the wards he'd set up earlier.

Harry shook his head, his belly quivering like loose gelatin. He was starting to sweat as the breeze seemed to stop everywhere around them except inside the ring where sand was starting to blow just a bit.

"Whatever this is man, I don't like it, whatever you got up your sleeve, you need to put a stop to it right now," he demanded with half a heart. He knew that when the eldest Emerson set his mind to something, the only person who could steer him onto a different path was dead.

"You asked if there was something you could do to help."

Harry swallowed hard, "Yeah."

Nick reached under the neck of his shirt, lifting a gold chain with a nickel sized bauble at the end of it, over his head.

"I told you this was my dads, it's the only thing of his I got besides his name."

Harry nodded, "right."

Nick nodded back, somehow not even seeming halfway in the present, "all the important stuff is in those notebooks... well, all of it that I could find out...or remember."

"Find out about what?"

"It's the one thing that can't be changed... his murder, I always wondered if there was some way to fix things before they went so bad," he slugged back on the flask again.

Harry could feel his heart thundering in his chest, "What'dyou mean *before* things went so bad? Look, I know you can do some funky-ass shit, but do NOT tell me you suddenly learned how to time travel."

Nick winced and gave a minor shake to his head, "no, not travel," but he chuckled, something unsettling in the sound as he mused more to himself than Harry, "course it's not like we all can't, or don't time travel every second of every day," he returned to the moment, "but no. I'm talking about resetting it. Resetting time."

Fighting a suddenly rolling bubbling in his tummy Harry couldn't stop his mouth, "Resetting? How is that NOT going backward in time?" He demanded after sputtering out a slug of the whiskey.

Pressing a small latch on the side of the pendant Nick motioned Harry closer and held the bauble up to the moonlight, flipping one tiny page after another, four in total before going back to one that had 13 pin sized marbles tracing lines out toward the edges of both parts of the page.

"You see this one?" Nick said pointing to one of two tiny spheres on the far left that were nearly touching.

"Yeah," Harry swallowed.

"This is us, it's Earth."

"Earth? What is this some kind space map or something?"

Nick next put the tip of his blade to a tiny nic just to the left of the bead that he said represented this world. "Don't move it any further back than this point... no matter how far forward you go, you can't go back further than this point."

"ME!? Why ME?!" Harry barked, "I'm not fuckin' with the goddamn time line of the whole fucking planet Nick!"

Nick's gaze flicked to the rising whirlwind inside the circle, "and you say I got a potty mouth," he huffed then looked back to Harry, "Listen there's still more you have to hear..."

"NO! GODAMNIT! NO!" Harry stormed as Nick took a deep breath and closed the pages.

"Look at me!" he ordered flipping open the top knob, revealing a chamber into which he squeezed several drops of the blood from the cut on his hand. When it was full, he closed that too then held it up before Harry.

"It only holds about 3 drops. All you have to do is lock the knob, righty tighty lefty loosey. Lock it then push it down. If you're not ready to rewind or haven't moved the world nothing will happen. The chamber has to be full, it has to be MY blood, no one else's will do."

"Nick no!" Harry whispered, the color drained from his face, his eyes saucer wide with disbelief.

"The notebooks... little details... all the things I could think of that could make a difference... thumb drives get erased... electromagnetic field I guess."

Somehow they'd wound up on their feet facing each other, Harry trying to back away, Nick's grip vice-like on his upper arm while the winds swirled even harder, throwing stones against the barrier the ring created, any of which could easily knock either of them out cold or maybe even crack their skulls.

"Don't do this Nick... you think Frankie'd want you to do this?" Harry whispered, unable to look the broken young man in the eyes, "You think he wouldn't want you t'keep livin? Let you just give up? Just chuck it all away 'stead'o fightin' the good fight?"

Nick flicked his gaze to the ring, everything inside suddenly holding, suspended in air, awaiting his permission to move forward in time again. His ability to hold the spell slipping away faster than he'd anticipated, he gulped, needing just a few more minutes. He just had to hold on a little longer, make Harry understand, then he could let it all go and return home.

"I can't..." he choked out, his lips quivering beneath a surprisingly gray layer of thick whiskers that kept the secret of his nearly skeletal face. His pale blue eyes pleaded with Harry's gentle browns, in fact Harry was certain Nick's eyes were so pale he almost couldn't tell they were blue anymore.

"I lost him Harry. I swore I'd protect him and I fucked it up, over and over again, I blew it. I froze over and over again, and then that pasty faced fucker shows up and..."

The older man nodded, his mouth suddenly desert dry, "I know man, did him just like he did your daddy, it's not like you could've..."

"Don't you get it!? I TRIED and TRIED to stop him! To stop him," he gulped, "and I couldn't! It didn't work and that same son of a bitch turned him inside fucking OUT! Just like it did our dad and nothing I did could stop it, nothing I tried! I can't live this anymore man," he sniffed and shuddered a heavy breath, "I tried but I couldn't, I can't. And I can't live with this... it's like my soul's been ripped out of me... please say you understand? Please..." He shook his head and wiped his running nose on his sleeve, "could be you'd be next, or Mickey, Charles, Ernesto, or any of us... anyone I care about's at risk, especially if I can't change what that fucker does! I gotta...well *you* gotta, the only way to get in front of this fucker is to stop it before it starts... and it's gotta be you... please!" he begged folding the pendant into Harry's hand.

Shaking the tears out of his eyes and stuffing the pendant into his jeans pocket, he asked, "Why me?"

Nick's weight dragged down on his arms as he leaned harder, his strength waning. "Because you're the only person I trust, and more important, you're not me."

He shook his head, "Nick... shit like this just isn't possible! If we could time travel..."

"It's not *traveling!*" Nick whimpered as he explained it yet again. His eyes closed as he rolled his head back and forth on Harry's chest before meeting his eyes again, "it's cutting open a closed loop. *I am* the loop. S'why I can't change it, it's MY history, to me it's immutable. You go back to the beginning, you set the orbit on the page back to where I showed you then push the stem just like setting a watch."

Holding the younger man away from himself Harry couldn't help it, he stood there, on the brink of the moment of truth, wondering if Nick had finally gone 'round the bend, if he'd always been crazy, or if he'd dragged Harry into his own craziness. "I don't know Nick... everything says you don't fuck with time!"

Lurching forward and breathing harder, the storm inside the ring returned to its previous and growing ferocity, Nick panted, "You are the only person on this planet that will ever know."

Harry felt his jaw drop, "the whole fucking planet?"

Nick nodded, "yeah."

"What if I fuck it up? What if I go back too far? What if I wind up back in the fucking dark ages or something?"

Nick smiled, a faint, tired, desperate smile that could still charm almost anyone into doing anything he wanted them to. "Just don't go past the mark."

"How much blood is it going to burn up doing this?" Harry asked then smirked and shook his head when Nick placed a small vacuum sealed jar into his shirt pocket.

"You need more than that, we're fucked anyway... you get to the last of it... whatever happens you'll have to let it run its course after all. But if you can find a good line... burn whatever's left," he ordered.

The swirling winds of the vortex continued to grow stronger, their howling making it almost impossible to hear when Harry asked his last question.

"How'd you figure this out Nicky?"

"What do you think I've been doing for the last six months," he choked, his face shining with sweat and tears that couldn't be stopped as he grasped Harry in a tight embrace.

"Six months?" Harry gasped.

Nick swallowed hard and nodded, "and I'm the only person who knew."

"That's why you look..." Harry mused as Nick nodded trying to ease himself from the older man's embrace.

Harry didn't want to let him go. He'd learned more about spells and magic and physics than he'd ever wanted to since he met Nick and Frank, but as much as he hated to admit it, his best friend's plan made sense.

"You can do this... you're the *only* one who can..." Nick whispered, finally managing to pull away. The last of his energy being drawn out of him and into the vortex, he managed to hold Harry still on the timescape while doing what he had to. He couldn't bring himself to look back as he walked into the swirling winds; sand and stones ripping the flesh from him as whatever fundamental part of him remained, managed to get through, making its way into a small center point of light before it finally disappeared.

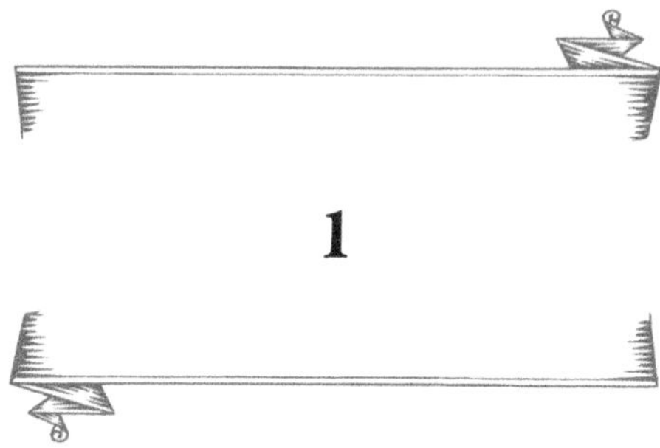

# 1

The bullies coarse, cruel laughter faded under a breathless 'whump' and a heavy steel clang. A plastic bag sharted detritus and the scent of rot into the dark.

"Eeew gross!" was followed by struggled rustling just before a thin bereft sigh escaped his lips. Tiny grunts helped him push, squeezing his slim fingers between the lid and the body of the dumpster, welcoming a blinding sliver of sunlight into the darkness.

Frank Emerson could've sworn he felt something brush past his shoulder, he looked around, *nothing's up that high.* He gulped as a shiver ran down his spine in spite of the heat and his belly started to bubble. In a whisper as tiny as he feels, and just in case the bullies were listening, he couldn't help but plead, "Please hurry Nicky, I think there's something b'sides me in here today."

As if in answer to his secret prayer a burst of heavenly golden light exploded into the void and a comparatively large, weathered, brown hand reached down. Frank's dark blue eyes locked onto the now weathered fifty-three-year-old face of the school janitor, Harry Armstrong. Behind the five year old, a ghoulish pale face disappears into a deep shadow inches away. Harry's expression hardened as he sighed a resigned mutter, "How that boy can be late every damn day?"

Frank Emerson didn't want to cry, he didn't like to cry; and even if Nick said it was okay sometimes, *he* never cried without good reason, and there was nothing more that Frankie wanted than to be like his big brother. But Nick never got thrown into a smelly, old dumpster either.

He pushed his tears down and smiled his gratitude up at Harry, taking his hand just as Nick's footfalls could be heard running across the asphalt.

"Thank you Harry!, Thank you, I think there was somethin' in there with me today!" he gushed, gasping a lung full of untainted air while Harry braced him enough to let him get a leg over the rim of the container.

"Big ass rat," he snarled, then shook it off and smiled at the boy who surrendered himself into his big brother's reaching hands.

"Nice o'ya t'join us Nicky, what was it t'day? Grades, a fight…"

"Someone said they saw me smoking in the john," he shook his head, "I mean who even does that anymore?" He guided Frank down to the ground and took a sniff then winced, "gross!"

"That's what I said," Frank nodded helping brush food goo off his clothes. Seconds later, he snared his big brother with a grip so tight Nick wasn't sure he'd be able to breathe any time soon, which was just as well considering the stink clinging to the little guy's clothes.

"What happened?" Nick asked, stroking the cheese encrusted silky brown waves pressed against his belly. His ice blue eyes looked questioningly into the janitor's warm comfortable browns, but the older man just shook his head with a hint of sadness.

"I'm sorry, Nick, I tried to hide." Frank rubbed away any evidence of tears into the belly of his big brother's shirt. "I knew you were gonna be late, you're always late," he explained without a hint of blame, "and they dragged me out of the bathroom, it was stinky, and they," his breath hitched. "I'm sorry. I tried, but I couldn't, Nick. I couldn't, and they just…" he sighed flicking his head toward the dumpster. "Well, you know."

And indeed the elder Emerson did know. No matter what he tried, no matter how thoroughly he planned, Nick never seemed to be able to get anywhere on time. He always managed to get Frankie wherever *he* needed to be, but when it came to getting somewhere for himself, something always seemed to stand in the way.

What made matters worse was that for the last two years, ever since *That Night*, Nick couldn't seem to shake the feeling that something, *something*, always seemed to be working against them.

From boys that thought they could bully him, to the ones who *did* bully his beautiful, timid and almost scarily smart Frankie, it was as if they were magnets for trouble when all they wanted was to be left alone.

He'd heard a phrase once, 'Born under a bad sign,' and he'd recently begun to wonder if there might be something like that at work in their lives, and if there was, was there anything he could do about it?

*Do what you want t'me, but so help me…NEVER touch my brother!* Nick cursed at the universe. Francis Michael Emerson was all that was left of what he'd once called 'normal' before their dad was murdered, and part of their mother seemed to have been too.

"S'okay, Frankie, I gotcha," he wrapped his arm around his little man and, not for the first time, was almost afraid to let go. Seemed like every time he was forced to, someone or something was trying to hurt the one person he'd come to think of as *his*.

He looked up into their friend's sympathetic brown eyes, one arm protectively draped over Frankie's shoulders as he offered his free right hand to the careworn older man. "Thanks, Harry," was all he could get out before his chin threatened to wobble and his eyes to tear.

Wordlessly and with that familiar, faintly sad smile, the custodian ran a gentle hand over both of their heads before wiping at his eyes and heading back inside the school.

"I'm sorry, Nicky," Frank apologized softly but couldn't bring his arms to unclamp from his big brother's waist. "I don't wanna be a baby, I'm sorry. I don't wanna make you 'shamed of me," he sniffed, the sound of snot bubbling back into his throat before he swallowed. "I wish I could be like you. I'm sorry," he said again.

Nick wrapped his arms around his little brother. *I'm the one that's sorry, Frank. I let you down again.*

"Hey, listen up, pizza for brains," he grasped his little brother's tear-streaked face in his hands, "first, you could never make me ashamed of you, got it?" He smirked when Frank sniffed and nodded. "Second, it takes a long time to get to be this kind of 'cool', you dig? And…" he looked around conspiratorially, then leaned in close, "as easy as I make it look," he looked around again, "it takes work, man." "Wha…" Frank questioned, taking a quick glance around. "Work?" he asked, clearly amazed by the confession.

"Who said you were smoking?" Frank asked as they walked under a fluttering green-gold birch leaf canopy.

What they currently called home was a run-down apartment their mom was subletting from her creepy boss. He ran the diner she worked in, and had insinuated himself into their lives just over six months ago, for two young reasons.

"Dunno, wouldn't surprise me if it was Tommy or Bruce tryn'a get me out of the way though, so they could get their mitts on you. What'd you do this time anyway? Get another gold star?" he grinned, pushing his little man across the puked-up-s'more-colored carpeting directly into the bathroom.

Nick knelt at the tub trying not to breathe the dumpster stink too deeply while he started the water running and frowned a curious half smile at his little brother.

Frankie shook his head, his sapphire blue eyes bright while little teeth chewed his full rosebud lips. He watched the hot water run until all the brown was gone, then grinned when Nick stopped up the tub and squirted a glut of shampoo into it making mountains of soft bubbles.

The older boy turned his attention back to his little brother, "No?" he asked, incredulous. "You didn't get a gold star?"

He slid his hands up the sides of the shirt, holding it open so Frankie could pull his arms out of the holes. After that, he simply opened the neck hole a little wider and pulled the filthy thing off.

The younger boy knew not to make a move without Nick's say so, especially after a dumpster dunking.

Once the slimy t-shirt was in a ball on the counter, Frank shook his head and stepped out of his shoes. With his big toe poking out through a hole in his sock, he slid them off while Nick undid his jeans.

"A silver one then?" the older boy asked, pushing down the filth covered denim. *I wonder if he's big enough yet for a couple of my older pairs of underwear,* he thought when his eyes fell to the holes in the little one's hand me down tightie whities. Again, Frank shook his head.

"What?" he frowned. "I can't believe it, we worked really hard on that diorama," he reminded his little brother then gave a swish to the water around in the tub, testing its temperature and stirring up bubbles just the way Frankie liked it.

Content that everything was okay, he motioned to the tub. "Okay, tiger, hop in," he grinned.

Grinning back, Frankie hurdled the rim, landing on his feet with Nicky's help, then slid under the bubbles until he couldn't hold his breath anymore. He lurched up, spraying them both with clean smelling foam.

A shift and a shimmy brought the raggedy pair of underwear out of the tub where a perfect pitch flung them with a slosh into the basin.

"Good shot," Nick nodded, impressed. "Alright, shrimp, so what happened?" he asked, rubbing shampoo into Frankie's mop while working the cheese out of it.

Frank held up two fingers. "I got TWO gold stars! And Tommy said he coulda done even better if he had a big brother to do all the work for him. But I said you didn't, that you just helped with the cutting out 'cause all we have is the big scissors, but I did everything else," he rattled as Nick stuck a finger full of bubbles onto his nose. "And, except for that, you just helped me hold things until they stuck." He squeezed his eyes shut, "I'm gonna sneeze..."

"Nope, not yet, shrimp, I ain't got b'hind yer ears," the elder brother smiled, adding another tiny ball of suds to the mound before sliding his fingers first behind the boy's ears, then into them, making him squirm, laugh and squirm some more as the tiny bubble-man rolled from his nose to his chest.

Smiling brightly, Frankie blew a palm full of suds into the air, at the same time tossing a handful of water into his big brother's face, then scooping up another handful to pile on Nick's head.

"Eeeew, shrimp, c'mon...cheese-water, gross," Nick protested half-heartedly but couldn't hide his enjoyment of their little ritual. A moment later, with the last of the cheddar-like goo finally gone, he nodded, "Alright, dunk."

Frankie took a dramatically noisy deep breath before sinking beneath the water again so Nick could work out the last of the soap before he came back up panting and sputtering with a smile.

FRANKIE LOVED HIS MOMMA, but sometimes when she was sad, he hurt inside because he couldn't change it, but sometimes Nicky could, just like sometimes he could make Frank smile even when he didn't want to. That was just one of the things that made the older boy shine like gold in his eyes.

Even when he got thrown in the dumpster, Nick managed to fix everything up just right in no time. As a consequence of two years worth of moving around with their mom chasing dead end jobs that barely kept bread in the fridge, and his big brother's seemingly effortless handling of the day to day needs, Frankie often felt that life was supposed to be just the two of them. Sometimes he forgot that there'd been a time when he and mom stayed home and spent their days together waiting for Dad and Nicky to come back and join them. But sometimes, at night, part of him remembered things the daytime tried to let him forget.

Frank knew this dream, he'd had it every night for a little while, but now it was only a couple times a week. He was being carried in Nick's arms, he's facing backward, looking into a long hallway lit in red with Daddy standing at the end of the hall, his hair was the same color as Nick's, and they had the same eyes too. His hand is raised, his mouth open, saying something but Frank can't make it out. From behind him a long, spooky Halloween kind of person rises up and turns him. It slashes his throat, then runs its blade down his chest and belly, before ripping his rib cage wide open in the blink of an eye as blood shoots and runs everywhere. From somewhere behind him, toward the front door a voice screams, "FOR FUCK'S SAKE DO IT NOW!" just before he startles awake to the sound of a gunshot ringing his ears.

Waking, feeling cold and shaking he sighes, looking at his big brother's comforting shape outlined by the light from the streetlamp outside the window where something strange catches his attention. *That's not right,* he thought, feeling the short hairs on the back of his neck stand up as the shape of a man slinks down into a shadow behind him. *We're on the second floor...* he whips around, his breath 'woosh'ing out of him when he sees there's nothing there.

He needed to get into Nicky's bed, but he was suddenly sure if his feet touched the floor, that same something he'd seen a second ago was going to reach out from under his bed and grab him, and drag him into the dark with it! *I gotta be brave, like Nicky would be,* he steeled himself, jumping across the three feet between their beds, and lifting the covers found his safety next to the older boy, whose arms closed reflexively around him.

For several long stretchy 'late night' moments, he lay still in the darkness, glad for his big brother beside him. With a faint 'pop', Frank took his thumb from his mouth. *Nicky won't like it if he wakes up and the pillow's all slobbery just 'cause I had to suck my thumb,* and he dried the digit on his pajama top, then thought about the dreams that scared him.

There wasn't much he remembered about the night that took his daddy away two years ago, but sometimes what he did remember, mostly sensations, smells and colors, scared him silly. *Big hard hands that didn't smell or feel familiar grabbed him out of his bed and shoved him into mommy's warm softness, but there was something wrong about her arms that night. Then, once more he was shoved into another pair that, this time, both smelled and felt the way they were supposed to.*

*"Get him out of here NOW!" Momma's voice shrieked in the dark.*

*"I gotcha, Frankie," Nick nodded, holding his little brother to his chest.*

After that, things moved real fast and there were so many angry adults around, yelling at each other, blaming each other, yelling and pointing at him and Nick in ways that made his tummy feel sick, that he let himself forget most of it. The one thing he couldn't forget though was that their Daddy was gone, and wasn't ever going to be back. After that, with mommy always sad, or crying, or gone to work, it was up to Nicky to take care of things.

But Nick was only ten, and sometimes he couldn't stop the bad things.

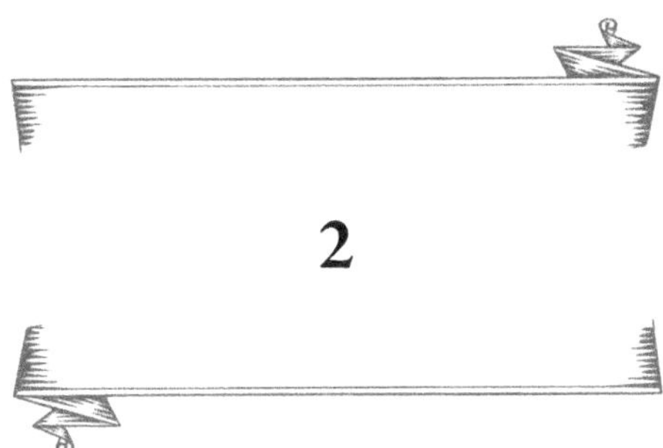

# 2

In the back of his office, Harry Armstrong leaned heavily against the old battered file cabinet, a bent and creased photo pinched between his fingers. It was a genuine photograph from a drug store drop box, not a home printed job. It was cracked, bent and torn, just as he often felt. In fact, it had been through almost as much. The photo was thirty-five years old to his fifty-three. *Love me some symmetry, even if it is back assward,* he chuffed, knowing full well the bit of memorabilia technically wouldn't exist for another four or five years.

Tears slid down his face, his big leathery hand pawed them away as he traced his finger, not for the first time, over two of the familiar faces embraced by his seventeen year old arms.

His breath trembled from his throat to his chest, "Ahhh, miss y'Nicky."

Steadying himself, he slid the war-mangled photo back into his wallet and his wallet into his pocket. His eyes fell on the clock, and with a nod, he gave himself permission to flop into his chair and remember.

His hand trembled faintly and squeezed his knee. Every time he'd been through these last five or six months, and every time he saw those boys as they'd been earlier, as they'd been before they all 'technically' met - free, innocent, and not yet scarred up by whatever those bastard schades really were, his heart cracked just a little more.

*Gonna up'n shatter pretty soon, then who...* but it didn't matter. There were no more chances left.

Instead, he reveled in the joy of the moment. Every moment he watched them, the hero-worshipping light in Frankie's eyes and the unabashed love for the little guy in Nick's was proof that neither of them was yet twisted or warped by circumstances that were truly beyond their control. But every time he went through this, as the target date drew closer, he'd almost swear he could see Nicky's spirit die just a little more.

Every time he re-set events, he'd wait for the boys and he'd watch over them, glad to see them once again free of hate, vengeance or love gone awry. But every time he had to watch them go through it all again was torture, maybe in some ways more for him than even for them, and yet for almost eighteen years he held tight to hope.

*I gotta get it right this time, we're gonna hafta go through it and see if we can still save Frank. If we can, maybe we can save ourselves, too.*

His hand slid into his shirt, fingers wrapping around the watch like pendant Nick had passed on to him so many years ago. *Please, God.* He sent the hopeful thought out into the world and let himself rest, but just for a time.

STANDING IN THE HALL outside the kindergarten classroom, Nick watched his little brother dash happily to the coat rack. He fastidiously hung his jacket on the hook with his name written in pencil on masking tape, and just as carefully placed his cracked, plastic, green Scooby Doo lunch box 'just so' directly above that.

He smiled faintly, remembering Frankie's delight the previous summer at finding the Second Hand Store treasure, how he'd held it to his chest grinning at the giant goofy look on the cartoon Great Dane's face.

*"Can I have it, Nicky? Pleeeeeease?" he whined, then straightened at the sight of his brother's spocked eyebrow and tried again, "Please?"*

*"How much is it, shrimp?"*

*Frankie turned it round and round in his hands, missing the red wax pencil marking, $0.75, through several passes.*

*"Never mind," Nick smiled motioning his happy little shrimp toward the register, "but you don't get no new socks till school starts now."*

*"It's summer," he reminded his older brother. Still, Frankie's sapphire eyes lit up and his face beamed a smile that could disarm even the crankiest adult. He nodded furiously, holding the box to his chest and hopping in place as he waited for Nick to join him at the counter.*

*"I'm gonna put my army guys in it, and it's gonna be their tank! Then, when school comes, he'll guard all my pencils, 'specially the magic one, y'know?..." he'd babbled happily all the way home, not daring to swing the box by the handle, but keeping it safe against his chest with one hand while he made sure to hold Nick's with his other. "I always wanted a dog! And Scooby talks, Nick! Did you know Scooby can talk?" he continued chirping.*

With a faint frown and a sense that the world was just slightly off kilter, Nick watched until Frankie found his assigned seat at the table and plopped into it, filled with a natural exuberance for the start of a new day.

Shaking his head, he turned away from the kindergarten classroom and toward his own first period class just as the tardy bell rang.

He bolted down the deserted hallway, "Fuck!"

*WHAT?* Frank wondered, glancing back at his classmates as he approached the whiteboard.

They were laughing, and he kinda had the feeling they were laughing at him, but nobody would even look at him.

*What?!* He looked at each of their faces, his smile faltering just a tiny bit.

Sarah Flemming, a shy but otherwise nice little brunette-haired girl, pointed at him.

Frankie looked down. *Nope, zipper's up. I didn't have a accident. What's so funny?* he wondered, looking all over at himself, craning his head around wondering if he had a hole somewhere embarrassing.

As he turned his head one way, pulling his jeans the other, he saw it. A big wad of pink, sugar-filled bubble gum stuck to the butt of his pants with long spidery strands striping the back of his jeans. *Oh, man! Nicky's gonna be so mad! These costed good money and now they're wrecked!*

It wasn't bad enough he felt his eyes starting to mist up with the prospect of making more work for his big brother, if the room hadn't erupted in wild cackling laughter at just that moment.

With fingers pointing at him from every direction and childish, crow-like 'caws' echoing in his ears, he felt his lower lip quiver, but he was pretty sure he could still keep it in.

"Hey, bubble butt! Frankie's got a bubble butt, Frankie's got a bubble butt," Tommy Haywood sing-songed, and before Frank could draw another breath the whole classroom picked up the chant.

Even with that, he thought he could have laughed, too, and done what Nicky always said to, *"…just play along and don't let 'em know they're getting to you."* And maybe he could have, but that was before he saw Bruce Evans reach up high on the coat rack and draw down his bright green lunch box.

"Hey!" Frankie frowned, pointing to the back of the class. "Don't you do that!" he hollered, somehow having the perfect view of Bruce sitting on the floor, eating *his* sandwich with his yucky yellow teeth then washing it down with *his* purple juice box.

As the chanting slowed and Frankie moved toward Bruce, Ms. Rubens rose from her chair, clapping her hands firmly for attention while striding quickly to the back of the classroom.

"Give it back, Bruce!" Frankie burst into a run, plowing into the bigger boy who blew a mouthful of purple squishy sandwich stuff into the smaller boy's face.

"Bruce Elmer Evans! You say you're sorry right now!" Ms. Rubens pulled the boy to his feet, unaware of the cruel glint in his eyes as he smashed his foot down on the bright green lunchbox. "No…" Frankie's whispered protest was a fraction of a second too late. The classroom fell silent just in time for the thunderous crack of the hard plastic to echo through it.

Another well placed boot before Miss Rubens got full control over the boy shattered that happy Great Dane's goofy smile into three jagged pieces.

"That's *it,* young man, you are going to the principal's office!" Ms. Rubens grasped Bruce by the shoulder and marched him toward the door. "Frankie, come along," she directed as he squatted down, gingerly picking up the jagged pieces and trying to get them to fit together again, to make that silly Great Dane something he could smile at again.

"Anybody moves out of their seats and every single one of you will have a phone call to your parents tonight!" Ms. Rubens threatened as Mr. Hollet, one of the monitors, was waved over to watch the class.

TIGHTLY EMBRACING THE three pieces of Scooby, Frankie stood still, letting the tears run down his face silently while the nurse pressed a packet of ice to the back of his jeans so she could peel the gum from them.

*Now my butt's cold and I'm gonna have a wet spot, too. My Scooby...* his breath quivered softly in his chest *...and I'll prolly go in the dumpster again today, too, b'cause I got him in trouble. Please be on time today, Nicky, please? I don't wanna be in the dumpster again.*

"... SO SNEAK OUT," JOSH Torres shrugged. "It's not like your mom's even gonna be there right?" he asked, snapping his fingers in front of Nick's wandering gaze.

After a quick perusal of the playground, he frowned, "You don't know squat, Josh. Besides she's working a double tonight and I can't leave Frankie alone." He craned his view around Harry who was tossing garbage back into the dumpster after some of the middle graders had decided to go diving for teachers' answer sheets.

"Dude, turn on the TV, wait till he falls asleep, then just go out. Look, it's only for a couple hours; he'll still be suckin' his thumb when you get back," Josh groaned.

"I dunno..." he hedged, knowing that once Frankie was out, not much other than an earthquake or nightmare was gonna wake him. But it was the thought of leaving his baby brother all alone that didn't sit right. It was one thing if he was in the living room watching TV and Frankie was sleeping in the other room, at least then, if need be, he could run interference.

There were butterflies in his belly at the prospect, but he couldn't tell whether they were a warning not to do it, or the tingle of excitement. He'd never been very good at making that distinction. "Tell you what, if I'm not at the corner by 10:00, figure I ain't comin', how's that?" he asked, scanning the group that his brother usually played with.

One of the boys, a butterball with lemon colored hair he was fairly sure was named Pete, was waddling their way.

Nick stepped out in front of the boy, watching his eyes grow wide in momentary fear, "Where's Frank?"

"F..Fr..." he stuttered, blinking hard. Nick nodded, "Yeah, where is he?"

"Nuh, nuh... nurse..." was all he needed to spit out before Nick wheeled around dashing into the building as if the hounds of hell themselves were at his heels.

HIS HANDS GRASPED CLUMSILY at the office doorknob trying to keep himself up as his feet scrambled round the corner.

"Where is he?" he panted at a pinch-faced man behind the desk.

"Frank Emerson, where is he?"

"Nicky?" came a faint, tentative voice that seemed to reach into his chest and grab his heart.

He dashed around the counter and into the nurse's office. One look at his little brother's tightly crossed arms and tear-streaked face had Nick on his knees looking into his little one's glistening eyes. "What happened?" he asked with his hands on Frank's shoulders while the nurse smiled at him from behind.

He snared the little boy's arm, drawing him away from the woman. "What're you doing to him?" he asked tightly.

She held up a paper towel filled with pink while smiling apologetically. Nick felt his face frown in confusion as he grabbed his little brother under the chin searching his tearful gaze.

"I'm sorry, Nicky," he sniffed, shaking his head, his lips bowing downward and trembling, "I didn't know."

"Didn't know what?" he glanced at the nurse. "Is that gum?" She nodded.

"I sat in it. I ruined my pants and now they're wet and my butt's cold and soggy and everyone's gonna think I made a accident," he sniffed, opening his arms, revealing the pieces of plastic. That was when his tears broke free, his lips quivered and his chest shook with tightly held hiccoughs. "An, and Bruce, he, he broke...he hurt Scooby."

*Aww, baby boy.* "C'mere, you," Nick grasped a gentle fist full of that wavy brown mop and held open his arms.

It was close enough to being alone, Frankie collapsed into the older boy, his arms clinging around Nick's neck, his hands holding fast to the plastic fragment that razored across his big brother's cheek, leaving a fine line of red dripping slowly down while he let the little one cry.

"They're only pants, shrimp. You'll outgrow 'em in no time, anyway," he sighed. "Really?" Frankie breathed.

Nick nodded, "Sure, didn't you know? That's what shrimp's do, they grow into bigger shrimps," he patted the young boy's back. "You'll be King Prawn in no time. And we'll find you a new Scooby, okay? A soft one that big clumsy ox can't hurt, okay?" he promised, feeling the warm wetness of his brother's tears nodding against his neck.

"You sure?"

Nick swallowed hard, wondering how he was gonna manage such a feat. Those soft-sided lunch boxes cost almost as much as two weeks worth of food and lunches for them both. *I can do it, I'll make sure; a few skipped lunches or dinners is all, no big deal.* He nodded,

"I'm sure."

*I'M NOT GONNA BE LATE today, I'm not gonna be late today. Nothing's gonna budge me from this spot until the bell rings and that door opens, and I'm gonna walk right in that classroom and walk right out with my brother, and so help me, God, if either of those sons of b...those bastards touches him again, they're gonna regret it!* He pulled his knees to his chest and watched the second hand on the clock slide greasily round the face. *Ten more minutes, then Frankie and I can go to the 7-Eleven and share a coke or a Twix. I can't believe I won almost a whole buck just on whether or not Derek would give Lucas a wedgie today. Always bet on the mean guy to just keep on being mean.*

"Hey, Nick," Harry called, stepping out into the hallway from his office, "can I talk to you a minute?"

Nick startled, but moved over to the man with a smile, then leaned against the wall, "Sure, Harry, s'up?"

"C'mon inside here, kiddo," he held open the door as the boy slid under his arm and into the darkened space.

In the world of Elementary School, having access to any adult's office could ratchet up popularity points very quickly depending on which crowd a person hung out with, and even a janitor's office was no exception.

"Have a seat, kiddo," he directed pointing at the shaky looking wire frame chair beside the desk.

Nick cocked an eyebrow, uncertain if the hammock of filthy coarse yellow fabric would be able to hold him. He pushed down on the seat experimentally, then sat as Harry flopped into his chair where something screamed in protest when he leaned back.

"Welcome t'my world, Nicky," he grinned openly, his hand waving over the cluttered but organized expanse of dimly lit mustiness. "T'ain't much, but for now, its home," he chuckled.

Nick shook his head with a faint confused smile turning half his mouth up. "Cool," he shrugged as Harry lowered the zipper on his jumpsuit then started on the buttons on his shirt.

Nick's palms turned slick as he shifted nervously in the seat.

"Harry? What're you doing?" he asked.

"I'm gonna show you something," he grumbled.

The boy started to push out of the chair with a faint shake to his head, "Uh, yeah, y'know, I promised Frankie..." he motioned to the door.

"Relax, Nicky, I'm not like that sick bastard your mom thinks she's gotta keep gettin' with t'keep bread in the fridge," he smiled sadly.

Nick's heart skipped heavily into his throat and he felt his eyes grow wide. "How..." he breathed faintly, feeling just a little sick as he sank weakly back down.

"S'not important," Harry shook his head pulling aside his shirt to reveal a six-inch long, half-inch wide scar over his chest. "See this?"

"Yeah." Nick, to his own chagrin, leaned forward, amazed by the size and thickness of the wound.

"Guy my mom was dating took after me one night. He'd had too much to drink and decided he was gonna *take* what my momma wasn't willing to give, if you get my meaning."

Nick's eyes widened for a second as he swallowed hard, nodding.

Harry nodded, "I got in the way. When my momma saw his hands covered in MY blood, well that was all she wrote for him. Courts ruled it self defense."

Nick shook his head, beyond stunned, "Why are you telling me this, Harry?" he asked, sitting back down as the man started buttoning his shirt back up. Before he was finished though, he looped his nimble fingers around a gold chain and slid it over his head.

Harry glanced sidelong at the boy, "I heard you and Josh talking out on the playground. Now, I'm not gonna tell you NOT to go tonight, but I *am* going to tell you this much," he faced the young man, opening the chain, and slid it over his head. "IF you do go, gettin' home tonight is gonna be the one time you can NOT be late."

"This was meant for you, Nick," he explained, holding up the gleaming bauble that seemed unusually heavy for something so small.

Upon close examination, Nick realized it was a tiny version of a pocket watch, or an old fashioned stop watch, he wasn't really sure which.

He watched Harry open the cover, gently pull on the knob at the top, then turn it forward until the hands showed ten minutes to two. The old man gently pushed the knob back down, then another gentle push set it a little deeper.

"What I just did was kinda like setting an alarm. Wherever you are, at ten to two in the morning, you'll know you have to get home. Whatever you're doing, you stop it! No matter what it is you're doing, you STOP as soon as that alarm goes off and you get home and into bed, do you understand me? I don't care if you've got your p.j.'s on or not, you get into bed, pull those covers over you both and close your eyes, do you get me?" he urged, his voice growing a sharp edge Nick had never heard from the man before.

Nick shook his head, Harry leaned in closer. "Pigg."

"No," Nick gasped, jerking backward.

"Yeah," Harry continued, "lemme put it like this, you DON"T get home and tucked in with him... the last eighteen years of my life, and the next twenty three of Frankie's are as good as shit down the toilet... NOW do you get me?"

Gulping hard, Nick nodded while his heart and mind raced, and a familiar fear shimmied through his insides. "Yeah, I gotcha," he nodded frowning deeply.

"Good," Harry slid a finger into the collar of the boy's shirt dropping the tiny watch down against his chest.

*It's not even cold,* he noticed in the periphery of his mind.

With a glance at the clock, the suddenly mysterious janitor clapped his hand onto Nick's shoulder, guided him to the office door and turned him so they were face to face, "After Frankie, that watch is the most important thing in your life."

Numb, Nick found himself drifting back across the hall. He leaned on the wall outside of Frankie's classroom just as the bell rang, bringing him back to the present with the exhilarating knowledge that, for once, he wasn't late.

"SO, SANDY SAID THAT Josh's brother Jeremy works at this place where there are *naked* people, and some of the big kids are gonna go there." He looked up at his big brother, frowning at the distant look in the older boy's eyes. "Why would people do that? Who wants to see anyone nekked?" he asked, tugging on Nicky's hand while the other crushed the paper bag containing the pieces of Scooby's picture to his chest.

"I dunno, shrimp," Nick muttered, trying to shake himself out of the funk he'd slid into since going into Harry's office.

"Would *you* go there?" he asked.

Nick's attention snapped back to the moment, he turned, looking down into his little brother's openly curious face. Smiling crookedly, he rubbed his hand through the kid's unruly waves, "not tonight."

AS SOON AS FRANKIE moved, Nick's eyes shot open. His breath stopped for a second as he listened to the sounds of the still empty apartment. Across the room, bed sheets rustled and his baby brother's feet hit the floor. He knew what was coming next and smiled, warmed deep inside by the joy of being needed.

A waft of cool came first as Frankie lifted the blankets back. Next, would come the dip at the edge of the bed as he rolled onto his side leaving them face to face for a moment before his little hand grabbed the edge of the blankets and drew them back over them both.

Usually Nick would wind up getting 'whapped' with an elbow or some poorly controlled body part as Frankie turned onto his right side, but he never minded, and tonight, with Harry's words circling his exhausted and overwrought mind, he would have been glad of it just to know his baby boy was safe.

With Frankie situated, Nick's arm rolled forward, pulling the little spoon tight into his big spoon, and breathed a sigh before closing his eyes and waiting.

Some time later, he was awoken by a strange sensation, as if there was some little man ringing one of those Christmas bells inside his chest. Everything came pouring back and he wrapped Frankie more snugly to him, wishing he could pull him under his skin, hide him from whatever it was that made yesterday, and everything up to now feel as if the world was waiting for something horrible to be born.

One by one, he watched the minutes pass on the blue face of the digital alarm clock between their beds. Each one seemed its own eternity until the digits read 2:00. Right on schedule, heavy, sloppy, shuffling footfalls scraped to the door. A hard clumsy hand turned the knob letting in a shaft of light. Not for the first time, Nick closed his eyes, holding tight to his soundly sleeping little brother.

Afraid to even crack his eyes open, he listened to those clumsy feet make their way into the room. What surprised him, though, was that they went to the bed opposite his. He heard the springs creak in protest as mom's fat drunken boss stumbled onto it, his puffy, beefy hands groping under the blankets and sheets.

Nick wasn't quite sure what was going on a moment later when, even though he knew his eyes were closed, he saw in his mind, *Mr. Pigg (as Nick and Frankie referred to Mr. Pickerd), kneeling on the floor beside Frankie's bed, and even though he knew his little brother was tight in his arms, he could see him sleeping, sprawled as he often did, on his stomach with his thumb stuck firmly in his mouth. 'I gotta get him to quit suckin' his thumb', Nick thought briefly as he watched Pigg pull the covers back from his little brother. 'No!' his arms clenched around the little boy.*

*'Frankie, wake up!' he urged inside his head knowing it was futile.*

*'No, not Frankie,' he squeezed, his eyelids shut tight until all he saw was stars, but he could still hear.*

Keeping his eyes squeezed tight against the terrible sights inside his mind, he reminded himself that Frankie was safe in his arms, NOT in the bed across from his.

*The sound of thick, congested breathing filled his ears and made him shudder.*

*"What? Hey? What's goin' on? HEY!" vision-Frankie protested, his voice still muddled with sleep.*

*From the smell of the shampoo they used to the scent of their detergent, all the way through to the warmth pulled protectively to him, plus Harry's warning were the only reasons he stayed put.*

*'Why? We had a deal, NEVER Frank!' he wondered while his face worked into a frown as in this nightmare Pigg started with his little brother the same way he'd started with him.*

*"I'll take good care of your momma, and your big brother, and you. But you have to keep our secret," he leaned over briefly before rising and slipping quietly out the door.*

*"Nuh, nuh, Nicky?" Frankie's voice trembled quietly as he got out of bed, his hands grasping between his legs as if he had to pee or had already had an accident.*

*With a painful sounding gasp, vision-Frank ripped his pj's off and climbed into his big brother's empty bed, wrapping himself around Nicky's pillow and sobbing with his thumb firmly stuck in his mouth until he fell asleep.*

*'I'll kill him, he EVER touches Frankie and I'll slit his fucking throat!'* Nick promised the universe as a confused Mr. Pigg turned, seeing the boys together, and shambled out of the room.

Nick unclenched the fist that was under his pillow, working the cramps out of his fingers before quietly slipping the kitchen knife into the drawer of the table between their beds. He missed the faint gray man-shaped silhouette slipping backward to blend in with the shadows.

OUTSIDE ON THE STREET, with classic Motown easing from his car stereo, Harry sighed, relieved as light left the window to the boy's bedroom.

"Good man, Nicky," he smiled, sliding the safety back on and tucking the semi-automatic pistol back into his battered briefcase before putting the car into gear, "...and when Evans and Haywood toss Frankie into the dumpster tomorrow, we're gonna start to rewrite the future kiddo, again. God knows tomorrow's already a better day than it usually is." He nodded, smiling faintly and humming along.

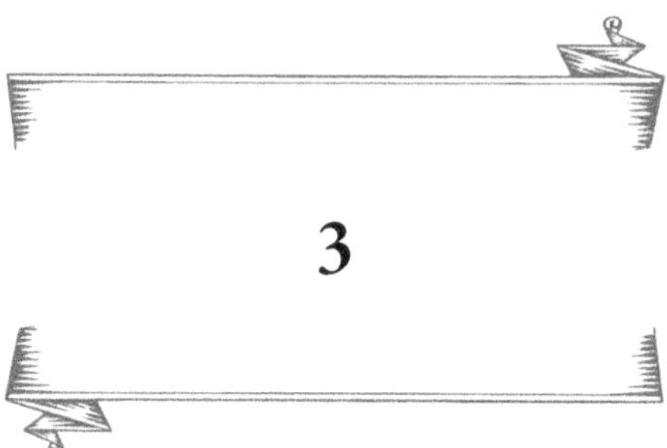

# 3

"Harry, you gotta tell me, man! How'd you know, huh? How'd you know that sick son of a bi..." he bit his lip and blushed madly while slapping a hand over his mouth.

Harry chuckled good-naturedly and swiped at the kid's shaggy brown hair, "I've heard worse, Nick, even said a few things that're worse than that." He sipped at his coffee, "Just don't be spouting it off in front of the other adults, okay? Most of 'em won't take kindly to it."

Nick nodded. "But how'd you know, Harry? And what about that eighteen years of your life and twenty three of Franks?" C'mon, tell me?" he pleaded again.

"Didn't take much to figure out he was just movin' down the line." Harry shook his head and shrugged, "Always bet on evil to keep on being evil."

Nick pulled the watch from his shirt. "You want your watch back?" he asked, already reluctant to part with it.

"T'ain't mine, boy, you KNOW that. It was meant for you, it's always been yours and always gonna be yours," he hedged.

Nick shook his head, "But I've never seen it before."

"Sure you have, you think about it, it'll come to you," the older man nodded sagely.

Nick felt his heart beating in his throat as he chewed his lip for a moment, then finally met those warm, liquid brown eyes, "You're not just a janitor, Harry. Are you some kind of," he swallowed hard and rolled his eyes to himself, "...guardian angel or something?"

The guffaw he half expected didn't come, and for a moment, the possibility left him feeling light-headed as he leaned back in the rickety wire chair, his head buzzing for the breath trapped in his throat.

"Me, an angel, huh? You've called me a lot of things, Nicky, but NEVER an angel," he shook his head and nudged the young boy until he gasped.

"Well, then who are you?" he finally panted. "And what do you mean? I've never called you anything, well, nothing bad anyway."

"Not in this life," the old man laughed, his eyes flicking up to the clock, lighting on the severed wire that, had it been connected, would have enabled him to hear the sound of the bell inside his office. *That should be enough time.*

He smiled into the boy's face, "I'm your friend, Nick, yours and Frankie's," he feigned a frown, "...and as a friend, I hate to say it, but you're late. And given the trouble those boys got into yesterday, it's a sure bet Frankie's headed for the dumpster again."

"Shit!" Nick leaped from the chair dashing from the office with Harry's heavier footfalls lagging behind.

Sure enough, Frankie's classroom was empty, and just outside the door he could hear his little brother pleading to be put down.

Harry stood in the kindergarten classroom's outer door leaning against the brick wall, his arms broken out in goose bumps. Smiling nervously, he watched as the boy who would one day become a brother to him ran across the blacktop, the pendant bouncing against his chest until he grasped it tight and hollered, "STOP IT!"

*What the hell?* Nick wondered as his steps slowed on approach to Bruce and Tommy who held Frankie between them halfway up the dumpster.

Unconsciously, he tucked the pendant into his shirt and crept warily toward the three frozen figures, taking a moment to walk around and observe them. He looked for a rise of the chest or a flick of the eye, even a tremble of a lip to try and tell if they were putting him on, but there was no such sign. For all he could tell, he might as well have been looking at life-sized dolls or wax figures. His stomach clenched and he suddenly felt very much like he had to go to the bathroom while a greasy sweat poured out of him.

*Is Harry doing this or am I?* he wondered a split second before something inside him desperately urged, *Get Frankie down!* So he reached up. His hands closed around his little brother's torso and he startled as the air split with the last half of the boy's plea.

"Nicky!" his cry turned gleeful with surprise while he squirmed and with his big brother's help, twisted loose from the grip of the two bullies. "What's with them?" he asked, sticking his tongue out at Bruce.

"You okay, Frank?" he asked, holding the boy closely as they stepped back away from the still frozen other two.

"Nick, what did you do?" Frank breathed, astonished by the sight of his tormentors actually still. He dared a step forward, waving his hand in front of the bully's face, then grinned and gave him a shove.

"Frankie, no!" Nick steadied the bigger boy before he could fall and wondered, *how long's he gonna stay like that?*

"Aww, you shoulda let him fall. It woulda been funny to see him wake up on his butt."

"He mighta got hurt, fell and cracked his head or something."

Frank's mouth dropped into a surprised 'o'. "I didn't think o'that."

"Yeah, s'alright," Nick breathed, wrapping his arm around the boy while his eyes scanned the back lot for any sign of Harry. *Maybe he'll know what's goin' on.* But the older man was no longer leaning against the wall, and something inside told Nick Emerson's firstborn son it was time to move.

"C'mon, shrimp, let's get outta here," he urged, grasping his little brother's hand firmly and jogging across the playground.

As their feet hit the sidewalk, there was an odd shift in the air followed by two surprised yelps.

Nick and Frank turned, the sight of the two kindergarten bullies sprawled on the pavement and scratching their heads in surprise and confusion bringing bright smiles to both of their mouths.

They walked in silence for a time, their bound hands swinging easily as the sun shined warmly into them from above, "Nick?"

"Yeah?"

"They were frozen like happens on TV sometimes, weren't they?" he asked.

"I think so," Nick nodded.

"Are you magic?"

"I don't know. I don't *feel* like magic."

"Then how'd you do that?" Frankie asked, more than just a little awed.

Nick shrugged as his hand dug into his shirt and he pulled the pendant out. "I just said 'stop' and they did," he said, almost afraid that his little brother would once again freeze, but their pace and swinging arms continued.

"Cool!" Frankie nodded.

A long moment later he turned to his big brother, "Hey, Nick?"

"Yeah?"

"Are you gonna be a superhero now?"

The elder brother gave a short uneasy chuckle, "I don't think so."

"Why not? I could be your sidekick. You could be Nick of Time and I could be Second Hand, get it? It's funny 'cause all we got's second hand stuff and there's a second hand on the clock. Its good, isn't it? You get it?" Frankie asked, bouncing just a little more at his big brother's side.

"Yeah, I get it."

"Nick?" he stopped, this time turning his big brother to face him.

"Yeah?"

"You can't tell anybody about this, neither of us can, okay? Far as anyone knows, we're just still us, okay?"

The earnest look in his eyes reminded Nick of the expression on his face last year when he'd brought Frank into his fourth grade classroom to watch their caterpillar emerge from his cocoon. He'd never thought to see that kind of wonder in his little brother's face again, but here it was.

He held up his right hand, pinkie out, "Pinkie swear, shrimp, just you and me."

Frankie scooped his pinkie into his big brother's and shook hard with a huge smile on his face.

Nearing their apartment, Frankie glanced up at Nick, happily swinging their locked hands back and forth, "Hey, Nick?"

"Yeah?"

"You think we're gonna need costumes?"

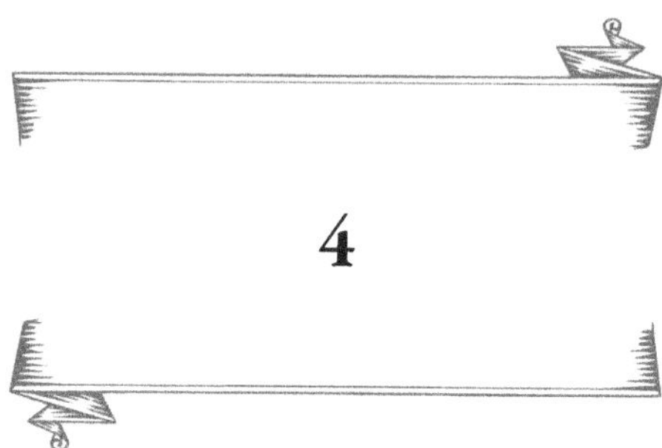

4

With a dull ache in his head and a sore feeling in his jaw from clenching his teeth, Nick frowned at the noises on the walkway outside the apartment. He quickly looked for the sliver of brass deadbolt between the door and the jamb. *Jeez it's noisy.* He rubbed the sweat off his face,

"That's enough for now, Frankie, okay?"

"You look like you're gonna throw up," Frank frowned. "You want the garbage?"

The elder brother shook his head. For over two hours he'd been trying almost every way he could think of to make time stop again. Holding the pendant tightly in his hand, he tried forcing it, willing the clock to stop, and even trying to be still like those yoga people on TV said to. But no matter what he did, he just couldn't seem to make it happen. In fact, he was beginning to doubt that it really happened at all, or that *he'd* had anything to do with it.

"Mighta been Harry," Nick suggested tiredly to his little brother, "Or maybe they were just stunned I actually got there in time, I don't know."

"No, no, Nick, see, it can't be," Frank protested, grabbing his big brother's shirt into his fists and shaking his head almost desperately. "It *can't* be. You saw it like I did, and you heard them fall down, and," he sniffed, his sapphire blues turning glassy.

"Hey, hey, easy there tiger, easy," Nick frowned, gently prying his little brother's hands open. "It's okay," he assured the boy before handing over the soda they were sharing. "Listen, Frankie, I gotta ask you a weird question, and I don't want you to feel bad, okay?" *I don't wanna. Please let me get this right so he doesn't figure it out. Do I really wanna know? Heck with that. What I want doesn't really matter now, does it?* Another voice from somewhere deep inside asked. *I GOTTA know, I gotta know he's still safe. I gotta make sure I'm doin' my job right.*

"What do you gotta know?" Frank asked curious about the strange look on his big brother's face. "What?" he asked wiping his eyes dry.

"It's about Mr. Pigg," the older boy prefaced.

Frankie stuck his tongue out and shook his head, "I don't wanna talk about him. He makes my tummy do ugly things."

Nick nodded, "Mine, too, but it's just one question, okay?"

Pursing his lips, the youngest Emerson sighed and nodded, "Okay, but just one 'cause talking about him makes a day yucky!"

Nick grinned, swiping his brother's hair, "Yeah, it does. Okay, here's the question," he took a deep breath, "and this is just between you and me, okay? Never gonna go anywhere but between us, okay?" he assured, hoping the soaring bats in his belly would calm down, though he knew they wouldn't until he heard the answer his deepest heart desired. Once he knew for sure that what he'd seen in his mind's eye last night was nothing more than a bad kind of waking dream, *or vision,* he thought, then he might be able to feel right in his belly again. "Okay," Frankie shrugged.

Nick pressed his hand to his little brother's chest, right over his heart, "From here to your toes, has Pigg ever touched you, Frankie?" "Touched me?" Frank asked, noting something 'sticky' in his brother's voice. He thought a moment, his brows furrowing together as the Labor Day barbeque they'd had just before school started came to mind. "Well, he patted me once, but it wasn't a spanking or anything. It was like when the baseball players do after a home run."

Nick's throat twitched inside and he almost choked on his own air, "When?"

"The picnic last summer, when we were playing whiffle ball and I scored for our team," he frowned, gazing into his brother's eyes.

"Why? Is this about your nightmare last night?"

The older brother felt himself swallow hard, "Nightmare?"

"Yeah, you were huggin' me real hard this morning like I'm a teddy bear," Frankie smiled. "But you only do that when you have nightmares. What were you dreaming about? Was it about Daddy? I dreamed about Daddy the other night. I miss him; do you know why the man did that?" he asked curiously, but definitely not for the first time.

"No, I just know if there was a heaven, daddy'd be there watchin' over us." Nick blinked back mist and reached for the soda, trying to shut out the memories, the sight of the shadowy figure grasping at his father in the hallway while Frankie's arms and legs clung to him. The sound of wetness and fear in their father's voice the last time he heard it as he called out to his wife to get the kids out of there. The memory of it sent chills through him.

"You miss him, too, huh, Nick?"

"Yeah, I do," he nodded, then shook his head back to the moment. "But, okay, so Pigg only ever patted your bottom just that once, right?" he double checked.

Frankie nodded, "Uh huh," then shook his head. "I think he was trying to be like a daddy 'cause he kept petting me a whole real lot, but then he didn't anymore. That's good. Can we be done talking about him now? You wanna watch cartoons?" he asked, hopping off the couch and dashing to the TV.

"Sure, shrimp," Nick nodded.

His lips turned up faintly as relief coursed through him, finally allowing his tummy to settle down. *He's still safe Dad, for now.*

LONG AFTER THEIR BEDTIME, Nick rolled over to check the time. *12:35. Mom gets off at 1:00, and Pigg's bound to come home with her, I mean it's Friday night - unless she goes over to his place. Please go to his place.* He gazed across the room at his brother and sat up, throwing the sheets off himself. *Could I stop him?* He grasped the watch around his neck. *Was it real? Did it really happen at all?* he wondered, looking at his little brother. *I know why I'd like it to be real, baby boy, but why does it matter so much to you? Will Harry think I'm crazy? Maybe I am crazy?* He glanced at the clock again.

*12:42. I can't take any chances.* He nodded to himself and crossed the room, throwing the covers off his little brother.

"I love you, Frankie," he breathed heavily, sliding his arms under the boy who lay sprawled, once again on his tummy, his head turned toward his brother, his thumb perched in his mouth. As Nicky turned him onto his back he watched his little guy work that thumb and flushed with warmth, remembering when he was fresh from the hospital and mom used to sit with both of them on the couch, Frankie suckling at her breast while she and Nicky watched cartoons during the baby's mid afternoon feeding.

"C'mon, little man," he smiled softly, pulling the boy into his arms.

Almost reflexively, Frankie's arms curled around his neck as he swept him into his own bed, gently climbing over him and righting the blankets over them both. Instinctively, Frankie turned, edging backward until he was comfortably embraced by his big brother.

Petting the unruly brown waves and pressing his lips to the back of his little brother's head, Nick pulled him close. Closing his eyes, he let a shaky breath settle between them as he drifted off to sleep.

"BUT ITS *Saturday,* Nick," Frank frowned, his expression a contrast to the easy skip beside his brother.

"Listen," Nick turned and crouched before his brother, "we need to talk to Harry. He knows something, he..." he shook his head, not knowing exactly what to say, "we just have to talk to him, okay? Just trust me?" he half pleaded, his guts turning, and though he was thrilled that Pigg hadn't come to either of them, he was exhausted by the fear that had kept him awake more than half the night.

The littlest Emerson tilted his head to the side and smiled just a bit, "Always, silly, it's just that..." he stopped and shrugged, *if you find out you should be scared like you think, then it'll all go wrong, and that scares me.* But with whatever it was bothering Nick, the last thing he wanted to do was add to it. When he woke up this morning with visions of Pigg searching under his covers for something, and the image didn't go away until Nick woke up, Frankie knew something was different. He'd never shared a dream with his big brother before. He couldn't say how he knew it was Nick's dream except that it just 'felt' like him, but given his cranky mood, Frank didn't want to start the weekend off bad. "It's school," he finished weakly while frowning and found that tears wanted to come out.

"I know," Nick nodded.

Early Saturday morning, kids were still inside watching cartoons and having pop tarts inside blanket and pillow forts in their bedrooms or living rooms. Later they would burst out into the open, into the sunshine, to explore the world that waited for them. But for this moment, the Emerson brothers had the world to themselves, and they were taking advantage of it. They slid around to the sunny side of the building and the door that was closest to Harry's office.

Nick raised his fist and banged on the kindergarten classroom's outer door, then peered under his hand, searching for signs of movement.

"Maybe he's not here, Nick. Maybe he doesn't come here on the weekend either?" Frank couldn't keep the hope out of his voice.

"Mmm, maybe," Nick nodded reluctantly. Beside him, Frankie sniffed and his breath quivered in his chest.

Nick turned. "Hey? You crying?" he asked.

"Mmm," Frank shook his head despite the tiny shimmers in the corners of his eyes.

"Are too."

"Am NOT!"

"Sure you are, shrimp-o," Nick smiled, trying to get his brother to either smile or tell him why.

"I am NOT, and you're a poop head!" Frank stomped and ran off into the playground where he plopped onto a swing pumping his legs as if he could just take flight.

Dismayed by his little brother's sudden mood swing, Nick was momentarily glued to the spot. A second later, he shook himself out of his surprise and jogged onto the playground, "Frank! Frankie!"

"Hey, at least let a poop head know what he did wrong, willya?" Nick asked, sitting on the next swing over.

"You PROMISED!" Frank shouted, dragging his shoes so hard to stop that one of them came off. "You PROMISED and you LIED, you even pinkie sweared!" he cried, dashing with his shoe to the climbing slide and disappearing inside where he crouched up against the underside of the stairs.

*Pinkie swear, oh man,* he remembered yesterday afternoon, swearing secrecy with Frank about what happened, and here he was breaking his very own promise. Nick sighed, jumping from his swing with his head hanging.

*He doesn't know, I forgot to tell him.* "I did NOT LIE to you, Frankie! I wouldn't do that!" he called, approaching the structure. If he entered, he was sure it would just send his brother running to some other playground piece.

"Yes you DID! You PROMISED, Nicky! And now you're gonna break that promise; you said it was just you and me!"

The sight of Frank's red jacket between the beams drew the big brother to a halt on the other side of the wall, "Frankie, listen..."

"NO!" he shouted, scooting across the inside so that now he was facing his big brother while keeping further away. "Poop head..." he muttered, laying his head on his arms as they crossed over his knees. "Grown-ups'll just ruin everything! That's all they ever do!" he mumbled into his arm.

"Frank, where the hell do you think I got the thing?!" Nick yelled, angered by his little brother's stubborn attitude.

"You said a bad word," he observed.

"Hell isn't a bad word, it's a bad PLACE. Harry's the one who *gave* it to me, Frank. How else do you think I could get something like this? Huh? You think it's gonna just magically appear out of nowhere? We aren't Harry Potter, man, and this ain't Hogwart's!"

At the mention of his favorite series of books, Frankie looked up, tear smudges on his cheeks already starting to dry. "But Harry *did* give it to you. Maybe he's magic too?"

"You really think that?" Nick asked, creeping toward the entrance, as a memory pops into his head. He was a toddler, maybe about three, he pulled the chain out of his dad's shirt and examined the bauble. His dad's chuckle vibrated through his chest, "it'll be yours one day baby boy."

The woebegone sigh that puffed into the air from the young boy brought a sad smile to his big brother's face as he entered the base of the slide.

"No, but why can't it be like that, Nick? Huh? Why can't it be? It HAS to be magic," Frank shuddered as his big brother sat cross legged in front of him.

"Why?" he asked. "Why's it so important to you that this is something special? That this really maybe did what we think it might have?"

"It just has to." Frank shook his head, his eyes downcast while less frantic tears made fresh smudges on his cheeks.

"Hey, Second Hand, a sidekick doesn't keep secrets from his big brother," Nick cocked his head to the side. *I think I know,* he remembered Frank's question yesterday about their dad, and where he would go when he died. It was a strange thing but it was like he sometimes forgot the things he and Nick would talk about. "This got something to do with Dad?"

"You'll think it's stupid," Frank pouted.

"Does it?"

Slowly, Frank nodded, "Maybe if we can make it work we can get him back. Maybe we can make things go backwards and get Daddy back, and then we won't be here and there won't be any more Pigg or bad dreams, and no more dumpster, and mommy won't cry so much." When Nick made no response, no ridicule, no corrections, no 'that's impossible', Frank looked across and felt his mouth drop open in shock. He reached over, his finger tracing the shimmer on his brother's cheek before the tear found its way into his mouth.

"That would be good," Nick barely breathed, his bright blue eyes sinking into Frankie's darker ones. "C'mere baby boy," he opened his arms then closed them around the little one. "Did you know that's what Dad used to call me?" he asked softly.

"Uh uh," Frank shook his head.

"Yep, he'd come home, plop into his chair, and when I could climb into his lap I'd just sit there snuggled up against him, and he'd pet my head all nice and warm and kinda like a little bit of forever, y'know?" he nearly whispered and felt Frankie nod against his neck. "And after a little while, when everything got just right, he'd ask, 'so what'd you do today, baby boy?'" Nick stopped, his chest quivering, trying to hold back his grief, to keep it from Frankie who already had enough pain in him. *I'd do anything to feel that again, Frankie, and to hear Dad call me his baby boy again. Yeah, I'd do just about anything for that, even if it was only one more time.*

FROM ACROSS THE PARK, eyes like school glue and milk watched the little boy run away from his brother and wished he'd run just a little further, maybe even into the very same slant of darkness those eyes were peering out into the day from.

He felt his mouth turn down when the child perched on a swing and simply seemed to wait for the elder boy to arrive. *Enjoy it while you can Vanwah Feya,* it thought, spying movement at the school as one of the side doors came open and the old man peered out into the park, watching the boys move toward the slide tower.

*Does he see me?* it wondered, moving gently back into the shadows. *Do not interfere old human.* It wanted to charge across the playground, to grab that aging nuisance by the throat and squeeze until his head came free, or turn him inside out like Ne'Min had done to the father just two years before. *Patience. Time, all in due time.* It drew back further still as the salt and pepper haired, black man moved cautiously toward the two boys in the park.

"Frankie? Nick? S'at you boys?" Harry asked, ducking into the doorway as Nick got to his feet, his monkey of a brother still clinging to his neck. "Hey, Harry," Nick smiled wanly.

"Wha'choo boys doin' out here this early?" he asked.

"We came to see you. Nicky says you gave him this," Frankie pointed to the gold chain around his brother's neck. "And he's been trying," he climbed down from his brother standing beside him, drawing his arm across his eyes then under his nose, "but he can't make it work, and he wants to, even if he says he doesn't b'lieve it."

"Well then," Harry smiled tightly, his gaze scanning nearby shadows as he guided the children out into the light, "I guess you fellahs oughtta come on inside for a bit, huh?"

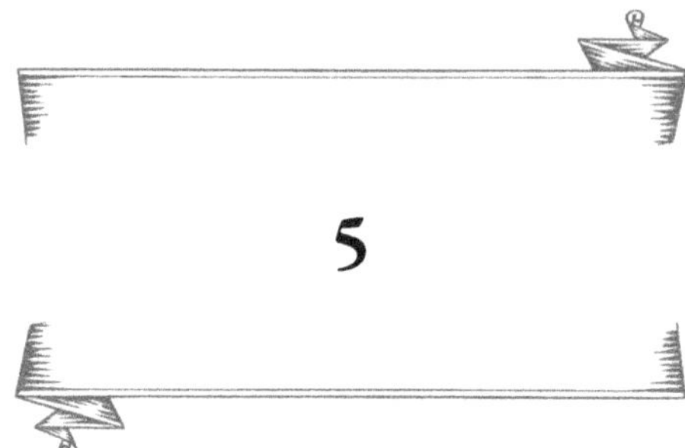

# 5

"Here you go guys," Harry opened a can of soda, handing it to Frank as he met eyes with Nick. "So what's got you all upset this early on such a fine Saturday morning, kiddo?" he asked the young Emerson.

Frankie shrugged bashfully sliding off Nick's lap to sit on the floor sipping noisily at the soda.

"Harry, how long did you watch yesterday afternoon?" Nick asked.

"Long enough," the older man hedged over the lip of his coffee cup, his eyes never left Nick's. "I saw Tommy and Bruce come up empty-handed once you had Frankie safe."

"Harry, what did you see? I mean, did you, did I?" he frowned, shaking his head. "Nevermind, this is crazy, it's..." he stopped, starting to push himself from the chair as his eyes slid downward.

Looking into Frankie's upturned face, he was blindsided by the innocent faith shining in those eyes. *Just 'cause I can't stand the pain of hoping doesn't mean I have a right to take it from him. He still needs his; he deserves to hold onto it.*

"You wanna know if you froze those boys," Harry motioned to the little boy on the floor as well, "... and your little brother here like on TV, don't you?"

Nick didn't even feel himself flop back into the chair, nor did he feel his head nodding while his mouth hung open in disbelief,

"How?"

Harry leaned forward, pulling his overstuffed wallet out of his back pocket and started thumbing through it, "We're gonna talk a little bit today about some things ain't anybody but a few ever gonna understand. But before we get into this, I gotta *tell* you boys something, and I'm gonna *ask* you something," he looked from one brother to the other, watching each one nod. *Two boys, one mind. I just want to give back, guys, for everything you did for me. I'm sorry.*

"Yes. You froze a moment of time, Nick," he started, then grinned as Frankie's eyes flew wide and a bouncing, clapping squeal of excitement slipped from him.

"I told you, Nick! I told you you're magic! You're gonna be a superhero!" he grabbed his big brother's leg wiggling it excitedly.

"Easy there, shrimp," Nick breathed almost inaudibly, his expression filled with disbelief and more than just a little fear as something he couldn't identify tumbled through his guts. "How?" he asked.

"I don't really know." Harry shook his head, "Listen, there's things you gotta know before you make any decisions about what you're gonna do here. It ain't all fun and games. I think you *saw* that the other night, right?" He looked deep into the older brother's eyes after a flick of a glance toward Frank.

The little one watched something pass between the two of them and frowned but held his tongue for the moment, there were a lot of things adults and older kids didn't want younger ones to know, and the boy knew it.

"We'll get to that later," Harry nodded, watching Nick's eyes flick to Frank and knowing he understood.

"There's no way around it, there's no other way to say it. You have power, Nick. I don't know how it works, except that it works WITH you. When the moment is right, when the need is right and the purpose is right, *that* is when it works. And I can tell you, boy, it ain't been an easy road for you to figure it out, 'course, you had a lot of other things on your mind at the time," he chuckled and his eyes went far away for a second, "...heh, time. But maybe now we've gotten your feet on a better road. What you'll be able to do eventually isn't a joke, it's not for fun; it's a double-edged sword. There's things you'll be able to do, Nick, that are gonna be bound only by your own imagination, *but*, there's a burden, and a price that comes with it." He handed Nick the photograph.

"Sad thing is, you're gonna get the burden no matter what you choose. It's part of who you are. So you gotta make a choice. Do you want the power and all the bullshit that's gonna come with it, or do you wanna just go on letting life shake you around the way IT wants, like a dog with a tug sock?" he asked. *Easy, you know he's gonna do it. He always has and he always will; it's his destiny.*

Nick watched his fingers tremble as he took the picture the older man offered. He felt his brows furrow and his mouth turn tight as Frank pushed himself to his feet, leaning over his brother to look at it, too.

He looked at Harry. "Who's that?" he asked. "He looks like Nicky, only bigger." Nick met Harry's eyes for a moment before the older man looked at Frankie smiling.

The young boy's eyes popped wide with understanding, "That IS Nicky? How'd you do that!?" he asked. "Did you do it on the computer?"

Harry leaned over, moving his finger over each image. "That's me," he pointed to the one in the middle. "I was around seventeen then," he huffed and shook his head, then moved his finger to the Nick yet to come. "That's Nicky five years from now," then back to the other side, "and that's you, Frank, ten years old."

Frankie frowned, "I look weird."

"You ARE weird, shrimp," Nick swept a hand over the boy's head.

"You look mad, Nick," Frank scowled then leaned even closer to the picture. "Hey! You got a scar!" he ran his finger down the scratch on the left side of Nick's face. "Look," he looked back and forth between Harry and his big brother.

"How'd you get that?" he asked, "is it from this?"

Nick turned his eyes up questioningly to Harry. "It ain't from that, but how you got it? You never said," the older man shrugged.

Nick shook his head, letting Frankie snatch the photo from his fingers and sit on the floor looking intensely at the images there. "Harry, this can't be. I don't..." he stopped to gather his windblown thoughts. "This isn't really real, this *can't* be real!" he panted against the tightness in his chest.

Slowly, the older man nodded, "I can't imagine ANYONE feeling anything different than what you are, but you're *meant* to be able to handle this, Nick. You may not think you can, but it's right, you are *meant* to have this, but you're not the only one."

He rushed forward before either of the boys could ask about others just yet. "But it IS real, and now, with what you did yesterday, so is the danger."

He watched Nick's hand stretch out to grasp his little brother's as the color drained from the ten-year-old's face. "Danger?" he whispered.

Slowly, Harry nodded, "Yeah. There're things out there that don't want you to use your power, things that move in darkness and shadow…" *and they want you both Nicky.* "…and they don't want you to learn to use it, to exercise it or to *grow* it."

"Grow it?" he asked.

"Inside you," his lips twitched in a way that told Nick he was hiding something. *What's he NOT telling me?* he wondered. *He said there were others, Frankie?* He startled as a memory leaped into his awareness.

*A piercing scream sent shockwaves through the corners of his body, making him shake and have to pee. Daddy's voice rumbled down the hall, "They're here! Get the boys!"*

*He was just sitting up, sliding his feet into his floppy dog slippers when the floor shook under his feet and downstairs. It sounded like the the time the tree that used to be in the front yard got hit by lightning and scared him bad enough to make him wet the bed.*

*Uncle Ryan, one of Daddy and Uncle Howie's friends from work, burst into the room with mommy running in behind him. Mommy's shiny white face and wet eyes were scared as she noted her big boy already up and on his feet. Ryan went fast to Frankie's bed, flipped the baby into his arms, then put him into Mommy's hands. Scared, and shaky, she looked at the baby as if she'd never seen him before, then shoved him into Nick's embrace.*

*Frankie's feet curled around his big brother's waist. "Mmm?" he moaned, draping his arms around Nick's neck.*

*"Get out to the car, NOW!" Mommy screamed.*

*"Nicky?" Frankie mumbled against his neck.*

*"I gotcha, Frankie." The older boy dashed out into the hallway, turning at the sound of Daddy's deep voice rumbling from the far end where a dark figure kept him from his family.*

"What kind of things?" he asked, barely able to draw a breath through his tightened chest.

The older man's eyes flicked to Frankie who was wholly focused on the photo.

"Things that want the world to be a different place, a different way, a way that can't ever be allowed. They're called schades."

The older man read the look on the boy's face, a sense of fear and uncertainty so easy to see at this age, so open and vulnerable compared to the young man Harry had known. He dropped a hand onto the child's shoulder and smiled gently, "You can't stop it, Nick, it grows *with* you, it IS you and who you're meant to be." He stopped, feeling his eyes mist up until he blinked them dry again.

Frankie hopped to his feet, pulling at his pants and crossing his legs. "Don't say anything m'portant till I get back! I gotta go pee," then dashed out the door and down the hall.

Once Frankie's footfalls softened in the distance, Harry leaned forward, "From what you've told me, well, WILL tell me eventually, the visions are going to get more intense the older you get."

Nick nodded, but that wasn't what was important to him. "Is Pigg gonna hurt Frankie? Does it *have* to happen, or was it just that one time?" Nick gushed against his racing heart.

Harry's eyes began to water, "I'm still not sure, but I do know that when it *has* happened 'cause you weren't home, a lot of things got worse…" he breathed deeply and reached for the boy's shoulder. "Nicky, you gotta *tell* someone boy." He cupped the boy's face in his gentle and calloused hand.

Nick's eyes bulged wide and he shook his head, "No! I can't! He'll make it bad, and mom," he shook his head and huffed, "he'll make it bad for her. He yells at her and calls her horrible things, and I think maybe he even hits her sometimes. I can't."

"How about your Uncle Howie? Can't he help?"

"We haven't seen him since," Nick shook his head.

"The night your father was murdered," Harry finished and nodded. "Nick, what killed your dad… you can't abuse this gift you have, you can't overdo it. You have to be very, very careful. It's not a game; these things are attracted to people like you, like they were to your dad."

"What about Frankie, you said there were others? Others like me? Is he one of them?" he asked, looking over his shoulder.

Harry frowned, his expression uncertain. "I don't know. When we first met, Frankie had already been hurt so much, you both had. If he has any kind of a gift, I never knew it for certain, and God knows you'd never admit it; but you once thought that maybe it was 'cause he was so broken inside." He leaned forward again. "Please, Nicky, don't let that bastard keep hurting you. Tell your momma. I told you what I told you because your momma loves her boys so much! If she knew, nothing could stop her from helping you." He watched the young boy shake his head, his eyes wide and terrified.

"No! Harry, I'm in charge! I'm the one she trusts to take care of things, to take care of Frankie and the house, and to get things done. As long as he's okay, that's all that matters," he tried to explain.

"Nick..."

He shook his head. "No! She gave him to ME, Harry! That night, *ME*! He's *MINE,* and I have to keep him safe! That means making sure she can do her job without worrying about US! Besides," he sniffed, "she'll cry, and she'll hate me for making things harder than they already are," he pleaded desperately, water filling his eyes, clouding his vision as something sick started to wind in his tummy. "She'll be so ashamed..."

"No she won't," he insisted. "She'll be proud her boy's been so brave, so strong. Strong enough to tell."

Nick shook his head, tears flowing freely now as the sound of Frankie's footsteps grew firmer the nearer he drew. "Please don't tell, Harry, *please,*" he wiped his nose on his sleeve and pushed the tears off his cheeks.

Harry shook his head, torn between honoring the wishes of his life-long friend, and doing what he'd done a handful of times before, even though it never came to any good.

"Please?!" Nick breathed again, his crystal blue eyes glowing desperately as he clutched the man's hand and sleeve.

*I got one more shot at this Nicky. If it doesn't work, if I don't do it right.* He sighed, then nodded, resigned for the time being.

Nick nodded, relieved when Harry's hand swept his head.

"Remember kiddo, I'm here, and you can talk with me about anything, okay?"

Nick nodded, wiping his face clean again as Frankie skidded into the janitor's office, the smile on his face twisting strangely once he looked between the other two.

"What'd I miss?" he asked, not at all sure he really wanted to know considering how tightly his tummy was twisting. Still, he slurped noisily at the soda, doing and acting exactly what he somehow knew they wanted him to.

Nick shook his head, "Nothing, I was just telling Harry about us missing Dad."

"I wish it was possible, kiddo, but with your daddy up in heaven, you gotta know he's watching over you both, and that he loves you both very much," Harry covered.

*'SUCH A TREAT, ISN'T he? The little one,'* the pasty-faced resident of shadows leaned forward, its lips almost touching his ear as he stepped out back to dump the garbage. *He's too young, at that age they talk, it's too risky. Better to stick with the older one,* he thought. *Speaking of which,* he pulled a small bottle from his pocket dumping the contents into his palm, *Only three left? I need more, can't have Mom getting in the way now, can I?* He huffed a chuckle and turned back, watching Lisa Emerson sway among the tables as she moved through her day.

The ancient and sinister creature slid back, sticking to the gray areas where those with closed minds would never see it, and waited. It would stay with Richard 'call me Dick' Pickerd, and it would wait until the shadows of the man's heart held sway, then it would try again.

"WHAT'D HARRY SAY THAT made you cry?" Frank asked while they waited for the light to tell them it was okay to cross.

"Told you, shrimp," Nick sighed, fighting the squirmy feeling in his belly. *Too much information, I can't. This stuff can't be real, I mean, it's just not reality. Maybe he's crazy? Does that make me crazy for listening to him? What about Frankie?* he wondered, looking down at their clasped hands, watching his little brother scrape stones from the crack in the sidewalk with the tip of his shoe. "It just hurt about Dad is all."

"Hey?" Frankie tugged on his big brother's hand. "We can go now," and pointed to the walk signal just as it turned orange again.

"Huh? Hey you want me to drop you off at Davey and Chris's?" Nick asked.

Frank shook his head, "No. We gotta practice so you can make it work whenever you want. I wanna help."

The sound of children playing emerged from behind them, drawing Frankie's attention to the playground that had only an hour ago belonged solely to them.

*I need information I can't get with him around,* Nick realized sadly. Even with the warm sunshine slanting right at them, showing off the deep reddish highlights in Frankie's chocolate-colored hair, the older Emerson found he couldn't shake the cold out of himself. *Harry knows, and he's gonna tell. He said he wouldn't, but would it really be so bad if he did? If he broke that promise? If mom hated me, could I take it? What if she left us? Or me? What if she took Frankie and left? No, I couldn't, I need him. She wouldn't do that, would she?*

As if they had life of their own, doubts spiraled dizzyingly through him, keeping his tummy clenching so hard he wanted to throw up, almost.

"Momma wouldn't leave you behind, you came first, I came last so it'd be me, but she wouldn't anyway," Frank shook his head having a hard time understanding the strange feelings that were rolling off his brother, "What'd you do that makes you think she'd want to leave us?"

A cold shiver ran up Nick's back, *he's reading me. How long's he been doing that?* "Nothing," he answered weakly, "just maybe she's not gonna wanna have to have a freak for a son," he muttered looking at the school building, he needed to go back.

"Don't say that! You're not a freak, it's special what you can do! Momma'd say so too!" tears slid down Frank's cheeks until he let go of Nick's hand to sweep them away.

Pushing the dark thoughts into a corner of his mind Nick turned back toward the school, hoping the sight of his little brothers' friends playing would be something the little one couldn't resist, "Yeah," he smiled softly giving the boy's mop a tussle, "You wanna help me do research?" he asked, arching an eyebrow. "'Cause that's what I'm gonna go do." "What do you mean?" Frank asked.

"Well, if this is something about time, don't you think it's smart to learn as much as we can about it?"

Frankie's slender shoulders bobbed up and down and a huff blew that one stubborn shank of hair out of his eyes, "What's to learn? It just *is*. I mean, you can tell time on both kinds of clocks, so what's else to know?"

"I dunno, that's why I'm gonna do some research."

"Sounds boring," Frank's gaze slid to the playground, his expression open and wanting to join them.

"I'm sure it will be," Nick smiled easily, then leaned down. "I'll be back in two hours, go play," then gave a gentle shove against his baby brother's back.

With the faintest hint of 'are you sure?' in his glance, the youngest Emerson barely waited for a flash of his big brother's smile before tearing off at breakneck speed toward the playground and his friends.

Nick smiled, somehow not quite surprised when the kindergarten classroom door opened and Harry waved him hastily inside.

With the door closing softly behind him, he wondered, *does 'time' even exist except in our heads? Man, this is gonna give me a headache, I can feel it already.*

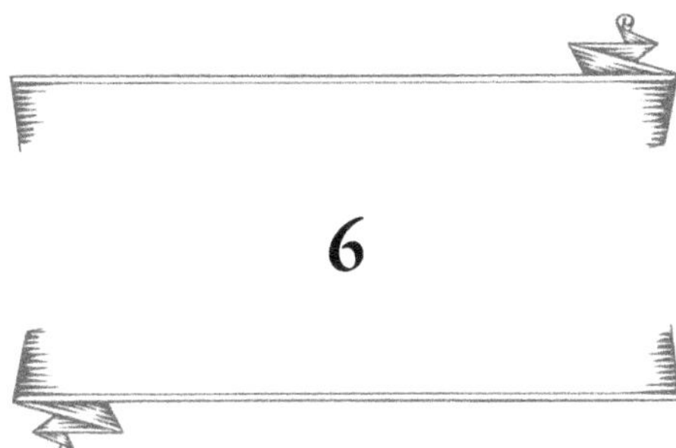

# 6

Chantal Mercury waddled behind the gimp mega-store shopping cart, her feet ached and her ankles itched they were so swollen. *Six more weeks and I can finally evict you my little love.* She thought with a soft smile.

Shoving the cart against the corner of her mini-van she pressed her hands into her low back, stretching out a kink that seemed to have taken up permanent residence there. She grinned as the baby stretched with her, saying hello in his or her own way. Neither Chantal nor her fiancé Julio knew what gender their first child would be, nor did they care. When it came to names for the little one, they were both adamant about their choices.

Julio wanted a Jesus or Jasmina while Chantal argued for either Abigayle or Anthony. Not for any particular reason other than those were the names she'd wanted for a child since she was one.

"I guess it really doesn't matter does it?" she asked, stroking the squirming bundle in her womb, "All that matters is that you're gonna be the most loved little one in the world," she promised, popped the back hatch and began unloading her purchases completely unaware of the milky white eyes that disappeared into the shadow beneath a shrub, then surfaced again beneath the rear fender of the vehicle.

The itch in her ankle turned into a tickle.

"Damnit, I gotta get these tired dogs up," she sighed reaching down with one hand while the other steadied her on the rear of the van.

When that frighteningly strong, dusty hand pulled her feet out from beneath her, cracking the consciousness out of her head on the edge of the van, there wasn't time to react. No one saw the beautiful bronze woman slide into the dark shadow beneath her vehicle. And surprisingly, no one bothered her purchases or belongings until the police arrived several hours later; and noting a streak and two spots of blood, took them into evidence.

*OH, MAN, NOT NOW!* Howie "Wee" Emerson felt the phone in his pocket vibrate, but had a bigger problem at the moment. "RYAN! Light!" he choked as those powdery yet gelatinous hands squeezed around his neck until purple polka dots danced in his eyes. He hated the feel of these things; they gave him the heebie jeebies. *It's like snot rolled in chalk dust! Gross! You'd think they couldn't be so strong!*

"Ryan…" he gasped before trying one more time to turn. He let his body drop at the same time he tried a frantic twist, and this time finally managed to come face to ashen face with the schade. *I am NEVER gonna get used to these things!*

"Coming!" his best friend, husband and business partner called, dashing through the darkness, his fingers fumbling to narrow the beam of the flashlight.

Balling his fist, he fought back the dark cotton edges that wanted him and swung, connecting viciously with the creature's jaw, the ferocity of his punch shooting flecks of shadow into the distance.

"Coming! I'm here, Wee," the older man gasped, shining the narrow beam into the milky dead-like eyes of the creature.

It screamed silently and flailed, forgetting the youngest of the senior Emerson's for the moment as it reached for the source of its inevitable doom.

"Say g'nite," Howie breathed harshly, flipping his favorite blade from the sheath at his hip up and out. In one smooth motion, he severed the creature's head before it finished screaming.

"Dang man! Where the hell were you!" he scowled, watching the fallen entity lose its cohesion until it appeared to be nothing more than a pile of sooty dust and debris.

"I went out for a burger, what do you think, man? I was saving my own neck!" Ryan snapped. "And what happened to your flashlight?"

"It's over there somewhere," Howie pointed into the corner where a glint caught his eye. "Damned thing jumped me from behind." He quickly tested the light, then stuck it back into his pocket. "You said it was just those two here?"

"Yeah," Ryan nodded, "just the two, well, that's all those kids saw anyway."

"What I don't get is where they've all been coming from? I mean, we haven't seen this many of these bastards since before Nick," Howie shook his head. "Its nuts," he muttered, wiping the dust from his blade before sheathing it again. He'd learned a long time ago that leaving the essence of one of *them* on the blade would corrode it, making it useless in very little time.

"I know," Ryan nodded, "and I don't know, but something's coming. I mean, even before Nick, it used to be what, one or two of these things a month? Now it's like one or two a week."

Howie nodded as they headed out to the car. "Yeah. Either there're a lot of people out there making a whole lotta different choices," Ryan snorted his retort, "or there's a whole lot more of these things than we ever figured on before."

"Well, since most folks can't un-do the choices they've made, I'm bankin' on door number two," the older man smirked as they tossed their blades into the trunk.

In the late afternoon light, their eyes met, each one knowing exactly what the other was thinking. They'd been taking these little trips together for so long there was very little they could or would bother hiding from one another.

"Beer?" Ryan asked.

"Saw a dive back at the edge of town," Howie nodded.

"You shouldn't worry, man," Ryan started a moment later as the tires cut through the sodden, slick mud road. "Dylan knows how to take care of himself, and you know damned well he's not out there looking for these things."

"He's my big brother, Ryan. Two nights ago his pregnant fiancée disappeared from their BED in the middle of the night. If he's not out looking for schades, then you tell me what you think he's out there looking for? Huh? Demons? Devils? 'Cause they're not *our* burden. What else is gonna be able to get past him?" Howie argued.

"He won't even acknowledge his own sight, and you think he's gonna go off chasing shadows? Huh? I tell you, you got the second most frakked up family I EVER heard of." Ryan shook his head, "Nobody LIKES being a psychic freak. I ain't met a single one that actually ever ASKED for it, but your boy takes the cake! Total denial!"

"Yeah," Howie nodded, "it's a shame it never made it easier on him."

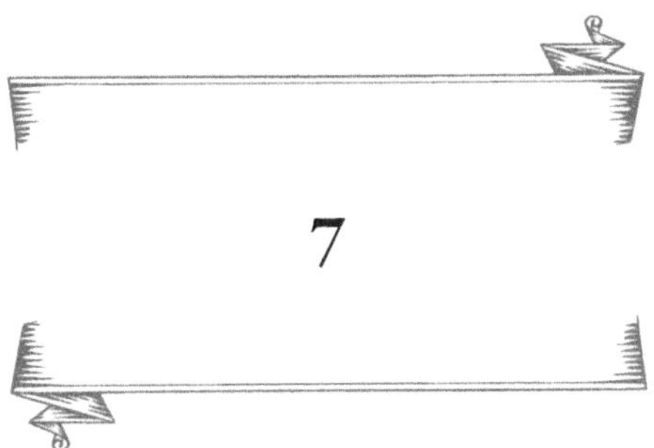

7

"C'mon, sweetie, help your brother get his bag packed," Lisa dashed back to her bedroom with her bathing suit in hand.

"Do we have to go, mom? Can't me 'n Frankie just stay home? I promise we'll just watch TV. We'll have sandwiches for dinner..." Nick followed her into the bedroom watching her pick through her lacy things.

"Honey, Dick went to a lot of trouble to arrange for us to have this night out. There's a show in the banquet hall and everything." She stroked his cheek, smiling brightly, a hint of the light that had attracted Nick Emerson, Sr. to her gleaming into the late afternoon.

"Mom says there's a pool there, too! So we can go swimming," Frankie grinned, spinning around in circles with his bag in his hand, making him wobble from side to side.

Nick felt himself smile at his little brother's exuberance, "Mom won't let you go swimming if you make yourself puke, shrimp," he warned, watching the boy stumble in ever slowing circles until he flopped down onto the rug.

Lisa turned, cupping her big boy's face and pressing her cheek to his temple. "You're such a good brother, Nicky; your daddy's so proud of you, I just know he is."

"Mom? Can I ask you something?" he asked almost breathlessly.

"Sure, sweetie," looking into her son's eyes she could feel the pull of their crystalline clarity. From the moment he was born, there was something deep in those eyes that scared her. It was something that if she'd had to name it, the only word she'd be able to come up with would be 'ancient'. But as ridiculous as it seemed to apply such a word to a child, let alone an infant, it was the fullness of it, especially in those first few days when many newborns still seem to be between worlds, and glimpses of it that sometimes left Lisa quaking with a visceral, primal fear. Nana Emerson, her husband's mother, was the only person on earth that she'd ever confided those feelings to, and all she'd done was smile indulgently, pat Lisa's hand and tell her, 'You'll get used to it, dear'. Sometimes Nana made Lisa furious.

As she looked into the sparkling ice blue eyes he'd inherited from his father, a lifetime's worth of love flooded her, speckled with the torment of that life cut short and the scars left on the children they'd made. Barely able to breathe for the weight of it all, she found herself on her knees before her eldest, her hands on his shoulders, in a way keeping him at bay in spite of the fact that she wanted nothing more than to clutch him to her breast while mist glittered in the corners of her eyes.

"Did...would you..." he struggled, honestly not knowing where to begin or how. *Harry seemed so sure.*

*"...would you," he took a deep, steadying breath as his mother leaned back, looking him deeply in the eyes, sensing something perhaps. "Could you still love me if I told you Mr. Pigg does things?" he blurted, touching his mother's eyes with his own before they darted away, full of shame.*

*"Wha...?" Lisa breathed, feeling a weight in her chest as her hands gripped her boy's shoulders, trying to keep her balance. "What kind of things?" she was barely able to ask.*

*Nick felt himself look down, burning with embarrassment and humiliation, then he thought of Frankie, of what could have happened, and so he muttered, "Dirty things, and he wanted Frankie the other night, but he was in with me so he couldn't, 'cause I kept him safe..."*

*When he looked back up, the room around them had changed, the light had grown to the rich gold that comes just before dusk and Nick was peering out into the living room from his slightly open bedroom door.*

*Mom and Pigg were yelling, Frankie was sitting on the floor with his knees in his chest, crying softly and so was Nick, just as it happened.*

*Mom raised her arm, pointing to the boys' bedroom with one hand, then to the front door, ordering him to "GET OUT, you sick bastard!" when something inside the man snapped.*

*Nick watched the back of his hand hit their mother in the face. He watched her turn with the blow, stumble over her feet and put her hands out to catch herself.*

*He watched her hands hit the center of the flimsy plywood coffee table and saw the top split, part of it folding upward as her knee came down on the edge. And when she was done falling he could see shiny red shafts of wood sticking up through her back while her body trembled for a moment before laying still.*

"*MOOOOOOOOOOM!*" he screamed.

"What honey?" Lisa asked again with a faint shake to his shoulders, all the while she kept her bright smile beaming into his eyes, hoping it didn't look as stiff as it felt. *Oh, God, what was that? Why'd he do that?* In the back of her head the word taunted her, *'seizures.'* It even sounded like Nana's voice, *'they started when he was entering his teens, but don't worry, they don't last long and he'll be over them in no time. At least that's how it was with Nicholas.'*

"Wou..." he cleared his throat, "would you uhm, be mad if I brought my book?" he gasped, feeling vaguely dizzy as the blood drained down to his feet.

Her own cornflower blues sparkled as she kissed the boy's temple. "Of course not, honey. What book are you reading?" she asked. "Something for school?"

Nick nodded stiffly, "Yeah."

"Must be important, is it for a report or something that's due?" she asked, the awkward moment between them dissipating in the way of a passing cloud on a summer day.

He shook his head weakly. "Just an assignment," he muttered, shuffling from her room back toward the one he shared with Frank. His chest was tight and crampy feeling, and for some reason he couldn't quite be sure of, tears pinpricked the corners of his eyes as he angrily shoved various pieces of clothing into his overnight suitcase.

"NICKYYYYYY! COME IIIIIIIN!" Frank called from the edge of the pool, grinning brightly.

Nick looked over at his mother lounging in the chaise next to his, he readily caught her wink and faint nod of permission. He really did want to go play with Frankie, and be splashing around in the water. He wanted to play basketball, and do cannon balls off the short little diving board, and since

Pigg hadn't come yet, and Nick didn't have to worry about the hungry way the cruel man might look at him, Nick put his book down and ran across the deck.

He leaped into the deep end and with his knees tight to his chest splashing a spray of water high into the air while Frank worked his way, concentrating on the right strokes, toward him.

"This side of the rope mister!" Lisa called, making sure her eldest was on the shallow side of the divider. She knew he'd never let anything happen to Frank, *but accidents happen all the time, otherwise they'd call 'em 'intentionals'.* Her eyes flicked to the book her son left behind and she fought a chill. *'Jonathan Livingston Seagull,'* she thought, glancing nervously at her eldest. *It's normal reading for a kid his age; thousands of kids read that book every year,* she tried to assure herself.

Filled with love, she watched Nick hold Frankie over head so he could throw the ball into the hoop. When he made the basket, her eldest gave a 'one, two, three,' then tossed the little one several feet away. Frank's squeal of delight, even with the short flight, brought her an instant of reassurance.

She glanced at the book again and chewed her lower lip. *Maybe I should call Nana, find out how old Nick was when he started having his 'moments'. No, why should I give her the satisfaction? They turned their backs on us when we needed them the most, left us floundering, left me. At least the boys, they never should have turned away from the boys. How DARE they!* Her temper flared just as it did every time she let herself think about their selfish retreat and abandonment. It was as if without Nick, she and their children didn't even rate. *Still, it's a matter of his health.* She tried to be rational.

Her mind turned to this afternoon, the waxy sheen on her son's face, the pallor as his blood fell to his feet, the faint almost electrical hum through his body as she touched his face then let him go. *Please don't let Nicky have got it, please let it have skipped my boys. Nick, I love you baby, but please look after our boys; help them be well.*

HOWIE FELT HIS MOUTH pull down as he replayed the voice mail message, "The boys need you now. It's starting," he heard again.

Seven words before a click. *Who the hell are you?* he wondered, his thoughts turning immediately to Nick's sons.

He hadn't seen them in over two years, not since the night of his brother's murder, not since the night that unnaturally strong schade had found them. He'd hoped that by staying away, Lisa and the boys would be safe, that their scent would be lost and they'd be left alone.

Math came to mind, leaving him thinking for a moment. *Nick's only ten! It can't be starting yet, but it could explain the increase.*

The memory of the night he and Dylan lost their eldest brother snuck up on him making his stomach recoil. The sight of Nick senior facing off with that unearthly creature, fighting for the lives of his wife and kids left Wee burning with fury. Then, to top it all off, putting them in the hands of the Emerson family's youngest in the hopes that Howie could somehow serve them better than *he* had, was a cruel joke that shamed him to his very toes.

*You gave your life, Nick; why didn't you point it at one of us?* His stomach squeezed when the scene replayed in his mind's eye, the wet gurgle that splattered through his big brother's throat as the front of his body was cleaved open. *I'm sorry, Nick. I froze, I didn't know what to do, man. But I helped her get the boys out. I helped at least that much.*

Knowing his nephews were in the car with Emily, and Ryan at the bottom of the stairs, his gun trained on Nick or that *thing,* all he could do was keep Lisa out of the line of fire as that creature literally unmade his big brother.

Nick senior was a man who'd dared to make the life he WANTED. He'd done his level best to teach Dylan and Howie that life was a gift wasted if one didn't SEEK what they desired and strive for it in the face of any obstacle.

And all the youngest of the senior Emersons had been able to do was watch him suffer. Howie'd been too stunned, too frightened by the unusual amount of power the impossible creature exhibited as it literally turned his big brother inside out, leaving the man somehow still alive, to do more than gape.

Later that night, Lisa forgave Ry when he told her he'd somehow missed the 'intruder' as she referred to the thing.

Wee in turn, forgave *her* for needing to think her husband had been killed by something mere and mortal.

He re-lit the screen on his cell and cursed the word, "Unavailable" that should have instead been a return call number. *Who the hell are you? What do you know?* He wondered as he scrolled through the phone book and called Lisa without so much as a glance at the clock.

ONCE HE KNEW THAT HE and Frankie were going to be sharing the second bed in the room, Nicky was able to find some enjoyment in the little excursion Dick had planned for them. He hadn't cared much for the floor show in the banquet hall, but the band that came on later to cover some of his favorite Beatles tunes was pretty good.

He grinned when after dinner, with a belly full of hot dog, fries and chocolate cake for desert, Frankie sorta flopped to the side, stretching out half on his own chair and half on Nick's lap, stuck his thumb into his mouth and fell asleep with his big brother petting his hair.

"You want me to take him?" Dick offered, opening his free arm though his other was around Lisa's waist as they made their way to the elevator.

Pursing his lips, Nick shook his head, "He ain't heavy."

"So what'd you think of the show, Nick?"

"I liked the Beatles band; they were good. The dancing and stuff," he shrugged, glancing at his mom leaning heavily on the older plump man and knew that soon she'd be very deeply asleep and even harder to wake. *He wouldn't do nuthin' with mom in the same room, not EVEN if she was passed out. He wouldn't dare!* he thought disbelievingly, but still felt the twisting, turning little creatures of doubt in his belly *gotta be being sad so much, she never used to sleep so hard before.*

"It was okay, but..." he shrugged, watching the numbers on the panel light up as the car came down for them.

Dick chuckled and ruffled the boy's hair. Nick barely even stiffened anymore, anything to keep that bastards hands off Frank.

"Yeah, well, as the saying goes, it's a long way from Broadway, but the cover band was pretty good. You three have a nice time today?" he asked.

Nick nodded, "Mom took us down to the pool, and me 'n Frank played basketball. That was fun."

"Sounds nice. Maybe we can go for a swim in the morning, huh? Just us guys?" he suggested, playing with the boy's hair again, then running his hand over Frank's head.

Numb and fighting that squirrelly feeling in his belly, Nick shifted his grip, moving his little brother's everything away from Dick and his sinister touch. "Maybe," he whispered while trying to crack a smile to keep the man's attention on himself.

From the corner of his eye, something darted through a shadow. Nick turned quickly, smacking his nose on Frank's head, but by the time he found the spot near the bend in the wall that led to the bathrooms, there was nothing. *A person?* He wondered but couldn't be certain.

"Why don't you let me take the little guy, huh?" Dick offered again, this time reaching toward them.

As the elevator door opened, Nick shook his head again. *You're not gonna touch him if I have anything to say about it.* "S'okay, I got him." He turned his head to look at the older man and backpedaled into an emerging guest, his eyes fixed on an ashen face that hovered between Dick and Lisa. Whatever it was calling skin seemed to be peeling in leafs. Tiny dusty bits of nothing rolled down over Dick's suit jacket and disappeared without a trace, shed by its mouth whispering at the man's ear. If it really *was* speaking, it was doing so too quietly for Nick to hear, but all the while it kept its milky white and gray mottled eyes fixed on him and Frankie.

"Besides, you got mom, she's tired today," he muttered, wishing he could find some excuse to not get into that elevator with Dick and that thing together.

*It's not real, it can't be real. Is it one of those schades? Is THAT what it is? He doesn't see it! WHY can't he see it! Why can't he. What's it saying? It's gotta be me; am I nuts?* He slid into the car and leaned against the wall opposite that *thing,* never taking his eyes from it.

"Yeah, that she is, the diner's been hopping all week," Dick agreed, pulling her close to sucker a wet kiss against her cheek.

When the doors opened on their floor, Nick dashed into the hall then watched the adults emerge, relieved beyond belief when the door started to close leaving that thing inside the elevator car. He dared a peek into the dim light just in time to see the gray peeling face fade back into shadows. It raised its dusty looking hand and waggled its fingers at him, but it was that sinister smile still hovering in the air while the rest of it disappeared that left him with shivers on the inside. *Just like that creepy cat. What the heck IS that thing? WAS it one of them? How did he not see it? Is it the same one that killed dad,* he shook his head, following Dick and his mother down the hall to their room.

"Why don't you let me help you get him into his p.j.'s?" Dick suggested, pulling out the pair of cartoon jammies Frankie packed.

"I gotta wake him up anyway so he can go pee," Nick explained, grateful for that bit of the truth. "C'mon, Frankie, gotta go potty before bed, okay?"

Slowly, the little boy's eyes came open, his feet moving along side Nick's toward the bathroom.

"DON'T YOU HAVE SOMETHING to say, sweetie?" Lisa yawned tiredly from the bed she and Dick were sharing.

*Thank you for NOT... nevermind.* Nick shook his head, "Thank you."

"You're welcome, son."

*I'm NOT your son!* The boy bristled, clenching his teeth. "Nite," he choked, turning so that his back was toward the adults and Frankie was nestled safely in front of him.

Nick knew he was dreaming, but it didn't matter; in fact, he wanted to stay. This was, after all, exactly what he wanted, one more chance to be with his dad.

In this dream, he was still ten and yet it didn't matter. *His dad was still larger than life as he leaned back in his recliner with his arms spread wide. At his age, he should have shaken his head, smiling sheepishly and chosen to sit on the arm of the chair or on the floor, or even beside his father. But he didn't. He looked around at the memory of their old house and thought about his talk with Frank this morning and about how much, how hard and how deeply he wanted just one more chance to be held by his dad. So he slid onto Nick, Sr.'s lap and laid his ear against his chest, listening to his heart beat strong and sure and his breath moving effortlessly into and out of his lungs.*

*"So, what'd you do today, baby boy?" Those sparkling bright blue eyes looked into his while his hand stroked Nicky's hair and back.*

*"I missed you. Frankie did, too, and mom."*

*"I miss you all, too. I'm sorry I had to leave. I never wanted to go, Nicky, you gotta know that, right? I'd've done anything to stay with you and Frank and your mom," Nick, Sr. sighed.*

*He felt tears wetting his cheeks, and as his father's arms closed around him, his breath burned in his throat. "Dad? Something's happening to me," he sighed against the older man's worn and warm flannel jacket.*

*A clatter from the kitchen brought his eyes open. He turned to look at his father and saw that gray, ashen, peely-faced creature with one hand around his dad's neck and the other over his mouth. His father's arms pushed out, shoving Nick off his lap and onto the floor as the man-like, but not even remotely human, THING pulled back, drawing the senior Emerson over the back of the chair.*

*"No! Dad!" Nicky shouted, lurching toward him. He hit the back of the chair, turning it over, tumbling down to the floor through an open trap door, he dropped down a hot, stony chute that burned his backside as he slid through orange, glowing, rough rock corridors, past half-curved windows barred with columns of stone.*

*"Nicky!" his father's voice called from somewhere up ahead. "Nicky, get out of here!"*

*"No, Dad, no! I gotta SAVE YOU!" he cried, willing himself to pick up speed, willing himself to slide faster.*

*"Protect your brother!" He heard as his body crumpled and tumbled, skidding to a stop once he dropped from the edge of the chute onto a hot, earthen floor.*

*Black shadows writhed and moved, whispering around him, drawing his attention. Fear thumped his heart, his lungs pumped and his eyes grew wide trying to penetrate the darkness. 'There're more of those things down here; is this where they live? Is this hell?' he wondered, noticing an opening just beyond an archway of darkness.*

*Looking back the way he'd come, he knew he'd never make the climb. The chute was far too steep and the walls too far apart to be of use. 'Only one way to go then.' He edged toward the opening.* The thought of trying to wake himself up never even crossed his mind.

"RYAN, GET UP," HOWIE shook his husband awake before slipping from between the sheets to dress.

"Mmm?"

"Get UP!" he commanded, sliding his jeans on.

"What!" Ryan stretched, squinting his eyes at the frantically dressing Emerson. "S'up?" he asked. "Vision?"

"No," Howie shook his head, slamming his belongings into his duffel bag. "No, I don't know, something... something's not right."

"The kids?" Ryan asked, practically jumping into his jeans.

"Yeah." Howie slid his feet into his shoes, double-checking the room as he started packing Ryan's few travel things as well.

"Nick?"

"I don't know!" Howie snipped then shook his head. "Maybe."

"Was it a dream or a call?" Ryan asked, far more familiar than he'd ever want to admit with the workings of a psychic mind, especially since that's what he believed was at least partly to blame for getting *his* brother killed.

Howie turned to him, scrubbing his face in his hands. "I don't know! He just, he was surrounded by them. They were holding him down, they were," he shook his head. "Lisa never returned my call. Nick's ten," he shook his head and shrugged. "*ONLY* ten. I don't know."

Ryan nodded, dropping a hand onto his shoulder, "Alright, okay, so we go then; we'll take care of it."

Shakily, Howie nodded, the gratitude in his eyes saying everything as they glanced over the room, and with bags in hand, dashed out into the night.

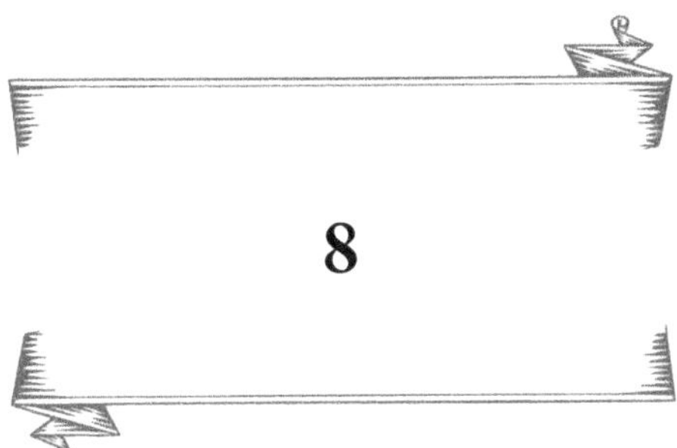

# 8

Nicky moved through the corridors, chasing shadows and the sound of his father's voice.

Echoing off the walls were whispers and whimpers, punctuated by the odd scream or yip of pain.

He dashed past half-circle windows at floor level. Layers of dark closing behind him, touching, petting, begging him to come back, to 'save me', crying for help, and though his lungs burned with air he was certain should have been hot, the mist over his eyes was icy cold as he blinked it away.

He cast a glance over his shoulder and ran headlong into a dead end.

"Nicky!" he could have sworn it was Frankie's voice calling to him. "Nicky, come back!"

'I gotta find Dad, shrimp,' he shook his head, turning around.

Two tunnels lay before him, one to the left and one straight ahead. "Nicky!" came the call again.

'No! Please, please! This is a dream, right? It's just a dream, then Frankie's okay. Frankie's safe; he's in with me, I got him. It's okay, nothing's gonna happen to Frankie. Nothing could wake him besides an earthquake or a nightmare,' he promised himself and dashed to the left.

'I just need to get Dad back, then you'll see baby boy. It'll be all right again. It'll be the way it's supposed to be.' His legs burned and the air in his lungs felt dry and cold, pinching in his chest. "DAD!

DAD! Say something!" he called.

He skidded to a halt in an abruptly open chamber. All along the perimeter of the round stony room at intervals were enormous fireplaces, each large enough to roast a man on a spit, with huge yellow and orange flames leaping and capering

63

*within them. In the center of the chamber lay a slab of stone, his father bound to it by chains at each limb and one around the neck. Nicky felt himself blush, realizing his father had been stripped and bound bare.*

*"Dad!" he dashed to the head of the slab, wrapping his arms around his father's head, kissing that face he loved so well. "I'll get you out of here, Dad," he promised, tracing the line of the man's arm overhead, to the chains that bound him.*

*"No, Nicky, listen to me! You gotta wake up, lil'man. You gotta wake up; you gotta learn to shut your mind, baby boy. Look at me, get up here and listen to me!" Nick, Sr. ordered watching his first born son's face appear before his, tearful and a little afraid.*

*"No, No, Dad..." he shook his head.*

*"LISTEN TO ME!" the man commanded furiously while tear filled eyes scanned the room, looking for the schades.*

*"You need to wake up, Nicky! You need to wake up NOW! You and your brother are all there is. You have to protect him! The two of you, nothing else matters."*

*"I do, I try, Daddy," he sniffed, wondering why he was gazing into the almost identical eyes he'd inherited rather than trying to free his father.*

*"You do so good, son." Nick, Sr. smiled against the water that ran down his face, his sorrowful smile deeply creased with evidence of abundant past joys. "No father could ask for more, but I have to. Wake up! Protect your brother! There's nothing more important than the two of you together, do you understand me?"*

*"No," Nick admitted, "but I will. Mom gave him to me, I keep him safe dad, I do. Well, I try."*

*"I know," the memory of Nick Sr. stroked the boy's head, "You do more than I have a right to ask."*

*Shuffling footfalls scraped in the hallway and the older man shook his head, "Howie and Dylan, Nick. Call Howie, get Frankie to do it, he'll come." He twitched his head toward the entryway his son came through, "Go. Kiss me goodbye, baby boy. Never forget how much I love you and your brother, okay?" His tears flowed freely as Nicky's eyes overflowed and he leaned forward, pressing his mouth to his father's cheek, wrapping his arms as tightly as he could around his neck and holding back a cry that wanted to split the dream wide open.*

*"Don't leave me, Daddy, please," Nicky sniffed, feeling himself pushed toward the hallway he'd come through, obscured by shadows as a handful of schades slithered into the room. They took up post around the slab, their forms turning solid while Nick, Sr. forced his tears to dry and his breath to even out, hoping the first of his life's best gifts was at least hidden from them, if not entirely safe. He was fairly sure he would have felt it if Nick, Jr. had woken up.*

*NICKY FELT HIMSELF pushed from the chamber just before the four schades took post around his father. The one at his head leaned over him, its hands on either side of his face, and before he knew it, the sound of his father's scream echoed and bounded around the domed chamber.*

*At the sound, so reminiscent of the very cry his father uttered on the night he died, Nicky shook and gasped. In a corner, he quivered, pressing his knees to his chest, arms overhead while tears streaked down his face and he shook his head. 'No, please, don't make my Daddy scream. Please stop hurting him!'*

*"Nicky? C'mon Nicky, please?" Frankie's voice called.*

*'He sounds upset. What's wrong, baby boy? What's the matter?' he wondered, feeling a tug, in his belly that felt like a grappling hook had been sunk into him and was pulling hard.*

*'Okay. Okay, Frankie. Nothing more important than Frankie and me together. Only for you, Dad. I'll be back, I swear I will,' he vowed.*

*As he traveled the barely lit corridors, behind him, peeling, ashen faces smiled slyly.*

"LOOKS LIKE HE'S COMING around now," a twisty sounding man's voice filtered into Nick's ears at the same time a sword of light ran through his eyes.

"Thank God. Nicky? Nicky, sweetheart, can you hear me?" Lisa asked.

"Mmm...om?" he cleared his throat, jerking his head out from under the hand that pressed against his forehead.

"Yes, sweetheart, it's mommy," she sniffed.

*She's crying? Why's she crying? What's goin' on?* he wondered turning his head toward her voice as her arms came around him, pulling him deep into her warmth.

"Frankie? S'Frankie, he was callin' me. S'he okay?" he asked, trying to focus in the strange over-bright room.

"He's fine, sweetie, he's with Dick..."

Nick's eyes popped open and he pushed away from her, "No! Not alone!"

Lisa's brows furrowed as she cupped her son's face, "They're out in the waiting room, sweetheart."

"Get me my brother! Please!" he pushed himself up on the cart as the doctors and nurses stopped what they were doing, one of them trying to ease him gently back down.

"S'alright, son, just lay back now," a man in blue scrubs tried to soothe. "You've had a rough night."

"NO!" he yelled, scooting back, feeling several different tugs against his bare chest then noticing the sticky patches and wires attached to them. At his side a monitor showed his heartbeat accelerate. "Mom!" he caught her attention. "Don't leave him alone! Please! Please get me, Frankie!"

Someone squeezed something into the tube that ran into the IV in his arm and almost instantly he began to feel sleep calling for him again. "Don't leave him alone with Pigg," he yawned as she slid him back down the gurney with a deep and puzzled frown on her face. Something in his voice had raised her neck hairs to attention.

Her darkly worried gaze touched Dr. Beckett's gentle brown eyes and noted the frown on his face. Before she could ask, he nodded,

"You can bring the little guy in here with you..."

Lisa was out the door with her heart in her throat before he finished his statement. Every other patient was beyond her notice as she drew to a stop at the edge of the carpet that delineated the waiting area from the triage.

"Frankie, hon?" relief coursed through her voice at the sight of her youngest sitting at a child's table working a silver ball through a labyrinth under the plastic table top.

He looked up and leaped out of his chair, dashing into her arms,
"Nicky's okay now, Momma? Did he come back finally?"

Tears pricked her eyes and sat heavy in the back of her sinuses as she nodded, squeezing her baby tight. "He did," she sniffed, "and the first person he wanted to see was you." She smiled then winced, holding him even closer as Dick approached.

"What'd the doctor say?" he asked.

Looking back at the doors that kept her son from view, she shook her head, "They don't know." *'Don't leave him alone! Don't leave him with Pigg?' Why not? What's my baby scared of? What have you done, you bastard?* she wondered.

"Can I see Nicky now?" Frankie asked, playing with the chain that held the St. Quirinus medallion Nick, Sr. had given her just after she accepted his proposal.

"Of course you can baby." She kissed his temple turning her eyes to Dick's, a glint of hard suspicion in there he wouldn't recognize if he was hit with it, even as she spoke to her youngest. "But don't be scared; he's gone back to sleep now, and the doctors put some wires on him."

Frankie nodded with wide eyes. "Oooh, like on TV? When the heart goes bip, bip, bip?" he asked.

"Just like that, sweetie," she nodded. "We'll be back in a bit," she said to Dick who wrapped his arms around her and Frankie, kissing her first then stroking the little boy's head before pressing his mouth for just a tiny bit too long to his temple. "I'll be here."

In the treatment room, Lisa put Frank on the cart with her oldest boy. "Just don't touch anything, sweetie, okay?" she smoothed his hair.

"'Kay, Momma," Frank nodded, sitting cross-legged beside his big brother while the doctor drew Lisa across the room to talk in hushed voices. Their eyes flicked back and forth between the boys and the waiting room.

Frankie leaned forward speaking with quiet enthusiasm. "S'okay, Nicky, you're sleeping good now. You scared me, poop head. I never heard you scream like that, but you made that ugly old ash-man go away. That's good, 'cause it looked like it hurt with his hands inside your head. You were all twitchin' and shakin', and your eyes did this funny thing back up in your head, but that's okay. I woke up Momma and then the ash-man was gone; so now you can sleep for real and then we can go for pancakes! Momma said we could, then you can have your hamcake sandwich. When you do, can I have some?" he asked, pressing one of Nick's eyelids open.

"Mm?" the older boy twitched his head away, the response leaving a huge, gleaming grin on the little boy's face.

"Okay, okay, you sleep," he stretched out next to his big brother, squeezing between his arm and his chest, then popped his thumb into his mouth just as Lisa and the doctor returned.

"How's your big brother, Frankie?" she breathed, only having the barest control over the hitching in her chest.

"He made a noise and I told him you said he could have his hamcake sandwich for breakfast after he gets some *good* sleep."

"Hamcake sandwich?" Dr. Beckett, the brown-haired, brown eyed man with a soft, easy face, asked, scooting to the side of the cart on a rolling stool.

"Yeah, he smushes a big piece of ham into a pancake, then rolls it up in syrup. Sometimes he can make it whistle before he eats it, like a big roll up!" Frank beamed, grinning at the kind eyes and gentle face.

"Man, that sounds good!" the doctor moaned.

"It's Nicky's favorite," Frank affirmed.

"Sweetheart, mommy needs to ask you a question," Lisa asked, drying her tears and steadying her breath.

"When Nicky woke up earlier, he said he didn't want you alone with Dick. Is there any reason you can think of that he would say something like that?" she asked, fighting the bats in her belly as a nurse came over with a needle and tourniquet.

"What's that for?" Frank asked, watching intensely as the woman filled several vials with his mother's blood, "Wow! That's neat!" he gasped, then looked at Lisa. "Does it hurt?"

She smiled as the nurse released the rubber strap, deftly taping a band-aid over the pinhole almost at the same time. "Not a bit," she smiled then turned to the woman. "Thank you."

"We should have the results back in a couple hours," Dr. Beckett nodded.

"I'm probably crazy," Lisa shook her head, "but..." she frowned, *it would explain so much, though.*

"Better to be safe than sorry," he smiled then turned his attention back to Frank. "So, Frankie, my name is Liam Beckett. I'm gonna be your big brother's doctor," he held out his hand to the young man.

"Liam?" Frankie asked, taking that warm, soft hand into both of his.

"It means William," he smiled.

"You call him, Dr. Beckett," Lisa advised, tussling his hair.

"I'm Frankie!" the young Emerson grinned proudly and introduced himself. "And this is Nicky. Well, Nick, but he lets *me* call him Nicky, just not other people mostly, 'cept Harry sometimes, and Momma."

"Frankie, hon, do you know why Nicky wouldn't want you to be alone with Dick?" Lisa re-directed the boy's attention back to the question at hand. With her eldest son's intense reaction, she felt something twisting in her guts. There were too many things that just made too much terrible sense if the puzzle pieces fit the way she thought they might. *All those nights I could barely make it to the bedroom after work, how just a couple drinks seems to just knock me out.* Her eyes flicked toward the waiting room. *If there's anything besides aspirin in my blood, and if you ever hurt my boys, I WILL KILL you!* she vowed internally. *Oh, man, Nick, please, please, baby, don't let me have failed our boys. Please!*

Frankie looked away from Lisa and Dr. Beckett and shrugged while he played with one of the ties for his brother's jonnie.

"I don't wanna talk about Mr. Pigg," he said with a faint pout.

Lisa stroked his back, "I know, honey, but it's kinda important."

"I already told Nicky, he makes my tummy do funny things. Nicky don't like him to be near me and that's good 'cause I don't wanna be; but it's hard on Nicky 'cause he says things are hard enough that we don't wanna make trouble for you, else he'll be meaner," Frank tried to explain while keeping the whine out of his voice.

Lisa felt herself turn crimson as her son's partial confession hit home, touching something deep inside that made her want to laugh and cry at the same time.

To the doctor's credit, his expression showed only understanding. "Frank, man to man here," Dr. Beckett leaned forward, motioning the boy forward, too, as if he wanted to ask him a secret question.

Frank sat back quickly and huffed, taking both of them by surprise. "Why does everyone keep asking me that?" he asked, looking between the adults. "Just that one time, and it wasn't a spanking or anything. I just made a home run at the picnic," he explained, noting that the look of relief that passed between them was very similar to the one Nick wore the other day after asking him the same question. "Why would anyone wanna do that anyway?"

Lisa was barely able to breathe as she asked, "Do what, honey?"

A sudden squirrelly feeling in his belly made Frank frown as he shook his head, "nevermind." *If it makes* them *feel all sticky like that, I maybe don't wanna know.* A moment later he sighed, turning his back on them so he could stretch out beside his big brother, returning his thumb to his mouth and snuggling in under the blankets, just as happy to leave adults and their tummy twisting questions behind.

A moment later, he turned over to find Lisa crying into her hands as Dr. Beckett spoke soft reassurances that helped calm her.

"S'okay, Momma. Uncle Howie's coming. He'll fix everything," Frankie yawned then let himself be drawn back down to sleep.

BEHIND THE CLOSED EXAM room door, Nick drew his knees to his chest and tucked the jonnie under his feet then pressed his back to the wall. "Can I have my brother and my clothes now? Please?" he sniffed weakly, dropping his chin onto his arms.

"Sure thing, kiddo," Dr. Beckett nodded, tossing the pair of latex gloves into the trash before leaning forward. There was a sigh in his voice as he reached for the boy, then with a barely perceptible twitch from the child, thought better of it and simply clasped his hands while leaning on the table.

"Listen, Nick, I gotta tell you, you've done a good thing here, the right thing," he leaned down, catching the young boy's eyes with his own. "There's no telling how many people, how many kids just like you and Frank, that you might have saved from him," he said softly, every instinct wanting to reach out to this young man before him, so stolid and very like his own son, he couldn't imagine what he might do if someone had hurt *his* child the way that evil man had hurt this boy.

Nick nodded. "I just... want... my brother," he said softly, then looked up with a hard ferocity within his glassy eyes. "Don't you tell him anything! And you tell my mom, too. NOTHING, NEVER. Frankie's never gonna hear ANYTHING about this EVER!"

Dr. Beckett sighed, "Nick, none of this is your fault; you didn't do anything wrong, you have to understand that, please, son,"

"DON"T CALL ME THAT!" he hollered angrily as the tears burst forth and he buried his face.

"You're right, I'm sorry," Dr. Beckett nodded, smiling faintly as the young boy lifted his eyes, surprised to hear an admission of a mistake from an adult.

"The point is, you can't blame yourself."

"I don't even want my *mom* to know; she'll look at me different. She'll feel bad, and I promised I'd never let her or Frankie get hurt! I promised I'd look after them, I should've been," he shook his head, his teeth sinking into his forearm, "better."

Dr. Beckett bit back a sharp breath while shaking his head, *where the heck did he get this sense of responsibility! It's NOT his fault!*

"'Kay, Nick, listen up. I'm gonna send in your mom and Frankie. I think she even brought back the makings of a hamcake sandwich for you,"

At this, Nick's eyebrows arched upward hopefully.

"Your mom knows something is up, she's a smart woman, and I don't know if you can get this right now, but as responsible as you feel for what you consider 'making trouble', she's being kinda smushed. She doesn't know for sure that he hurt you, and *not* knowing is gonna hurt her something awful. So, I HAVE to tell her what you've told me." He held up his hand as the boy bolted up straight with a horrified look on his face.

"Not the details, just that the man hurt you and that he tried to go after Frank the other night. This isn't going to be easy for any of you, but I'm gonna make you and your mom both a deal," he cocked his eyebrow, waiting to make sure he had the little boy's interest. "We'll let one of the nurses look after Frank for a few minutes while I lay a few things on the line between you two, and before I leave this room, you're both gonna agree that when either of you needs to talk about anything, what you're feeling, what happened, anything, any part of it, you'll do your best to just listen." He paused, letting his words sink in before continuing, "And YOU are going to talk privately with one of the counselors both before you leave the hospital and three times a week for a month once you're discharged."

"In *private*?" Nick asked.

Dr. Beckett nodded, "Anything you say stays strictly between you and the counselor."

Slowly, Nick nodded, "I want Frankie now, please?"

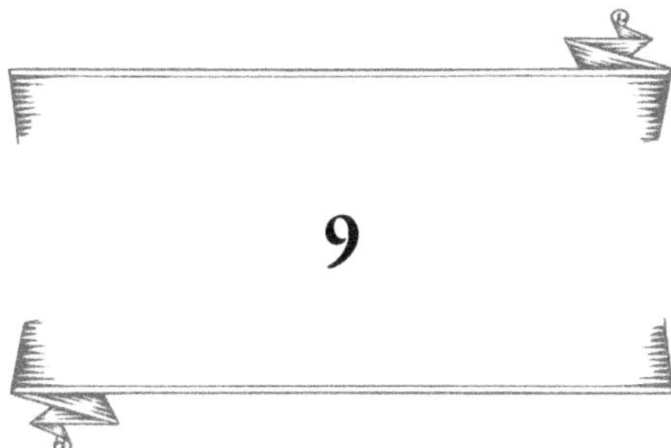

# 9

"I didn't think I would be, but I'm really glad you're here, Howie," Lisa smiled sadly, touching the back of his hand.

"I never should've stayed away so long, Lees. I just thought it would be better for the boys, easier on 'em," he flipped his hand over, grasping hers gently as he looked into her eyes, frowning. He'd been thrilled to see Nick and Frankie, and though Frankie'd almost tripped over himself to get to him, grinning hugely and hugging him as if there was no tomorrow, Nicky was a different story. Something dark had touched the boy, and through the desperate intensity in his hug, Howie felt him struggling against it.

"What's going on? What's happened here?" he asked, his stomach turning, deeply at odds with, or maybe because of, the elevatorized eighties power ballads the pianist was over-dramatizing just a few yards away.

Lisa's eyes slid toward the elevator. "Are you sure you can trust Ryan?" she asked in a hushed whisper.

Frowning, Howie nodded, "Lees, he's my *husband*, we've known each other since we were kids; he's family. What the hell's going on here? What happened to my nephews?"

"Nicky had a seizure last night; at least, Dr. Beckett is pretty sure that's what it was. It lasted almost four hours," she began.

He nodded, though he truly didn't seem surprised. A moment later, he smiled sympathetically and looked into her eyes asking, "Are you alright?"

Chewing her bottom lip, she nodded, then glanced away, shaking her head. "No. I failed my baby, Howie. I failed Nick, *and* Nicky," she sighed, squeezing his hand. "I just thank God he never got his hands on Frankie, too."

Her husband's youngest brother felt his heart leap in his chest, "*Who* never got their hands on Frankie? Lees, tell me everything."

"C'MON, NICKY, PLAY," Frank grinned, tapping the pile of cards between himself and Ryan.

"In a minute, shrimp, I'm almost done," he checked the book and smiled tiredly, glad to be out of the hospital and back into the hotel. "Just a couple more pages."

Ryan glanced at the seagull soaring on the cover, "You know, that was your dad's favorite book at one time."

"It was?" Nick asked, looking up.

"Yep, he was a big believer in the idea that there isn't anything we can't do."

"Like when I wanted Uncle Howie last night?" Frankie asked. "Got any threes?"

Ryan smiled and nodded, catching a glimpse of the older brother's puzzled look, "Pretty much like that," then handed over two cards just before Frankie laid down three 3's on the floor.

"That's what Dad said," Nick muttered.

"Got any kings?" Ryan asked, glancing from the cards to the older boy. "What's that, Nick?"

"He said Daddy said I'd call Uncle Howie," Frankie muttered absently while checking his cards meticulously before looking up.

"Go fishing," he grinned, looking between both of their openmouthed and surprised faces. "What?" he asked.

"How'd you know that, Frank?" Ryan asked before the elder brother could.

"He had a dream when the ash-man had his hands in his head and Daddy told him I'd call Uncle Howie, so I did," he shrugged. "Got any 7s?"

"Frankie!" Nick hissed.

"S'okay, Nicky, he's Howie and Daddy's friend. Uncle Dylan, too, but he won't say about his sidekick thing 'cause he don't want it," he looked expectantly at Ryan who, despite his sudden lack of color, fished out a 7 and handed it to the boy.

Nick slid off the chair and peered into his little brother's dark blue eyes, "Come with me, shrimp."

He didn't wait for Frankie to follow, he just knew the little boy would, as he led him into the bathroom and closed the door, then opened it again. "'Scuse us," he said quickly before closing it again. Nick felt plenty comfortable around Ryan, having known him all of his life, he was another uncle to them, but considering the sucker punch Frank just hit him with, he needed a moment to get things straight in his head.

Ryan signaled a thumbs-up, then after Nick closed the bathroom door, pulled his cell.

"Frankie's lit up 2," he texted to his partner, then stuck the instrument back in his pocket while eyeing the group of cards the youngster left on the carpet. With a quick glance at the bathroom door, he scanned the boy's hand and smiled.

"WHASSA MATTER, NICKY? Did I do something wrong?" Frank asked softly. He couldn't understand the strange look on his big brother's face.

"No! God, no." Nick grasped the little one's shoulders gently.

"No, I just," he swallowed, "I just wanna ask you somethin' in private, 'kay?"

Frank cocked his hip and huffed an unruly shank of hair from his eyes, "Is this about Mr. Pigg again? 'Cause with him going with the p'lice at the hospital, Momma said we don't hafta see him anymore."

Nick smiled softly and shook his head, wondering one more time if it could really be as simple as that. "No, it's not about him, it's about the ash-man, the *schade*," he corrected. "You saw him?"

"I saw him with his hands in your head, I told you that already. That's when you started gettin' all..." he jumped and wiggled in place. "Dr. Beckett said you had a Caesar, but that's 'cause Momma couldn't see the ash-man hurting you."

"Schade. But you knew about my dream, Frank? You knew what

Daddy said to me?"

"Uh huh, that was a scary dream place, but I didn't see it after I stopped huggin' you. I'm sorry, Nicky. I wanted to see Daddy, too, but then I got scared and I didn't want you to go 'way and stay with him and leave me all alone." He ducked his chin to his chest, unable to look his big brother in the eyes. "So that's when I got Momma and started yelling at you to come back," he glanced up. "Did you save Daddy?"

Nick shook his head, fighting a salty tang in the back of his throat.

"S'just a dream, shrimp," he sniffed then angled Frank's face so they were eye to eye. "If I've told you once, I've told you a gazillion times, it's you and me, Second Hand. S'always been that way, s'always gonna be that way."

"You fellah's alright in there?" Ryan asked through the door.

"You're the best big brother EVER, Nicky!" Frank tossed his arms around his neck, squeezing until Nick couldn't help but laugh despite his bloodshot and tear-glassed eyes.

"We're alright," he called, opening the door, waddling out into the room with Frank dangling from his neck.

"Ooooh, I gotta pee." Frank let go to race back into the bathroom.

"You alright there, Nick?" Ryan asked, splitting a soda between three cups for them. "Y'look kinda, not good."

Nick shrugged, perching on the edge of the chair. "So…"

Ryan cocked an eyebrow and nodded, "So."

"Soooooo…" Nick led. "You're not gonna ask what happened last night?"

"I kinda figured we'd let you tell us together, maybe once we get back to Nana's. Howie wants to bring you back there, you, Frank and your mom," he offered, wondering what the boy's reaction would be.

"We got school tomorrow," Nick shook his head.

"Mmm, my guess is you're gonna be out of school for a couple days."

As the boy sighed, a glint of gold shot off his neck. Without thinking, Ryan reached toward it, but to his surprise, Nick shied away.

Frowning at the shimmer of fear that crossed the boy's face, he pointed to the chain, "Can I see that?"

"Sure," Nick covered quickly, and drew the pendant out of his shirt, then leaned close but didn't take it off. He'd nearly gone crazy when he realized it was gone in the hospital.

"Where'd you get this, Nick?" he asked, something that croaked in his voice drawing the bright blue eyes to his.

"It was my Dad's," he shrugged, not wanting to rat out Harry.

"Yeah, but where'd YOU get it?" Ryan asked against the quivering in his belly.

Nick opened his mouth, but closed it quickly and sorta shrugged with a shake of the head.

The older man drew a deep breath, "Okay, if you won't tell me *that,* answer me this: WHEN did you get it?"

"A few days ago," he answered slowly.

The man took another deep breath, closed his eyes and bit his lips for a moment before asking, "Have you done it yet?"

Long seconds later, when there was no 'done what?' in return, Ry opened his eyes and let the air out in a rush, "You have. What'd you do?"

"What'd you do?" Frankie echoed, returning from the bathroom. Nick dropped the watch back down his shirt.

"I ran to the nurse's office and found you with a pack of ice pressed against the butt of your pants," the elder brother swung the conversation closed for the time being.

"Oooh, that meanie Tommy Haywood!" Frankie made a fist. "I just BET it was his! He likes those big, sugar block gums. I like the little bricks; they squeak against your teeth when you chew 'em really fast," he assured them while picking up his cards. "Hey, Nicky? Can I still get a soft Scooby that Bruce can't crunch?"

The older boy struggled to paste on a smile, "Sure thing. I made you a promise." he said, pinching away the mist that sat in the corners of his eyes.

RYAN WATCHED NICK'S head roll forward onto his chest with his exhausted body slumped snugly into the corner of the red brocade, winged-back chair.

Turning his attention to one of the beds, with matching brocade spreads no less, where Frankie sat with the remote control scrolling through a list of Free Movies the hotel offered. He gave a confused smile, *Nicky boy, you're giving me the heebie jeebies here. Aside getting lit up, what's goin' on with you? Is it just seeing schades? And maybe even more important, where did you get the pendant? And who told you what they're called?*

Knowing full well, as a big brother himself, that getting Nick to divulge anything was going to be harder than pulling healthy teeth, he decided to try another route, "So, Frank, what can you tell me about the ash-man?"

"I didn't see him long, but he was just standing there smiling all creepy and Halloween style with his fingers inside Nicky's head. That's when he jerkin' around and I got scared and got Momma, but he was gone when she turned on the lights, so she didn't see him," he explained absently while searching the channels.

In the chair, Nick gave a troubled grunt, his brows squeezing tight, drawing Frank's concerned attention before he settled down again.

"Do you know what he's dreaming?" Ryan asked, watching the boy's body language closely, watching his eyes dart back to the TV while his shoulders shrugged tightly.

"That's not a happy sound," he shook his head.

"No," Ryan agreed, "but you said earlier that his dream last night was scary. Could you *see* his dream?"

"For a little, but I got scared Nicky wouldn't come back, so I got Momma and I wished real hard for Uncle Howie just like Daddy said to." His face lit up and he flipped onto his tummy to watch the live action version of Scooby Doo who drew the little boy into a world where monsters were men in masks and dogs could talk.

Ryan, on the other hand, found himself contemplating the world of monsters that wanted to hurt two little boys that were part of the only family he had left.

A glint of light caught the chain around Nicky's neck, bringing to mind questions he tried to never ponder since the possibilities tended to give him headaches. *I'm not made for this stuff; what the heck good can I do?* he wondered, returning to the nightmare that had come to the Emerson family two years ago.

*He'd stood at the base of the stairs, frozen as Howie tried to wrestle Lisa from his line of fire. The schade had come out of nowhere, well... nowhere he could see and it was tearing Nick open like splitting an orange. He winced and felt his eyes fill as the man screamed in pain and another spray of red arced across the wallpaper.*

*In the light of the hallway, dimmed by the coating of red on the fixture, as Howie got control of Lees, he caught a glimpse of gold at the same time the creature laughed. A serpentine flash of metal and the pendant that had been passed through untold generations to Nick, and was destined for his own first born, disappeared into the shadows as the schade destroyed the eldest Emerson brother.*

*'For FUCK'S sake do it NOW!' Wee willed his thoughts to be heard just before Ryan gave his oldest friend peace.*

*All through that night, Howie, Ryan, and even the ever-elusive Dylan, combed the house and property for the pendant, coming up empty and finally calling the police, claiming to have stumbled onto the grisly scene when coming to pick their brother up for lunch.*

*In the front seat of the car, Lisa's shock-pale face seemed to almost glow as Emily eased the woman and her sons out onto the driveway. Ryan reached across the seat and closed the door between them. "Soon as she snaps out of it she's gonna freak," he warned the woman. "Just make sure Nana..."*

*"I know, Ry, we'll take care of it," she assured him as he backed down the drive to return to the search. "Just find it if it's there and pray they didn't get it."*

*"I'm prayin', baby, I'm prayin'," he nodded, leaving them behind in the still of the night. Emily was similarly slaughtered later that year.*

*Where did you get it Nicky, and where'd THEY get it?* His eyes slid to Frankie. "Y'know that pendant was your father's at one time," he mused. "It's been in the family for generations."

The littlest Emerson nodded, "I know. Harry said it was s'posed to always be Nicky's."

"Oh yeah?"

"Uh huh."

"Who's Harry?" he asked just as Scooby took off into the woods, hot on the trail of a sack of hamburgers.

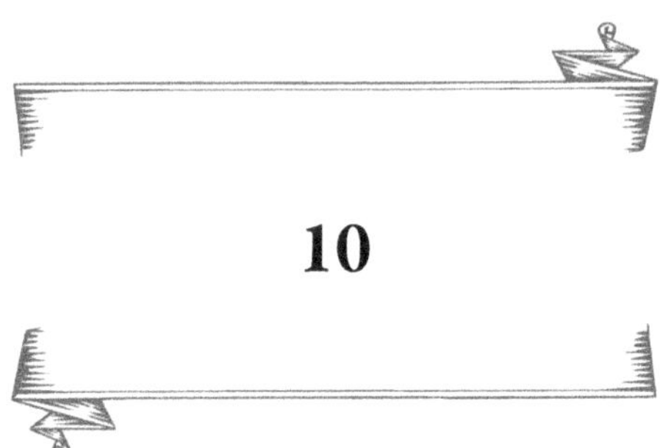

# 10

Lisa shook her head despite the war drums beating in time with her pulse. "They have school tomorrow," she protested limply, fighting the drowning sensation that seemed to be clogging up the channel between her mind and body. "It's not possible," she breathed, "things like, like, don't, they can't...and people can't just..." she shook her head, "...things like that just CAN'T exist!"

Howie fixed his gaze on hers, "I'd give anything to be able to tell you you're right. That the thing that killed your husband, that took *my* big brother out of this world, was nothing more than a man." He leaned forward, sliding a shot across the table to her. He watched her down the drink then look at him. "But I can't. Nicky's come into it, and Ryan just texted me - Frankie's lit up too," he frowned, shaking his head, something in his expression telling her he was worried.

"Lit up?" she asked.

"It shouldn't have come this early, to either of them; they're too young for this." *We have to get to mom, maybe she'll know something,* he hoped.

"If they're too young, then why? How?" she stammered. "I mean..."

"I don't know," he shook his head. "That's why we need to get the boys back to the house. Maybe mom'll have some answers."

"I can't believe this," she shook her head almost frantically.

"You're crazy, both of you, ALL of you! And if you think I'm going to subject my boys to anything more than what they've already," her breath caught in her throat just as she pressed the napkin to her mouth, using it to hold her sobs.

"I'm sorry, Lees, I'm really sorry. I thought there'd be more time, and I'm sorry these last couple years have been so hard on you. We should have been there, all of us." He felt like filth after hearing what she'd told him, after hearing what she'd discovered had happened to her eldest boy. *If I'd been a better, hell, if I'd been a presence at ALL in their lives, maybe the fucker never would have had a chance to touch him.. I was just trying to save them, to spare them, to keep them hidden. Who left me that message? Who knew what was going on and didn't help them?*

"Why?" she shook her head. "At the hospital, Frankie said you were coming."

"If he's lit up, then it was probably his call that woke me up this morning," Howie nodded.

Her brows furrowed. "He called you?" she asked. "When?"

"Up here," he tapped the side of his head. "I think his ability is probably similar to mine. See, Dylan gets visions, sometimes they're premonitory, and sometimes they're of the past. I don't really know the whole range. Dylan doesn't talk about 'em. They scare the crap out of him, so he pretty much lives in denial, but sometimes when it's bad, it's like he calls out, and I know he needs me." He sipped his beer, watching closely as she digested the information.

Her question poked timidly out, "And Nick?"

Howie smiled sadly, "Nick was the most powerful of us. He could stop time, but only in small increments."

"No," she shook her head, chuckling nervously against the tears. "No. Nana told me he had seizures when he was a teenager," she muttered.

He nodded, "That's how it started with him. We figure the hormonal changes at puberty are probably what activate, for want of a better word, the ability."

Her chuckles burst into laughter, edged in potential for hysteria. "Nicky's only TEN! He sure as hell isn't going through puberty yet!" she hissed.

Howie leaned forward, somber and unflinching, "Exactly, which means he'll probably wind up more powerful than Nick, Dylan AND me put together, especially if it's starting this early, Lees; and believe me, you really, *really* WANT that to be the case, 'cause the alternative is something you DON'T want to think about."

"What do you mean?" her words lay taut with fear between them. He shook his head, sitting back and taking a steadying breath.

"No, Howie! You tell me right now what the hell that's supposed to mean?"

He leaned forward, his teeth clenching through his harsh whisper, "How do I tell you, Lees? How do I tell you what Nick always thought there'd be time to tell you, but he wasn't able to? How do I do that to you?"

"Me? You're worried about *me*? Worry about my *sons*! Your nephews!"

The corner of his mouth turned faintly upward, "This is their legacy. Look, I'm not the one to try and explain it all to you. Mom really has so many more answers than I do, at least, I hope she does." He took her hand into his. "Please, come back to the house with us. We'll get the boys enrolled in school by the end of the week; they can finish out the year at the house while they learn how to use their abilities," he pleaded.

RYAN PEEKED UP FROM the computer screen as Frankie's head snapped toward Nick when the older boy's moan curled up into a squeak at its tail end. The movie was almost over and Scrappy Doo had just been unmasked and deflated. The youngest Emerson watched his favorite Great Dane flick the bad puppy into a wall and grinned, his feet waving in the air until something that sounded vaguely like

'Mmno...' slid out of his big brother.

*Wow, I didn't know a five-year-old could look that worried. Do you know what he's dreaming, kiddo?* he wondered, making sure to at least look like he was continuing his search while he watched the boy scoot off the bed and climb into Nick's lap. He straddled his big brother's legs, sitting on his knees, and leaned forward, petting his sweat slick forehead with more care than the average five year old usually exhibited.

"S'okay, Nicky," he assured before he sat up ramrod straight and gasped, his eyes rolled up into his skull and he started to fall backwards.

"Oh hell," Ryan dashed from the table, reaching the young boy just as Nick's arms closed around him, saving him from a fall.

"gotcha, shrimp," Nick grunted as Frank took a deep breath and seemed not to realize that anything in particular had happened.

"You okay now?" Frank asked, leaning forward into his big brother's chest with his thumb firmly situated in his mouth.

"Yeah," he breathed, "just had a little nightmare. Thanks for waking me up." He smiled awkwardly at Ryan while petting Frank's back.

"Welcome," he wiped his thumb on his shirt. "You wanna watch Scooby? I just saw the first one, but they got Scooby Two here, too, and it's free."

"You wanna talk about that nightmare, buddy?" Ryan asked, returning to the computer, but just like he knew he would, Nick shook his head. *Of course not.* He looked at Frank, *wonder if I can get it out of him later? Hmmm,* then turned his attention back to his search for any background information on a Harry Armstrong who worked at Robert Townsend Elementary School. What he'd discovered so far was unremarkable until he got to the beginning of the man's identity trail, which began just about six months ago.

The brothers situated themselves on the bed and a moment later, Ryan moved through the room, turning on enough lights to effectively banish most shadows and dark places from sight. "Hey, guys, you wanna order a pizza from room service or do you think you'll want to go out for dinner? There's a Game Lane right up the road."

He couldn't help but grin at the nearly electrical crackle of excitement that passed between the boys at the idea of going out.

"Game Lane? Really? With the skee-ball and dance mat and video games and the Wii?" Nick asked with the first sign of what Ryan would consider 'bright' emotion since their arrival.

"That's the one."

"Can we?" Nick asked Ryan.

"Can we, Nicky?" Frank asked at the same time.

"Absolutely," Ryan grinned. "If your mom and uncle Howie aren't done by the time the movie's over with, we'll go down and get 'em, drag 'em away from all that boring old adult business and feed 'em on soda and pizza until they puke. How's that sound?"

It was as if the room had been waiting for just the right moment to come to life. 'Whoo hoo's' and 'whoop's' of happiness bounced around while they 'high-fived' each other back and forth, which turned into a dizzying game of tag over, under and around almost every piece of furniture, then finally morphed into a tickling match that only Scooby could un-do.

*Thanks, Cal. I miss you, baby brother.* Closing the lid on the well of his loss, Ryan turned his attention back to the screen and the DMV photo of a fifty-three-year-old man, who six months ago seemed to have 'popped' into existence. *Who are you and what do you think you're gonna bring down on these boys? 'Cause, dude, I double DOG dare ya' t'try somethin'.*

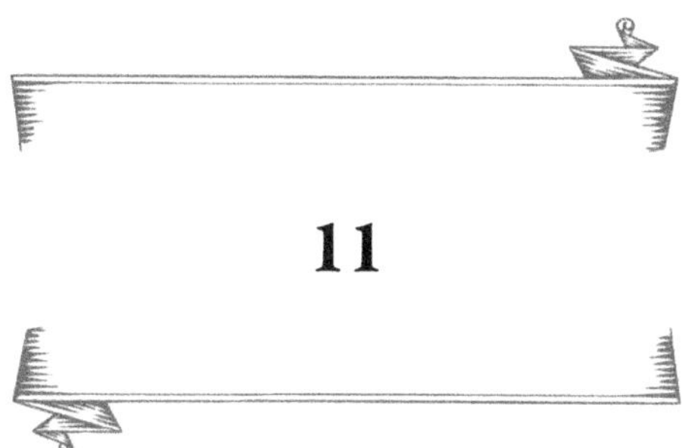

# 11

Laughing and panting hard, Nick guided Frankie into the bathroom, "You're good at that, shrimp! You'll be better than me in no time!" He leaned down, looking for feet in the stalls and guided Frank to the center one while he took the one on the far side.

"You think so? Really?" Frank asked hopefully, glad that there were stalls here. He didn't like using the open ones where anybody could walk in and see.

Nick peeked over at his little brother's swinging feet and smiled, "Yeah, I do."

When he turned his head, returning his attention to the business at hand, he shivered for a second upon noticing just how dark it was.

"What do you think about going to stay with Nana and Uncle Howie, Nick?" Frank asked.

Faint motion up close to the ceiling caught his eye. The elder brother slowly tilted his head looking up into gray outlines pushing forward from the darkness. He wasn't sure what he was seeing was real until that same 'damned creepy' smile that disappeared in the elevator last night spread through the ashen face.

He zipped up quickly, already starting to shiver inside. "Frank? You done?" his whisper trembled.

"It's almost here," the little one closed his eyes and tried to focus.

Before he could step back from the shadow, the face came clear and, though he wasn't certain if it was the same one that was whispering into Dick's ear last night, it looked like it might've been. Nick found himself mesmerized by the sight of the creature. It looked flaky and like it'd been dunked in gray dust.

As the fingers on that ghoulish looking hand bent and clutched toward him, it also seemed to shed something, but Nick couldn't be bothered with looking down long enough to tell what, if anything, actually ever landed on the floor. He was too caught up looking into its watery, milk and school glue eyes.

His head cocked to the side as he looked into those strange orbs, certain that just under all that sticky whiteness he could see something moving. It could be shadows maybe, or shapes, but he knew that if he just concentrated a little more he might be able to see inside, to see what that thing wanted to show him.

*I really should move now; I should just grab Frankie and run, that would be a really good idea. That thing's gonna grab me and it's gonna touch me and I'm gonna maybe be sick, but I'll never forget how it feels and it's gonna be cold,* Nick thought and actually felt one of his feet move backwards. At the same time, a change in pressure told him the bathroom door had just opened. *I should check on Frankie. Someone came in; what if he went out without me?* But what he *wanted* to do, and what he felt able to do, were two very different things.

He couldn't look away from that face, the dry curled leaflets of its lips seemed to crack and shed flakes as it mouthed something under that creepy smile. *It wants me,* he knew and he could have sworn it was trying to say something important, something that looked like the word 'father' when whispered.

In spite of himself, his hand began to climb through the air.

"Son of a bitch!" the curse came from behind, along with a powerful narrow beam of light that hit the creature's eyes dead on. Its face twisted in a horrible, soundless scream that vibrated through the floor as it was forced to retreat back into the last sliver of shadow in the stall.

When he was sure it was gone, Howie tucked the flashlight into his jeans pocket and crouched in front of his dazed nephew. "Nick?" he grasped the boy by the shoulders, *he's freezing!* And wheeled him quickly around so they were face to face. Barely inches away from his big brother stood Frankie, almost as pale as Nick, nearly terrified and looking like he was on the verge of tears.

"Nick!" Howie demanded with a little shake then started rubbing the boy's arms. "Talk to me, buddy."

Frankie lurched forward sniffling and wrapped his arms around Nicky's waist. He pressed his face to the older boy's belly while his hands rubbed briskly up and down his back. Howie watched the older brother's hands come reflexively around the little one and his gaze seemed to return to the moment.

"Frankie?" he asked, though his eyes remained on his uncle's. "What happened?"

"The ash-man came, Nicky! He came and you didn't do NUTHIN'. It was like you were hippotized and you wouldn't wake up!" he muttered into Nick's t-shirt.

"Schade," Nick croaked, backing out from Howie's grip but still holding Frank snugly. "Yeah it was, uhm," he breathed and frowned, *trying to show me something.* "How'd you make it go away?" he asked just as a sigh of relief puffed hard out of Howie and he clutched both of the boys to him, his gaze fixed in the corners of the stall. He was fairly sure it wouldn't come back with him around, but with the change in their behavior lately and their numbers, nothing he'd known before was certain anymore.

"Light," he shuddered then caught Frankie's gaze. "Was that the same one that came last night?" he asked.

"The *same* one? That means there's MORE than ONE?" Frank asked, clutching his brother all the harder.

"Yeah, there's more than one," Howie nodded. "Was it?" Frank nodded but wouldn't let go.

"Hey, shrimp, it's okay. It's over, it's gone," Nick soothed after a deep breath that seemed to bring him all the way back to the moment.

"You called it a schade a second ago, Nick. Did Ryan tell you what they're called?"

Both boys shook their heads, but didn't say a word. It was quickly very clear to the youngest of the senior Emerson's that these boys were going to be a challenge.

Nick was used to handling way too much on his own already, and Frankie wasn't about to make a move or say a word without his big brother's 'say so'. He looked at Nick, noting the pallor still holding tight to his neck and upper arms.

"You *look* like you've seen a schade. Twenty jumping jacks, guys; you don't want to upset your mom by looking all pasty, right?" Howie asked, fighting down a creeping sensation in his guts as the boys hastily flapped their arms and jumped until they were both a nice bright pink.

While the boys jumped, Howie washed his hands. He wasn't happy at all with how easily Nick seemed to be drawn to the thing, nor was he happy with how difficult it seemed for the boy to come back even after such short exposure. *What did it do to you, kiddo? What kind of nastiness did it plant in your head?* he wondered.

A moment later, all three men nodded that they were ready to leave the restroom, "Let's get back to the table, the pizza's bound to be there by now and we don't want your mom freakin' out in public, right?"

"Right," Nick nodded.

"Right," Frank echoed once he looked up into his big brother's face to judge for himself if he was really alright.

To keep his hands from shaking, Howie kept them in his pockets all the way back to the table.

"Everything alright?" Lisa asked once they returned.

"Yeah," Howie grinned, almost right-enough to fool Ryan. Almost.

Still, Ry kept quiet, until a genuine smile was coaxed out of him by the boys' enthusiasm as rattled on about how great this place was and how they both wanted their birthday parties here. Their playful pleading with Lisa was almost enough to drown out the rest of the noise that seemed to flow from every direction.

He shook his head, heartened by how quickly children could shrug things off and still find joy in the moment. When he'd seen Frankie's pale, scared face bouncing in the bathroom doorway, he was certain there was going to be something catastrophic. Fortunately, Howie saw him at the same time and excused himself.

Though it didn't appear that way, the boys' entry into the bathroom was the first moment they'd been out of sight all evening, and just like Howie and Ryan both feared, it looked like the schades might be stepping up their game. *Yeah, but why?* he wondered yet again.

"WHAT ABOUT THE STUFF at the apartment?" Lisa asked.

"Momma, are we moving?" Frankie asked, skipping between Ryan and Howie, then picking up his legs and letting the men swing and carry him for a step or two before skipping between them again.

"Yes, sweetie, we're moving."

"Tonight?" he asked.

"Not tonight," she smiled, shaking her head as they filed into the room.

She watched Howie lead the way, flicking the lights back on quickly then heading for the bathroom in a pattern of movement that felt far too practiced for Lisa's liking and reinforced the jarring sense of unreality that kept it's vice grip on her shoulder.

"Are we moving in with Nana?" Nick asked, startling her with his sudden appearance at her side. He watched his uncle's move through the room, absorbing it all, drinking in this new way of moving, of thinking and observing, all of which meant a new way of life for him, for his mother, and for Frankie.

*Mom's scared.* His eyes flicked to his little brother who made a bee line for the bed and the remote control as if he had no idea, *but he does, I can feel it. He knows. What are you seein' in your head, Second Hand? They think I don't get it, that I don't understand, but I do. I get it. They'll teach me how to keep mom and Frank safe.*

"For a little while," she stroked his hair and cupped his face. "What do you think about that?" she asked.

*Does SHE know? Or did they keep it from her?* Nick shrugged, "It'd be okay, I guess."

"Would you miss your friends?" she asked, guiding him to sit beside her on the bed.

"A couple," he nodded and shrugged, watching Frank flip the TV on and scroll through the menu to see what was on.

"I'd miss Harry. And Pete and Sarah, and Chris and Dave, but I wouldn't miss Tommy or Bruce! And I REALLY won't miss the dumpster, but I'd miss Ms. Rubens, she's nice," Frank tossed his two cents into the conversation.

"Dumpster?" Lisa asked, frowning.

"Yeah, Tommy and Bruce like to throw me in the one by the cafeteria. Sometimes I can still smell the spoiled milk for a long time after, too, especially on really hot days," he scuttled across the bed and patted her easily on the shoulder. "But then Nicky comes and makes me a bubble bath and then we do homework," he grinned, clinging to Lisa's back.

"Oh, baby," Lisa sniffed tearfully, the impact of just how little she knew of their daily lives striking her forcefully once again.

"Don't cry, mom," Nick said softly, leaning into her embrace while Frank pet his head.

Lisa sniffed, kissing her big boy and forcing out a smile, "You're right honey. Tomorrow we'll go get settled at Nana's and we'll start fresh, okay?"

"Can we see Harry before we go?" he asked.

"That janitor at the school?" she asked curiously.

"Mmm hmm."

"He fishes me out of the dumpster sometimes when Nicky can't get there fast enough, but that's not gonna happen anymore is it, Nicky?" Frank asked with an exaggerated wink at his big brother.

"Nope, it's not," he smiled, rising to his knees and throwing his arms around both Lisa and Frank together. He ruffed his little brother's hair, but favored Lisa with a kiss to the cheek that brightened her smile just like he'd hoped.

"So, what's the sleeping arrangement?" Lisa asked, looking between her boys. "Are you guys okay the three of us squishing in for the night?"

The boys grinned and somehow another wrestling match ensued that pretty much tore the bed apart, but left them both solidly crashed in each other's embrace before the nightly news had even half finished.

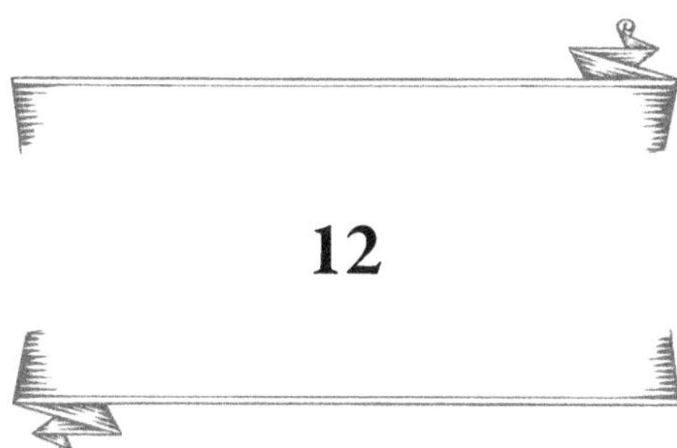

# 12

"C'mon!" Frank yanked on his big brother's hand.

A glance at Lisa who gave a quick nod had them tearing down the halls toward Harry's office, both of them grinning hugely with their fantastically 'legal' hooky.

"Okay, Mrs. Emerson," the school secretary slid a stack of papers in front of the distracted woman, "just sign your name by the highlights and we'll forward the boy's records to Douglas Adams Elementary- it's in district 51 and is the school they'll be attending," she stopped abruptly and stood up straight. "That is, if you want them to stay in public school?" she asked.

"Yes, that's fine," Lisa nodded, signing the papers.

"I hope Nick's gonna be alright; he's a good boy, they both are," the older woman smiled sadly. "But they can do wonderful things with medicines these days, and it's not uncommon for children who have seizures to grow out of them, too," she moved at a snails pace, checking and rechecking the documentation necessary for student transfers, then handed the stack of paperwork to one of the assistants to make copies.

"And he loves that brother of his. Do you know, I've never seen such a look of terror on a child's face as I did the other day when he found out Frank was in the nurse's office?" she gushed then quickly covered. "Oh, he just sat in some gum, there was nothing wrong, but," she sighed shaking her head, "it just does my heart good to see him look after Frank so well." She leaned forward and whispered, "Breaks it a little bit, too, sometimes when he's not able to pick Frank right up from the classroom. That poor dear."

Howie's arm around her shoulders was the only reason Lisa held her tongue. As well-meaning as the secretary was, all Lisa wanted was for her to stop talking about the boys as if she knew them better than their own mother did.

"But boys will be boys, now won't they?" she asked as a student assistant slid a manila envelope across the counter to the visibly stressed mother.

"Everything you need for both of them is in here, Mrs. Emerson. I've faxed over a copy to the registrar at Adams, as well as their arrival date set for two weeks from today." The young, sandy-haired woman smiled and offered her hand, "We're sorry to see you go, but the best of luck to you and the boys."

"Thank you," Lisa nodded, shaking her hand then the older woman's. "Oh," she turned back, "where can we find Harry?" she asked.

"Left out the door to the first corridor, then another left, and his office is the last door on the left-hand side before the "T" junction," the younger woman directed easily.

Trembling nervously, Lisa nearly bolted from the office.

"Lees, calm down, the boys are fine," Howie assured her while ignoring the fact that he was just itching to get to this mysterious janitor's office, too, especially after Ryan filled him in on his suspicions last night.

"I just want to get this done," she nodded then turned to her brother-in-law. "How could they let him out!?" she whispered, her eyes full of fear.

"I don't know," Howie shook his head, half boiling in his own anger. "But we're getting out of here, and we're getting all of you out of here; it's going to be okay. Ryan'll have the apartment empty in no time."

"I thought they were supposed to deny people like that bail!" she clenched her teeth.

"Funny, I thought they were supposed to..." he started but didn't want to aggravate the woman any further. "Nevermind, let's just go get the boys. We're here, they're here, Harry's their friend," *some friend, didn't lift a finger to stop that son of a bitch,* "it's going to be fine."

Just outside the office marked Custodian, he drew them to a halt, pressed his finger to his lips and leaned against the wall, listening to his nephews and this stranger, who six months ago didn't even exist.

"ARE YOU SURE?" NICK asked. "I didn't wanna say anything without asking you first."

Harry grinned, sweeping the boy's head, "Y'know, I really appreciate that, Nicky. Howard's your uncle though, he's family. It's okay."

"So are *you,* Harry. You said we're gonna be like brothers."

"'Cept you're adopted 'cause you're so old," Frank nodded knowingly.

The man burst out laughing and shook his head.

"Harry? Did you change things by giving me this?" Nick asked, fingering the pendant. "Where'd you get it?"

"Uncle Ryan and Uncle Howie are real curious about where you got it from, but we didn't say nuthin'," Frankie crossed his arms over his chest and smiled.

Harry chuckled knowingly, "I'll just bet they are, but that's a question best left for another time." He smiled, "You fellas go get yourselves and your momma settled in at your new house." He handed a piece of paper to Nick, "Here's my number. If you need anything, or want to talk about anything, any time, you come right ahead and call, alright?"

Nick nodded as Frankie unfolded the paper and read the numbers on it. "Harry? I think Howie and Ryan know, I mean, Frankie's pretty sure they know, you know, stuff," he tapped his chest where the pendant sat.

"'Course they do, kiddo, it runs in the family. And ain't nuthin' more important than family. They're the ones that're gonna teach you what you need, you just remember that," the older man nodded.

Nick nodded with him, "Are we gonna see you again?"

"C'mon now Nick, you know me better than that. May not be like this though," he admitted, patting his chest to indicate the man he was. "This is a brand new future for all of us. No tellin' what time has up its sleeve, it might not want two of me here."

"When are we supposed to meet you, Harry? If I screw up, it could undo all this 'cause then we wouldn't have met," Nick frowned, deeply confused.

Harry smiled softly "Well, after all my years," he stopped and chuckled, "I'm not entirely sure that's true."

"Listen, I don't want you to worry about any of that right now Nick. What is truly s'posed t'be, it's gonna be, so don't you sweat the details; they'll come as they're meant to," he nodded, then sighed, trying not to sniff back his uncertainties. "B'sides, I'm gonna give your uncles all the information you're gonna need for when the time is right. They're probably gonna come by and talk with me soon, so don't you worry about anything. You just go learn everything you can about controlling and using this gift of yours." He looked at the youngest brother, "You, too, Frank. You need to learn to control your abilities, too, make sure no one can use them against you." He leaned over, pressing his forehead to Frank's, his body was quivering and tears shone bright in his eyes, "or your brother, okay?"

"I promise," Frank nodded, feeling kinda stuck inside the moment. There was something in Harry right then that made his tummy wiggle, but not in a 'Pigg' kinda way; this wiggle was deeper, the kind of wiggle that said maybe Nicky's inside hurt was bigger than any of them knew just yet.

Harry nodded and stroked the boy's cheek, breaking the spell of the moment, "Okay then."

Nick nodded, "Okay then. Harry?"

"Yeah?"

"Can you still be our friend? If fate let's you stay here I mean?" he asked, feeling pretty sure he sounded more than a little childish.

Harry couldn't stop himself. His arm snaked out and grabbed the boys, pulling them both close while he snuffled between them. "You're not gonna get rid o'me that easy. Long as I'm alive, I will always be here for you, both of you. We been through too much for anything else t'be true!" He cupped each of their faces in his hands, "The Harry you know today, no matter what happens in the future, *I* am the one you can count on. Never forget that, okay?" He looked from one brother to the other, decades of horrors and victories and narrow escapes flickering through his memory.

"I promise," Nick nodded, resting his forehead against the older man's.

"Mm hmm, me, too," Frank shrugged out of Harry's grip, distracted by all the posters and general 'stuff' that decorated the office.

"I'll make sure," Nick nodded. "But you said there're things, you said they're attracted to... A schade came yesterday," he leaned forward to whisper, "he scares me."

"Mmm," he leaned back, the shriek of the chair making both boys wince.

"How come he doesn't come here? There's lots of shadows in here," Frank asked, leaning forward and looking into the desk drawer the old man was rifling through.

"I know a few tricks to keep 'em out, thanks to you boys that is," he nodded at them. "Now where the heck are those dang…"

Dust balls, paperclips and rubber bands seemed to almost leap from the desk drawer as he pawed through it, pulling it further and further out while digging all the way to the back.

"The couple I saw disappeared in shadows, and Frankie said that when mom turned on the light the other night it was gone," Nick mentioned.

"They travel through darkness, it can hide them, camouflage them, but light hurts." He smiled and withdrew his hand, "Ahhh, here we go."

"Why don't people see them?" Frankie asked absently, twining a rubber band around his finger and taking aim at a poster on the far wall.

"Long and short of it?" Harry asked as Frank let the band fly. The piece of rubber smacked the fuzzy UFO right in the center, leaving Frank with a huge smile on his face.

"Good shot!" Harry clapped. "Anyway, most folks don't see 'em 'cause: one, they work real hard NOT to be seen by regular folks, and two, regular folks don't WANT to see 'em." He held up his hand, "There we go."

From the drawer, he'd dug out two miniature-sized Mag-lites, linked through key rings. He tested each one, shining the bright beam one at a time into each of the boy's eyes. "See how big a surprise that is for you guys? Well, light hurts them. A light this size won't hurt them much, but it can buy you the time you need to get out of one's reach." He handed one to each of the boys then dropped a hand onto each of their shoulders, his eyes darting between them, his expression serious enough to keep their attention. "Until you're big enough to kill them, try not to let them touch you if you can help it."

"Why?"

"Why?" they asked together, sharing a nervous look.

Harry shook his head, "They can get in your head, and once they've done that, it gets easier for them to do it again."

"Is it bad?" Frank asked, squeezing his big brother's hand.

Harry bobbed his head side to side in a yes/no gesture. "Well, it won't hurt you right away or anything, but once they get inside your head, then if they get another opportunity, it's easier the next time, so you don't wanna give 'em a chance to start with, y'know?"

The boys looked nervously at each other again and Harry frowned, looking between the two of them. "Tell me what happened."

FIERY TONGUES OF RAGE seemed to lick inside his brain as he hung back in the shadows near the apartment watching Two Brothers Movers heft boxes down the stairs at the direction of a broad, tall man he'd never seen before, but desperately wanted to hurt.

*"He's stealing what's mine!"* something seemed to breathe into his ear.

While he watched strangers empty out what was HIS, he could almost feel the hunter's eyes searching for him, searching for anything that might give that natural born athlete an opportunity to use those muscles of his. *And THAT is why I like 'em when they're too young to fight back,* he smiled darkly.

*I'm lucky I looked out the window when I heard that truck,* he thought, balling his hand over and over around the pair of underwear in his jacket pocket. *It's only one pair. They're so well worn, he'll never miss them.* They were a keepsake for him to hold onto until he had the boy. *"One will bring the other; children are easy to control, but these children are smart. I have to be smart, too."* The breeze seemed to remind him.

*Yeah, I gotta be smart. Bide my time. Yeah,* he nodded, hanging back, wrapped deep in cool darkness.

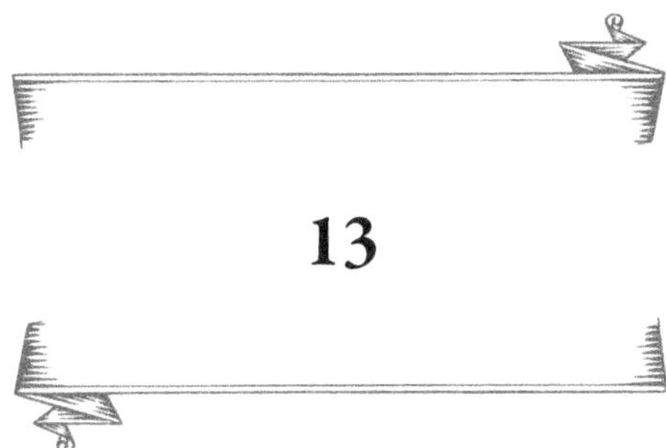

# 13

"Well now!" Nana Emerson leaned back on her knees with her arms open to her grandsons. "Look how you boys have grown!" she quickly swiped away her tears.

"Nana," Nick seemed to sigh into her embrace. There was something pressing on his heart making him want to cry when the woman wrapped him into her vanilla-scented presence.

"My Nicky, you look more like your father every day, you handsome young man!" she sniffed.

"What about me, Nana? Am I ham-some, too?" Frankie asked, sticking his tongue out at his big brother with a smile.

Her nearly violet eyes twinkled. "Of course you are! You're the spitting image of your Uncle Dylan," she grasped the little one into her arms as well and blew a raspberry against his neck that made him squeal and squirm before she grinned up at Lisa. "*Just* like Dylan was at that age!" Holding the boys away from her while Howie and Ryan carried their suitcases up the stairs, she sniffed again, "I've missed you all so much! It's been so horribly long!"

"Why didn't you come and see us, Nana?" Frank asked, "Did you stop loving us after Daddy went to heaven?"

His innocent question set the older woman's cheeks ablaze with shame while she fought a full onslaught of tears.

"No, baby, God, no! We were just trying to keep you safe," she stroked his face, meeting Lisa's eyes and finding only a hard glint in them.

"Right," the younger woman snapped tightly, drawing Nana to her feet.

"Alright, boys, go on upstairs and find Howie and Ryan. You'll be bunking in Dylan's old room, and your momma's gonna be in your daddy's old room," she cocked her head questioningly at the younger woman. "Unless that's not good?" Lisa shook her head, "Its fine."

Nana reached over, gently taking the distraught young woman's hand into hers. "We have a lot to talk about tonight. In the morning, we'll get the boys started with some rudimentary concepts of control after a good night's sleep."

"It'll have to be in the afternoon. Nicky has an appointment in the morning," Lisa shook her head.

"Sweetie, the doctors can't help him with this. I thought Howie already made that clear."

"Three times a week for the next month, at the very least, he needs to go see a..."

"MOM!" Nick barked tightly, his eyes blazing at the woman while he gave a faint shake of the head. He caught sight of Nana's curious expression. "They just wanna make sure everything stays okay, Nana. We can start as soon as we get back."

Slowly, the stylish older woman nodded, "Sure, sweetie, that's fine."

Nick watched his mother mouth the word 'later' and wanted to scream. Instead, he caught her attention, set his mouth into a firm line before he shook his head and mouthed, 'NO'. For a moment, the clash of wills was almost audible, and in the instant her eyes flicked to the side, Nick believed she understood. After all, he'd done his job. He'd kept Frankie safe and now that Pigg was out of their lives they were getting a clean start, he could let himself forget.

"C'mon, shrimp, let's go see our room, huh?" he turned Frank toward the stairs giving him a tiny push before looking back at his mother. "Promise."

With her hand over her mouth and tears running down her cheeks, she nodded.

"Goodness gracious! So much to do over a simple little homecoming! C'mon, dear, let's get some tea and you can tell me how things have been over the last couple years." Nana wrapped her arm around Lisa's fragile-seeming shoulders, guiding her through the living room toward the kitchen, "I'm so sorry we've stayed so far away, but it's been for your own good, and the boys'. Nick would never forgive me if I let anything happen to any of you."

Breathing deep his relief, Nick followed Frankie up the stairs, nearly plowing the little boy over at the top of them where he'd stopped and turned to look at his big brother. "Nicky, what's the matter?"

The older boy shook his head, but Frank knew better, "No, really, why are you mad at Momma?"

"I'm not, shrimp-o," he sighed, for the time being letting the fear slide out of him, knowing his little brother was far too attuned to him all of a sudden, and in ways that were new to both of them. "I'm just…" he shrugged.

"Off balance," Frankie nodded knowingly while standing on the edge of the top stair with his arms outstretched to the sides.

"Yeah," Nick nodded, grasping his shirt and forcing him onto the landing, he was surprised by the concept coming out of a five year old, even as exceptional as he knew this particular one to be.

Frankie shrugged, "Me, too. I kinda remember Nana, but I kinda don't, and uncle Howie, too. But I remember Uncle Ryan from the night Daddy went away."

"Do you remember that night, Frank?" Nick asked, sitting on the top stair.

"I remember some things, but I don't wanna talk about it 'cause I miss Daddy and I get scared," Frank shrugged sitting beside his big brother, his fingernail scratching at a rough spot in the knee of Nick's jeans that would soon become a hole. "Do you still get scared sometimes anymore?"

Nick nodded, "'Course I do, sometimes, but that's okay. We get afraid of stuff so that we keep ourselves safe, it's normal." He rose with an easy smile now on his face, "C'mon, let's go check out our room!"

"UNCLE HOWIE SAID THE ash-man can't get us at the house?" Frankie asked, swinging between Nana and Lisa while they walked off their dinner, and at the same time got the boys, in particular, a little familiar with the neighborhood.

"Haven't had one get in yet," Nana nodded.

"Schade, shrimp," Nick corrected, already smiling in anticipation of the raspberry to come. When it did, he chuckled, but turned his attention back to Nana. "How come you can keep 'em out, but that one got into OUR house?" he asked from behind the trio, once again his voice coming through a tightness in his chest and throat. "Why wasn't OUR house protected?"

Nana winced at the accusing bite in the pre-teen's voice. She was more than a little surprised by his awareness that it was a schade that killed Nick, but she'd sworn to tell them the truth, as much of it as she knew, no matter how much it might hurt to do so.

With her heart weighted by guilt and sorrow, she nodded, "It was." She looked at each inquiring face; they all wanted the same question answered, "Your father did everything right to keep them out that night. From what the boys told me later, when they went back there were just too many of them. That's how it got through in the end."

"Why did it kill Daddy?" Frank asked before the elder boy could. "Oh, boy," Nana sighed, "that is a very long story, my little love," and rubbed the boy's hair then, looking between Lisa and Nick, added, "and one best kept indoors."

"I assume you have some way to keep these things away from my sons?" the angry mother asked.

"What are they exactly?" Nick asked.

"And why did he put his fingers in Nicky's head?" Frank added, stopping the adults breathless in their tracks with the question.

"What?" Lisa gasped.

"When?" Nana asked.

"Good job, shrimp," Nick shook his head with a half-smile and shouldered his little brother.

The little one cocked his head to the side, frowning at Nick's crankiness, "What? I wanna know! Don't you? I mean it looked yucky. And the way you were gruntin' and whining and stuff, well, it sounded like it hurt. Don't you remember?" Nick shook his head, "Uh uh."

"What do you remember, sweetheart?" Lisa asked, crouching before her boy.

He shrugged, "I remember saying g'nite, turning over and," *sitting in Dad's lap in the big chair. I remember how warm he was, and the feel of his arms. I remember he told me I have to learn to shut my mind to them.* The nightmare unfolded in his head once more, detail by detail, *and I remember those THINGS hurting him while he somehow shoved me away.* He shrugged again, "That's it." He looked between all three of them, feeling a little like a bug about to get squished, "Then waking up in the hospital." He elbowed Frank again, "Glad you were there, shrimp, thanks."

Grinning hugely, Frank pushed his big brother, then leaned into him. He didn't know why Nick didn't want to talk about the dream. Frank *knew* he remembered it, but after thinking it over a bit, decided that maybe Nick didn't want to talk about it for the same reason he didn't want to talk about the night their father was killed. Maybe it just hurt too much. After all, he'd seen the dream through Nick's mind. The aching pain in his big brother's heart and the sense of emptiness he'd felt was what had woken him up. Then he'd seen the schade leaning over Nick with his fingers in his head.

Frank's shiver caught his big brother's attention just as the flicker of darkness that crossed his face made him frown. *Enough,* he thought, reaching out to tap the youngest Emerson on the shoulder.

"Tag! You're it!" then he took off down the sidewalk, keeping just a tiny bit ahead of his little brother.

"Don't go out of my sight!" Lisa called urgently.

"It's daylight Lisa, let them play. Night's the time for worrying," Nana pet the young woman's shoulder, smiling brightly at the sight of the boys playing.

"I want to know everything." Her tone left no room for argument even though her eyes never left her sons.

HARRY STOOD AT THE kindergarten classroom door, waiting until the two men came just a little closer before opening it to them.

"I knew you'd be back," the older man met Howie's eyes, then introduced himself to Ryan. "I'm Harry Armstrong; I'm a friend of Nick and Frankie's."

Ryan offered his despite his scowling partner. The young man had been on edge since meeting up with Lisa and the boys, but Ryan hadn't pressed the issue. He knew Howie would let whatever was bothering him out when he was done chewing on it. Even so, Ryan was taken aback by the solid wall of ferocity that the young Emerson became as he grabbed the man by the shirt and drove him backward into the cinder block wall.

"You call yourself their FRIEND and you LET IT GO ON! You LET that son of a bitch keep hurting him!" Howie stormed through gritted teeth.

*What?* Ryan felt his heart skip a beat as all the corners of his body turned sparkly at once. *'Let that son of a bitch...' WHO? Who hurt him? Which one? Nick.* His instincts responded, *Who hurt those boys?!* He glanced at Howie, *Why didn't you tell me? I'll kill 'em!* He felt his temper ignite as he closed the distance, as always, ready to lend whatever fists might be needed.

The old man's eyes filled with water. "I didn't have a choice," he tried to explain. "Every time I tried to stop it directly, things just," he shook his head, "came out worse!" he explained as Howie's fist drew back. "You think I didn't kill that son of a bitch myself once or twice!" he demanded. "All it got was either or both of 'em hurt," he shook his head again, his hands grasping the younger man's wrist, but not trying to stop any punches that might come. "This is the *last* chance; I got to do it right, Howie. The *only* chance left to save those boys and give them a fighting chance against what's coming."

Ryan caught the arm in mid swing, "What do you mean 'every time' you tried to stop it?"

"What do you mean 'against what's coming'?" the irate uncle asked.

"I mean, this isn't the first time we've had this conversation." Harry breathed a tad easier as both men seemed to simmer down.

"Ain't the first time you've tried, or taken, a pop at me either. Never could blame ya for it," he muttered, knowing that for the moment, the boys' uncles were willing to hold off on beating him to a pulp.

Harry reached over to the table and grabbed the jacket neither man had noticed there.

"C'mon, you guys are gonna need Ernie's. Gotta get y'fed first, *then* y'can have your beers. Just stay away from the shooters till y'get home," he looked between the men. "Please."

The hunters looked at each other, neither of them in the mood for so much as a beer all of a sudden.

IN THE DARKNESS OF the hallway, Nick scooted down another step and leaned gently against the wall, keeping his ear angled toward the light from the kitchen where Nana, Howie and Ryan had been waiting for the boys and Lisa to go to bed so they could talk.

*"They went to see Harry today; he told them things." Frank whispered as Nick sat beside him on the edge of the bed, re-tucking his blankets the way the little boy liked it, not too tight, but up high on the neck on one side, then down under the arm on the other. Mom didn't know so she just tucked the blankets up high on both sides.*

*"How do you know?" Nick tried to scoff.*

*Frankie's slim shoulders rose up to his ears in a shrug, "I just do. Howie was madder 'n hell at Harry, but that stopped."*

*"Then what?"*

*He shrugged again, "I dunno, once Howie wasn't mad no more I kinda woke up."*

"Do you boys believe him?" Nana asked, refilling their coffee cups. "Kinda hard not to when he knew that much," Ryan muttered.

"Which brings me to how the hell did he manage to make so many attempts? Is he of the line?" she asked.

"No," Howie shook his head, "he's not, but for the loyalty he showed, he might as well be. Blood, by the way. Nick's blood, I mean, Nicky's from the first line."

"He's been trying to save the boys for about eighteen years. Closest he could ever get was about six months from the catalyst event, as he called it, so he's always had to wait."

"Which was what?" Nana asked.

"Seems he zeroed it down to last Thursday night," Howie's head was still reeling.

"He had file cabinets filled with handwritten notes. He tried using flash drives, but something about using the pendant generates a field, probably an electromagnetic one, that wiped 'em clean," Ryan explained.

"So what was supposed to have happened last Thursday?" Nana asked watching the color flow out of both Ryan and Wee.

*So, we really DO have a fresh start.* Nick scrubbed his face with his hands and drew a shaky breath.

"Nooon't goooooo..." Frankie's thin, high voice slithered out into the hallway.

Nick leaped up the stairs, skidding into the bedroom just as the chairs in the kitchen scraped the floor.

"S'okay, Frankie," he sat on the edge of the bed, petting his little brother's sweat soaked hair off his face. "I gotcha, shrimp-o, I gotcha," he soothed, watching Frank's eyes slowly come open and fix on him.

"You didn't go?" he sniffled, looking around the room curiously before remembering where they were.

"Go where?" he frowned. "Where'm I gonna go without my sidekick?"

The littlest Emerson sniffed, his chest quivering with uncertainty,

"You promise?"

"'Course I promise."

"'Cause you're Nick of Time and I'm Second Hand?" he nodded, watching hopefully until Nick did the same, then ruffed his hair. "I can still be Second Hand, can't I, Nicky, even with Uncle Howie around?"

Nick frowned, confused. "What's he got to do with the price, Franks 'n' beans? Him and Ryan got their own super-heroing to do.

Besides," he smoothed the sheets over his little brother's chest, "they ain't us."

Nick was pretty sure that Nana, Howie and Ryan were now listening in on his conversation since he hadn't heard the chairs in the kitchen scrape the floor again yet, and he smiled.

Frank looked up, "I dreamed they wanted you to go be with Daddy."

"Who *they?*"

"The ash-men," he sniffed softly as his eyes darted around the room.

Nick shook his head, "No, Frank, you heard what Dad said in my dream, right?"

"You and me, nothing else is more important," he yawned. *But it wanted you and you almost held its hand. Don't leave me, Nicky. Stay with me.* "Scoot in with me?"

Nick glanced at the bedroom door. Just because he couldn't really see Frankie's pleading-puppy eyes, didn't mean he couldn't feel them on him. His eavesdropping done for the night, he climbed carefully over his little brother sliding under the covers behind him. He nestled the little one tight against his heart, curling his body protectively between the windowed wall and the most important person in his life.

"Just till you're asleep."

"Mmm," Frank's head nodded faintly as his breathing settled deeper and his thumb slid into his mouth.

"Alright now, baby boy," he whispered, sliding the digit out of Frank's mouth, "you don't need that anymore." He rested his cheek against Frank's head holding his hand.

"I THOUGHT YOU SAID he didn't remember the dream?" Howie asked softly once they were seated back at the kitchen table.

"That's what he told us." Nana patted her youngest son's hand and, frowning, fought the mist coming up in her eyes. "It's my fault."

"No," Ryan protested.

She nodded tearfully, "Yes, if I hadn't been so scared of leading *them* right to the boys, and Lisa," she shook her head and calmed herself. "There's no reason they should trust us. All we can do is hope to earn their trust from this point forward." She rolled her eyes up toward the ceiling,

"My God, what have I done? I thought I was doing the right thing; all I wanted to do was protect my boy's children." She breathed shakily then checked her emotions. There would be time for self-recrimination later, or so she hoped. After all, they'd gotten through the wards at Nick's house two years ago. Who could say if they'd be able to penetrate the same ones here, only time would tell and only Nicky could control that.

"What'd you tell, Lisa?" she asked Howie.

"Most of what little I know, ma, we're..." he motioned between Ryan and himself, "in uncharted territory here. The way these things are almost literally coming out of the woodwork." He shook his head.

"It's like nothing we've ever seen before," Ryan finished. "What can you tell us?"

Nana shook her head and looked at Ryan. She reached out and caressed his cheek, loving him as much as any of her sons. He'd come into their lives a heartbroken and lost soul without an understanding of what his little brother had lived with before being murdered over it, his throat slashed by the host of a very angry demon. In time, he'd allowed himself to heal and, though he never acknowledged it, allowed himself to give the understanding he hadn't been able to share with his baby brother, if not the love, to his surrogate family.

Making a decision, Nana rose and kissed both men, "Go to bed boys. When Lisa and Nicky get back from his appointment, we'll go over it all."

"Good, that'll give me time to run a little errand in the morning," Ryan nodded, leaning his head instinctively into Nana's warm palm against his temple.

"You'll stay far away from that son of a bitch, Ryan."

"I can't believe they let him out on BAIL! I thought they were supposed to throw guys like that into pits with starving wild jackals," Howie gritted through clenched teeth.

Ryan looked up at the Emerson matriarch, "If he shows a toenail on this street, I *will* kill him."

Nana nodded, "Okay. But unless that happens we need you here, NOT looking to get yourself put away." She shook her head then motioned them out of the kitchen, "Alright, boys, get... both of you, up to bed."

At the entryway, Howie turned, "I'll be taking Nicky to his appointment tomorrow; you need to deal with Lees. Explain it to her, help her see the big picture."

"What'm I supposed to do then?" Ryan asked, wrapping his arm around Howie's neck and rubbing a burning nuggie into the top of his head as they tripped up the stairs.

"Quit it, dork," Howie smiled easily. "Work with Frank. See how far his powers go."

"Dude, don't you think that's a little more YOUR area of expertise? I'm about as psychic as a brick wall."

"You transmit just fine once someone knows what to listen for, you'll be perfect," Howie assured him, closing the door softly behind them.

"You're worried 'cause neither of 'em should be lit up yet," Ryan sighed, flopping into the far too tiny twin bed on the far side of the bedroom.

Howie nodded, trading his jeans for a pair of sweats, then flopping on his own bed, "Yeah."

"What do you think it means?" the older man asked, staring at the ceiling with his hands behind his head.

"You don't have to be psychic to know what I'm thinking man."

Ryan nodded, but didn't look across the room, "Yeah. You're thinking it's gonna be them."

"Yeah," Howie sighed, raising his foot along the wall and flipping the light switch with his big toe. "I love you."

"I know," Ryan grinned, holding Wee's hand across the gap.

"You wish you were Han!" Wee teased.

"Mmm don't we both," he returned before they both fell silent, lost in fear that *this* really was the time those of The Line had been waiting for.

NICK ROLLED ONTO HIS back, clutching the pendant in one hand, his eyes fixed on the watch face he'd set up on the windowsill. The timepiece was a gift from his dad, something he'd had, it seemed forever, the crystal was scratched, pocked and laced with satin friction ribbons. It'd always been on his wrist, even at its tightest setting it was loose, a bracelet almost, but it never stopped. He wound it once a day, while he was on his morning potty, it'd always been that way, and as far as Nick was concerned, there was no other way it COULD be. The face was angled just enough for the street light outside to show him with certainty that the second hand was indeed moving, just as it should be.

He focused his eyes on that ticking sliver of steel. *Stop,* he thought. *Freeze?* He tried again then frowned.

*Okay, I was scared.* He forced himself to remember how he'd felt, how his heart had raced, how his body's corners had tingled when he realized he was late AGAIN, and how his lungs burned as they filled suddenly with air as he ran down the hall. He remembered that shaft of red-hot anger as, through the window of the kindergarten classroom door, he could see his baby brother being crudely grappled up the side of the dumpster. Tommy Haywood draped over the top, his hand pinching around Frankie's bony wrist, while on the ground Bruce Evans had the little boy around the knees and was pushing him up. *Stop,* he whimpered inside, recalling the sense of helplessness, the fear that he wouldn't be able to stop it and, in a way, gratitude that yet another dumpster dunking was the worst those boys did.

He knew that all too soon they'd learn how to terrorize their peers with their fists.

In his mind's eye, he examined the scene. *It felt like a ball coming out of me, it was strong. I, I was strong for just a second.* His internal gaze fixed on the image of Frankie's face - *My brother! MINE!* - and the tears making tracks on his cheeks in spite of his lips tight with resignation. *NO!* He felt it again and dared a glance at the watch face. The second hand held firmly still at twelve seconds after the minute. *Oh my God, oh my GOD, I did it! I DID it! It's real!* He glanced around the room wondering if he was dreaming. Against his side, Frankie's light, even breathing was no help. They were touching. *How long can I hold it? AM I holding it? One, one thousand; two, one thousand; three, one thousand; I AM doing it! Four, one thousand; how do I undo it?* A sliver of light shot off the second hand as it returned to its journey around the watch face.

*Oh my God,* Nick sighed as a layer of sweat broke over his skin, absorbing into his pajamas. His breath came hard and deep, ending with a yawn that didn't seem to want to end; and before he knew it, his eye lids started to slide closed. Smiling faintly, he turned onto his side, pulled his little brother into his arms and rested his cheek once more against those chocolate colored waves. "I think I did it," *'cause of you, Frankie. I love you, shrimp,* he sighed, then slipped away for the night.

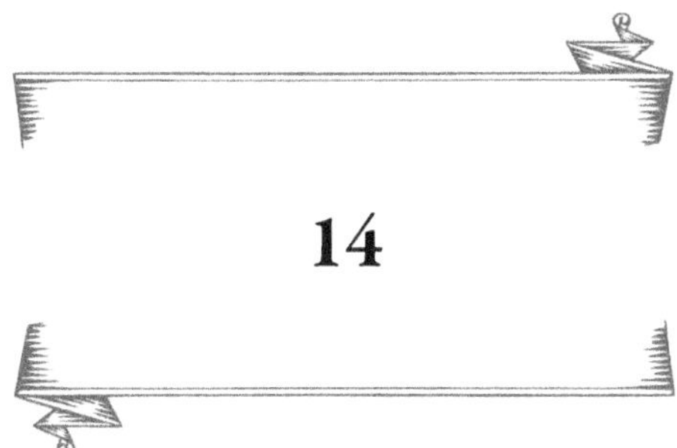

# 14

Howie took advantage of the stoplight to look at his nephew.

"You *both* will," he assured the boy.

"I want to start today. No matter where we go, there's always gonna be folks that are gonna need a good old-fashioned smackdown, and if I can't get there in time, then he's going to have to be able to take care of himself. The sooner the better," Nick muttered.

"Is this about those couple bullies that used to throw him in the dumpster?" he asked.

The boy nodded, "Partly. Mom won't like it."

"Mom's never do," Howie smirked and watched his first nephew stiffen uncomfortably as he reached over to ruff his hair. "Nicky," he started.

"Light's green," the kid motioned with his chin.

*Well then, I see the front door's locked up tight. Let's go peek in one of the windows, huh, gently though,* the youngest of the senior Emerson's thought. *Talk to me, Nicky, please.* "You know these guys can't help you. The changes, your powers, Frank's powers, it's part of who you are."

"I know," Nick nodded. His shoulders rose and fell heavily with the deep sigh that rolled out, "I don't want to talk to these people, Howie. I did my job. Frankie's safe, we're out of that hole." His breath quivered in his chest as his uncle pulled the car into a shady spot in a parking lot near a park. "And," he sighed, "it's over."

"Got something in your eye, squirt," Howie used the sleeve to wipe the faint shimmer off the boy's cheek. "Listen, there's something you don't know," he scowled, turning to face his nephew. "Pickerd was let out on bail yesterday."

He watched the little boy's expression go from tense to terrified before he swallowed hard and nodded as if he was preparing to resign himself to something.

Waves of conflict battered Howie as his nephew leaned back and closed his eyes. He rolled his head from side to side and simply whispered, "Please no."

"I'm sorry, Nick," he whispered, dropping his hand onto the boy's shoulder, though he jerked away.

"Don't touch me," Nick gasped, shaking his head and turned in his seat so he was facing the side window with his knees in his chest.

"I thought they said he was going to, that I wouldn't ever have to..." he turned back and looked at his uncle. "Who else knows he's out? Does mom know? Ryan? Nana?"

"Yeah, they know," Howie nodded.

"How about Frank? Anyone tell *him* yet? Take away what little bit of *his* innocence I managed to keep safe?" he demanded, trembling through a sudden burst of fury.

"No," Howie gasped, almost floored by the intensity of the young man's anger. "Nick, you won't, you won't ever have to deal with him again. Ryan and I, your mom, and Nana, no one's gonna let him get near you, I promise."

Nick shook his head, "No one had a right to tell any of you anything! She promised she wouldn't!" He shook his head and sniffed hard, not sure what to be more angry about- that his mother didn't respect his wishes, or that Pigg was out on the street.

"We're your family, we can't protect you if we don't know what to look for. You, of all people, know that. If you didn't know to look for guys like Bruce or Tommy, then you wouldn't know who to protect Frankie from, right?"

Slowly, Nick nodded. He definitely understood the logic, but the humiliation was almost too much to bear. He felt like all anyone would see when they looked at him was the dirty things Pigg did in the dark instead of the boy who kept his brother safe.

"You have nothing to be ashamed of. You didn't do anything wrong. You protected Frank; you did exactly what any big brother worth his salt would do. Nothing Pickerd did can change the young man *you* are, or the man you're going to be, do you understand me?" he asked, wanting to grab the boy and hold him until he could let the pain out. But Howie relied on his instincts when it came to reading the people around him, and he knew if he did it right now, Nick might not be able to take it. He needed to be ready for it on the inside.

Breathing deeply, Nick glanced at the older man. The remark about them being *family* didn't go unheard, but at least Nick understood why they'd stayed away when the danger was schades. At least *that* made sense. "When did you find out?" he asked, his emotions still pummeling at his uncle.

"Yesterday morning." Howie looked into the smear of pain on the boy's face. "You look so much like your dad did at your age." He reached for his nephew's cheek then winced as he pulled away again. "You're my brother's son; you can't hope to keep this from Frank unless you can let go of the hurt. I promise, that son of a bitch will NEVER get his hands on you again, and he'll NEVER ever, *ever* touch Frank." He took a shaky breath feeling how much the boy wanted to hope, how much he wanted to trust in that delicate lattice of faith that already trembled with every breath.

*Last week, me 'n Frankie were normal, weren't we?* "I can't do what Frankie can. I can't feel other people like he can." He looked into his uncle's eyes, "I don't know how I can keep it from him. He's already so scary smart, y'know? For all I know, he might already know." He shook his head, "I don't think he does, but he could soon. I need it gone and forgotten. But mom won't let me, and if I talk to these people, I can tell, they're just gonna keep it running around my head, too. They'll make me think about it and tell them things, and what kind of people wanna hear that sick shit anyway, huh?" He frowned just before his voice turned even quieter and his sniffle seemed to stutter, "if they make me go over it again and again and again, well..." he glanced at his uncle, glad for the expression that was on his face. It was open and curious, and there was even a hint of amusement in his eyes from when he swore. Nick could also see that he was a little sad, but at least his face didn't shout 'pity'. "Well, that's just not right. He's in the past. As long as mom doesn't go back with him, then it's over, y'know?"

"You are some kid," Howie sniffed, nodding and smiling gently, "What if I told you I'll talk to them for you?"

Nick nodded, "That would be good if you would." *There's stuff that's more important than what can't be changed 'cause its past, like what CAN be 'cause it ain't happened yet.*

"Consider it done."

Nick glanced at the older man, grateful that he at least seemed to understand. Slowly, he turned to face forward in the seat again and, with another glance, tried to smile just a bit, letting himself give in to hope just one fraction of a second at a time.

A moment later, with his hand wrapped softly around the pendant through his shirt, he asked softly, "Ryan told you I did it once already, right?"

"Mm hm."

"I did it again last night after you all went back in the kitchen."

Howie grinned hugely, "So you *were* listening. I thought I felt you out there. Nick and Dylan used to sit on the stairs and listen in on stuff, too. You paused it?" Nick nodded.

"For how long?"

"About a five count," Nick nodded. "I need to know more about why you thought that by staying away you'd be keeping me 'n Frank safe. Was it really only 'cause you didn't wanna bring schades to us?

Or was it 'cause you're afraid they want something from us?"

Howie felt his jaw drop open in surprise. "Did Frank tell you that?" he asked.

Nick shook his head, "The one in the bathroom at Game Lane. It felt like it wanted to show me something, but I think it really wanted something different."

"Do you know what?" Howie asked.

Nick shook his head, "I don't know."

Taking a breath to clear his mind and give himself a moment to digest his nephew's insight, Howie looked at the clock in the dash. *Too bad its digital.*

"What's say we go get us a couple of hot dogs, some french fries and go talk for a little while? Just you and me?"

Nick shrugged and smiled shyly, "Okay."

"Two things first."

"What?"

Howie grinned, *"What?" he asks... sheesh.* "Smart boy, Nicky. You are one smart boy. You do your Dad proud, y'know? First, you want to get past what that son of a bitch did to you?" Silently, the boy nodded.

"Trust that I'm not going to hurt you and give me a hug. You can't go through life being afraid to be touched and you'll never be able to hold your own in a fight if you're afraid of contact. More often than not, especially where schades are concerned, you HAVE to get in close, and that means contact."

"What's the other thing?" Nick asked.

Howie smiled slyly, "You're gonna pause time again and hold it as long as you can."

"What if I told you I just did?" he asked, spocking his eyebrow expectantly.

Howie chuckled and tried not to get too excited when the boy stiffened but allowed him to ruff his hair. "I'd say, I don't think so."

Nicky chuckled, "Could Dad? When I did it the first time, Frankie froze, too."

"And was he immune last night when you did it?"

"Yeah, but I was tucked in with him."

Howie nodded, "Yeah, he'll probably be mostly immune to it unless you *mean* for him to freeze, too."

"How much do you know about what's going on that you haven't told us?"

Howie smiled gently and shook his head. "Ahh ahh, dogs first."

"C'MON, GIMME SOMETHING hard," Frankie grinned, sliding the deck of cards back into the box.

"What? C'mon now, you didn't get all of 'em right, y'know," Ryan eyed the little boy.

"Right enough since you were trying to trick me anyways,"

Frank's head tilted and he frowned. "It's pepper."

"What?" Ryan asked.

"It should be 'pickle my pepper', not 'pickle my pecker'."

He frowned as Ryan sputtered his soda and coughed hard, turning rosy red.

"What? I'm supposed to be practicing, right?"

"Well, yeah, but..." the older man stammered as Nana and Lisa came chuckling out onto the porch.

"Frankie, sweetheart, some thoughts are private and listening to them is like eavesdropping on a conversation," Lisa tried to explain.

Frank's eyes lit up with understanding, "Oh, you mean like when they were listening in on me and Nicky talking last night."

"Oooh, caught with our hands in the cookie jar," Ryan winked at Nana who smiled and nodded.

"Cookies?" Frank's head whipped around to his mother. "Can I have cookies, Momma?"

"Sure, sweetie. In the meantime, maybe Ryan should try to keep his thoughts a little more..."

"Scooby Doo! It *was* a fun movie, wasn't it?" he nodded, smiling. A moment later, the smile traded places with a small frown.

"Nicky didn't go see Dr. Beckett. Him and Uncle Howie's at the park. Nicky was scared."

The trio of adults shared secretive glances that Frank knew he wasn't supposed to see, so he pretended he didn't.

"He's right," Lisa nodded. "Howie texted me about half an hour ago." She crouched at her little one's side, "Sweetie, can you feel what Nicky's feeling now?"

Frankie pursed his mouth and looked up a bit as if in thought.

"Mmm, he's got some sunshine in him now, like before Daddy died." His gaze snapped to Ryan and he frowned. "*Could* you have saved him?" he asked.

Ryan shook his head, fighting an unexpected covering of mist over his eyes, his mouth opened and closed a couple times, he'd spent the last two years asking himself the same question. "No, it was... it was too fast."

One thought led to another in a domino run of blood and loss, and before he could let himself drown, Ryan got up out of the chair, crossing out onto the lawn to fill himself up with the golden warmth of late morning.

"Hmm," Frank frowned and followed. In the sunshine, he stood poking him in the side until Ryan looked at him.

"Sorry, Frank. I'm thinking it might be time for you to practice keeping folks *out* of your head for a while, okay?"

"Okay. Who's Cal?" He looked up into his suddenly stricken expression as the answer came clearly, "Oooh, he was *your* little brother."

With a sad smile, Ryan scooped the boy up into his arms, "Yeah, he was."

"He's in heaven with Daddy now though, right?" Frank asked just before his body jerked straight up and his eyes rolled back into his skull. If Ryan hadn't seen it happen at the hotel, he would've been scared silly.

"Frank? Frankie? C'mon back now," he commanded gently as Lisa and Nana returned to the porch with sodas and a box of cookies.

He felt the little boy's body soften just as his lungs reached for a deeper breath, and when his eyes rolled back down they fell onto Ryan's with unexpected intensity. "If you'd been there, the mean lady woul'da killed you, too. She was from hell," he said simply, then pointed at the porch. "Ooooh, cookies!" He leaped out of the man's arms, dashing across the yard, leaving Ryan pale, shaking and soaked to the skin in sweat.

"Ryan?" Nana crossed through the sunlight to him, "Honey, what's wrong?"

"Howie and Harry were right. It IS going to be them." He turned to look down into her eyes, "Their lifetime, their time, their war."

He watched the older woman's color wash away as she glanced back at the porch then almost seemed to snarl at him. "How do YOU know?" But even as she did, he knew she believed him.

Frankie paused with the cookie halfway to his mouth, "I know you don't like what me 'n Nicky can do, but Daddy said it's important."

Fighting a chill in the cool shade, Lisa swept his hair out of his eyes, "When did your daddy say that, sweetheart?"

"In Nicky's dream, when he was tied down on the rocks, before the ash man, I mean schade, made him scream. Momma?" he patted her knee and looked into her face and the fear written on it.

Something in his lower belly turned icy and he was pretty sure he had to go pee all of a sudden. He put his cookie back in the box, looking between

Ryan and Nana on the lawn and Momma's fearful expression and suddenly didn't feel very much like eating anything at all.

*I didn't mean to make everyone sad,* he thought, feeling a little like he'd spent too much time on the merry-go-round in the park, the way Ryan was feeling, as if he was being pressed in on from all sides by the memory of his little brother and how much he missed him; and Momma's round-about thoughts going from fear for her boys to anger at Dad for not telling her things, and to something that made her belly twist tightly about Mr. Pigg. *I thought he was in jail?* he wondered. Despite wanting to know more, something kept him from looking into anyone's mind for more information on that subject. *Nicky's gonna get all tight again if he knows he's out though,* he realized as his belly flipped. He leaned forward just enough so that the splatter hit the floor of the porch instead of landing in his lap.

"Sweetie?" Lisa snapped out of her reverie as her little one's breath started to hiccough just before the tears came followed by the tight whimpers that, just a few years ago, would have been sobs. He stuck his thumb into his mouth and curled on his side with his head in her lap.

"I'm sorry, Momma, I didn't mean to make a mess," he hitched around the digit.

"Oh, baby, its okay," she kissed his clammy forehead and rolled him snugly into her arms. "C'mon, sweetie, you wanna lay on the couch for a little bit and watch some cartoons?"

He nodded, already close to fully asleep as she took him inside.

# 15

Dick Pickerd leaned back in his chair with a smug grin dancing at the corners of his mouth as he glanced down at Lisa Emerson's employment application. Her emergency contact information practically screamed at him from the page, and with it, the location of his boys.

*Gotta be careful, though, if that side of beef at the apartment was her brother-in-law, he looks, "the bigger they are the harder they fall, yes?"* That little voice seemed to whisper in his ear, *"get rid of the muscle and the others will fall away. Your path to the children will be clear."* But how do I get the others *out of the way?* he wondered. He'd been back to the apartment and knew there was nothing he could claim to have that would bring them out into the open. Absently, he pulled the almost worn through pair of underpants from his pocket and sighed, smiling at the softness against his cheek.

*I know, I need to watch them. Get a sense of their routine, but I'll have to be VERY careful. "Don't even THINK their names; they might hear it,"* the voice warned. *Yes, very special children,* he nodded, glancing at the waning day outside his window. He'd been smart enough to keep his father's locker at the Stow-N-Go where he kept all his 'private' records, addresses, notes, descriptions of all the women he'd worked with or hired over the years and their children. It was also where he kept his toys. *I'll have to wait until dark, though.*

Sitting back with that soft pair of underpants caressing his cheek, his mind ran riot with the joys yet to come, he didn't see the movement in the shadows as the schade slid back into the darkness, grinning.

HOWIE SHOOK HIS HEAD, amazed. *Just over three whole minutes?! Nick never got past five at a time. Wonder how long his recovery's gonna take.*

A gush of breath burst out of the sweat-soaked ten-year-old as he slumped over his knees and panted, "No more."

"No more," Howie agreed, reaching out to stroke his hair. He fought a rising tide of frustration as the boy ducked away. It seemed that even exhaustion wasn't going to let him get through his nephew's walls.

Nick glanced at his uncle from under his eyelashes. *I know, I know, I just...* he thought scooting to the older man's side. It was the only conciliatory gesture he could make at the moment. "How long did I hold it for?" he asked.

Waves of frustration rolled out of the boy, breaking over Howie like a storm tide washing inland. His nephew was being torn in two. At ten years old, he wanted nothing more than to be able to feel the comfort of a loving embrace, but the safety of such a thing had been challenged. He could feel the boy's fear and shame over what memories might come spilling out, but the worst of it was that, while Howie KNEW Nicky had the strength to move beyond the events of the last few months, Nick just didn't know it yet. He *hoped* he did, but he wasn't sure enough of himself yet.

"Three minutes two seconds," Howie shouldered the boy, somehow knowing THAT was a safe thing. It seemed that a hand coming toward him made him shy away most quickly. At least, that's what Howie sensed spiked his fear the most. *That bastard better hope I never get within gun range of him, and PRAY I never get close with a knife.*

"Wow, that's good," Nick nodded, lowering himself to his side on the grass and yawning hugely as his knees drew up tight to his chest.

*Oh yeah, I forgot about that.* "Sure is, kiddo. Hey now, c'mon before you fall asleep," he started and hesitantly reached out.

Relief stormed him and his breath trembled as his hand settled on the boy's upper arm. A sob choked him, partly grateful, and part blackly despondent as the child's turmoil stabbed into him. It was a profane mixture of pride and self-loathing, and as he gently shook the boy, he prayed the pride would end up the stronger of the feelings. *You protected your brother, Nicky. You did everything it took to save him. You're his protector and his hero.*

"Mmm," Nick sighed, already out.

Howie sniffed back a deluge of self-loathing and tearful anger and forced himself to focus on the moment, on what his nephew might need right NOW. He nodded smiling tremulously. "Used to burn your dad out, too, especially in the beginning or if he tried to push it." He slowly rose to his knees, "I'm gonna pick you up and take you home for some rest, baby boy. Just don't freak out on me. We don't need a scene in the park," he explained before gingerly sliding his arms under the boy and rolling him tightly to his chest.

Once he was on his feet, he shifted his grip, holding the ten-year old as if he was half his age. With every step toward the truck, he prayed the boy would continue to sleep, at least until they got home.

Once they were back on the road, he allowed himself a sigh of relief. *Over three minutes at THAT age.* He checked his watch, wondering once again about how long it would take the boy to recover. Would he be faster than his father? Or would it take that much longer because he'd pushed so very hard. *Only time will tell I guess.*

"NICKY!" LISA CRIED, running across the yard to the driveway as Howie wrestled him from the passenger seat. "Howie? Oh, my God! What happened? What's wrong with my son!?" she demanded.

"Holy crap," Ryan chuckled, "he's out cold, huh?" then took the boy from his partner. "Relax, Lees, used to happen to Nick once in a while, too." He turned his eyes to Howie, "How long did he go for?"

"Three minutes, two," he breathed.

"Are you kidding me?" Ryan held the boy close and kissed his temple, clearly amazed.

"What? Just over three minutes? What? Did he," Lisa waved her hand in the air, "you know...?"

"Yeah," Howie nodded, guiding her back to the house and nodding at Ryan. "How'd you do with Frank?"

"He's crashed on the couch. Little guy did great until he started getting MY baggage."

"Ooooh," Howie winced. "PPO?" he asked, smiling as Ryan nodded. Noting Lisa's curious expression, he explained, "Puked and Passed Out. Used to happen to me a LOT. At least until I learned how to keep my emotions separated from the incoming. Sometimes, if it's too strong, I can't keep it separated and still get nauseous. But most of the time I don't puke anymore."

"Did you say over three minutes?" Nana asked, emerging palefaced from the kitchen as Ryan laid Nick down on the couch behind

Frank. All four adults watched the older boy's arm wrap instinctively around his little brother, and likewise Frankie pushed back until he was snuggled tightly in the familiar comfort of the first born.

Back in the kitchen, Nana set the roasting pan in the middle of the table while Lisa stormed at her brother-in-law.

"You had no right to make that agreement with him! He's NOT your son! And he's a *ten*-year-old boy, for God's sake! He doesn't know what's best for himself!"

"Yeah, Lees, I think he does. People don't give kids enough credit anymore." Howie held up his finger to pre-empt her interruption,

"Listen, if these kids were in any way, shape or form *average* or *normal* children, I might be inclined to agree with you, MIGHT, but they're NOT. Nick knows he can't change the past. The only thing he and Frank can hope to change is the future. He can't change what that SOB did to him, but in his mind, it's really, at this moment, a 'nonissue'. Right now, it hurts US more than it does HIM. He protected Frankie, THAT's his job, and as far as he's concerned, he succeeded. The job is done, and if we let him, he WILL be able to leave it behind."

"And you think spending a few hours with him means you *know* him?" she sneered.

He shook his head, "I *know* what I feel, Lees. I *know* what I felt from *him*. These are *his* sentiments, *his* wishes, *his* priorities, not yours, not mine and not some doctor who has to look at the chart to know his name! What kind of good do you think it's gonna do for him if he goes three times a week for some," he breathed deep and checked himself, "counselor to keep all the memories running around his head? What do you think he's going to feel when one day Frankie asks him, 'Why'd Pigg do that?', when the only thing that matters to him is keeping that little guy as safe and innocent as possible?

What do you think that's going to do to Nick? Huh?" he argued, actually managing to vocalize Nicky's point of view.

Lisa paced, running her fingers through her hair. She looked accusingly from Howie to Ryan and then to Nana, "And you *all* agree? Just let my baby pretend he wasn't..." she sniffed and covered her mouth.

"No, sweetie," Nana draped her arm around the woman's shoulders. "Not pretend it didn't happen, just let him let go of it in his own time and his own way. He *will* have to deal with it, it *will* haunt him, but it would haunt him whether he was seeing a counselor or not. What you're waiting for *will* happen, but on *his* timetable, not ours," she tried to explain.

"And better that it comes when he's with people who love him than with some stranger," Ryan's experience with his little brother adding weight to their arguments in spite of the fact that Lisa didn't know his particular circumstances.

Tearful and hiccoughing with silent sobs, the young mother lowered herself into a kitchen chair looking forlorn and deeply out of her element as Howie crouched at her side dabbing at her tears.

Dazed, she shook her head, "I can't do this."

"Of course you can. For your sons? You can do anything!" he smiled. "Look, Lees, Nick always thought there'd be time to bring you into this nice and easy, and not a single one of us ever thought the boys would come to it this early or this strongly, and that can only mean one thing."

She shook her head as Nana slid the rolls into a basket and brought them to the table. Finally, everyone sat serving, reaching, and digging in absently, Lisa alone, unable to stomach a single bite. "Why? I mean, how? How does something..., why MY boys? Why not Joe Blow's kids? Why MY sons?" she asked, forking the tidbits on her plate from one side to the other.

"That, my dear, is a very, very old story," Nana smiled. "One that starts a few thousand years before Christ was born, when gods and men walked the world together, at least, some of the time. There were doorways to other worlds almost around every bend, and night time and darkness were not just times when light was scarce. They were living entities in their own right, conscious and conniving and hungry to rule the world for all time..." she began.

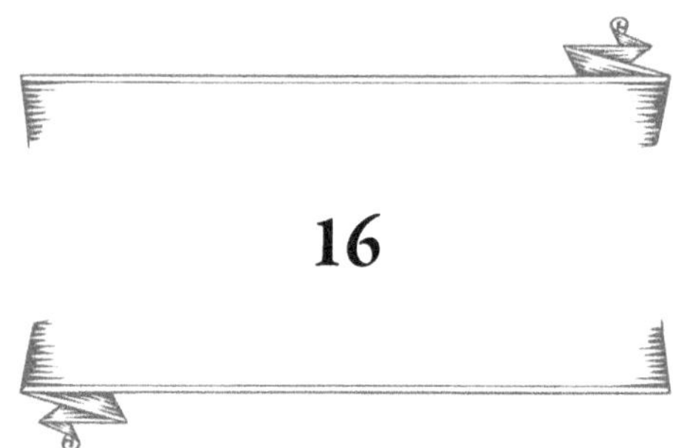

# 16

Moments later, Nana returned to the kitchen table with a large, leather-bound tome retrieved from somewhere in the front room. The cover was branded with several Gaelic words written in the Roman alphabet that had blurred and run together and become largely unintelligible over the centuries. In fact, the only word that stood out was "OEMIR".

"I was told that the cover says, 'The Origin of Oemir,'" she began then sipped from the wine cooler Ryan set before her.

"The Celts didn't have a written language until the Romans infiltrated and conquered them," she sighed. "The story on these pages was handed down through oral tradition for at least a thousand years, more likely two, before it was documented."

"Can you read it?" Howie asked with wide-eyed curiosity as she respectfully opened the tome to the first page. On it, there had been meticulously drawn what was clearly a gigantic and sacred oak. A dozen roots of the tree delved deeply into an obvious mound of earth, two of them bearing writing- one labeled Oemir, and the other Cathbad.

"What does this mean?" Howie asked, pointing to the names.

Nana smiled, "Well, Oemir was the first hero of your boy's line." She shook her head, "From what your father and I were able to find out about Cathbad, he was the druid who discovered the treachery and drew the Heroes together. He was the High Priest of Conchobar's court at the time, as well as his father, or so legends say."

"I've heard of Conchobar," Ryan nodded.

Howie smiled, though his eyes filled quickly, "Probably from Nick; he knew history."

"Conchobar was a mighty and often ruthless king; 'course, back then, one had to be. His nephew, Cuchulainn, was said to have been a son of the god Lugh and imbued with a great many godly warrior talents." Nana picked up the thread again, "He also is supposed to have fought against the darkness. From what some of the notations have intimated, the descendants of every line that fought has one of these books that tells the story so that, should the time come again, they'll all know what to do. But in order to keep the descendants protected, only *their* name and Cathbad's is on the book, just in case one of them should ever fall into the hands of the First Schade, the Master."

"So is all this," Lisa gently fanned the heavy and brittle pages, "is just a Celtic who's who in the zoo?"

"No. Actually, this tells the story of the war that reached its culmination almost two thousand years before the Romans conquered them and began a thousand years before that." Nana chuckled, "'Course, the timing in the book is off, probably in order to make sure the Romans didn't have reason to destroy them should they be found. So, if you believe the written word, Conchobar, who was supposed to have been High King at the time of the Great War, wouldn't be born for another thousand years."

"But we don't believe that time line, do we?" Ryan asked.

"No."

"Why not?" Howie asked with his eyebrow cocked and his lips turned in a smirk.

"The giveaway to the actual timing is the fall of the tower of Babel, the second one. Despite the fact that calendars varied, too, around the same time that the tower fell in Babylon, half a world away, Cathbad had a vision of the worlds sliding apart." Gingerly, she drew forth a few sheets of loose parchment from the rear of the book.

"Sliding apart?"

"And how would something happening in Babylon have anything to do with..."

She shook her head, "As far as we know, it doesn't, except to nail down the actual timing of the event. So, since Cathbad was probably *not* over a thousand years old, and we know he was the one who drew the Heroes together to fight WITHIN his own time, it stands to reason that the timing inferred in the book was falsified to hide the reality of the situation from the Roman. Probably, also, to hide the identity of the Heroes, most of who were bearers of divine blood."

"Ahhh, so that's the crux of it. Keep the lines and the Heroes safe from Roman persecution."

"Pretty much," Nana nodded then tapped a couple of the separate pages. "The visions that Oemir and Cathbad each had that they knew were going to take place far after the end of their lives were handed down as all other tales and knowledge was, orally. At least, until the arrival of the written word. Apparently, many of both men's visions extended centuries beyond their own lifetimes. Cathbad's, possibly several millennia," she motioned toward the living room with her chin.

"How do you," her son started to ask as she turned the parchment toward him and pointed.

"What'd you think I was doing while all my babies were off at college or exploring the wild world? Sitting here knitting?" she smirked. "Apparently, one of your ancestors was quite the translator," she indicated the other pages. "These few pages are all that's left of whatever visions were had. We don't know whose is whose. Maybe they're all that were passed down your line. It's possible they might have been separated by family like the books were, I don't know."

"Others?" Lisa asked.

"They're referred to as Heroes of the Line. They were the army that, approximately five thousand years ago, literally saved the world. Each blood line that fought pledged its descendants to return to duty should they be needed," Howie explained.

Nana smiled and stroked her son's hair. "Oemir was both a seer and a warrior. It was said he was born of one of the children of Danu and could see the strands of time. The children of Danu lived in the realms between worlds. Because of his role in the battle against the living dark, his line, starting with Mac-Oemir, was graced with the knowledge, will, and ability to protect this realm."

"'As heaven's spire falls in its cradle, so shall the otherworld's veils be sealed and the living dark cast down for all time, their world made separate and alone.'" Ryan looked up, "Mmm, ominous but telling, I mean, the tower of Babel DID fall."

"Twice," Howie nodded with a smirk while holding up two fingers.

As Ryan's voice drifted into the living room, none of the adults heard the faint grunt roll out from Frankie's throat as he squeezed further back against Nick and remembered with the older boy the swirling visions of their earlier lives.

*In the churning dark waters of the cauldron, nestled in a burnt bowl of desert, a fiery tower trembled and shook, the walls cracking and leaning as its base crumbled into a billowing, rolling wall of blood-colored dust. He felt his eyes pull away from the terrifying visage, rising to peer into the brownish greens across from him.*

*"I know this place and yet it's not a place I could ever have been."*

*"Its legend will survive the ages."*

*"I don't understand; I've had this dream more times than I can count, and...," he pointed, feeling his heart pounding in his chest.*

*"There! Look!" he directed as a billowing dark crossed the cauldron. "The living dark. My blood runs cold at the sight of it." He looked up as the vision ended and the cauldron calmed.*

*"A great war is coming, Oemir. The dark will rise and consume the world if we do not act to stop it."*

*His belly shivered deep inside and his heart thundered, "How do we stop shadows?"*

*"They were born of night and use darkness to move unseen through our world, but they can be fought, driven back and held banished for ages," his eyes shone fiercely in the dim light.*

*"How?"*

*The druid chieftain gazed penetratingly into his eyes, "It will take a special line. There must be one to whom all others will look, for guidance, for wisdom, for the strength to do what must be done, and there must be one within whom resides the power upon which to draw should the need arise."*

*"No."*

*"No," those of the line gasped.*

"Noooooooo!" Frankie mewled, turning unconsciously in his brother's embrace, pressing his face to the crook of that neck he knew so well even as the older boy choked on his own denial. His mind also filled with swirling mysteries, possibilities and travesties both past and future.

Nick breathed deep, his arms clamped around what was his. "I gotcha, baby boy, I gotcha," he soothed, stroking the little one's hair and back, pressing his mouth to the side of his head. "T'sokay, I gotcha." He rocked them both back and forth, and without bothering to raise his eyes to the faces he knew were in the kitchen doorway, retreated to the world his baby had pulled them both from. A place that felt safe because it had so long ago passed.

*"WATCH THEM, WATCH THEM all,"* came the whisper again. *I am, I am, but it's hard from here.* He couldn't help but shudder with a mix of fear and excitement as he raised the binoculars to his eyes and looked through the front room window. The curtains were still wide open and the boys were sleeping on the sofa against the right-hand wall.

*Yes, God, look at them, so close, so...* he clutched frantically at the nearest branch as his balance wavered. *Careful.* "Yes careful. *There is much to be done."* *Lots to do, so little time, time to watch though, watch them all.* "Shhhh, quiet your mind, quiet now, just watch." Nodding, he tasted salty drops of sweat from his top lip.

From across the street he seethed. His heart pounded out a rhythm filled with sinister promise as Lisa crouched before her boys, scooping the little one into her arms and out of his big brothers' embrace.

*No! Lisa, wait!* "Shhh, quiet!" *But, but, oh, God, so sweet!* He thought, disheartened as the woman disappeared from view with the prize he sought.

*There's two guys. Which one? Mmm, doesn't matter. They both gotta go. The big one first.*

The larger of the two sat on the couch in front of Nick. *No don't! Don't you touch him. He's MINE!* He breathed deeply, almost able to taste the sweetness.

Apparently, the kid was zonked though. The 'side of beef', as he thought of Ryan, scooped the child into his arms. The smaller of the men frowned deeply, dashing around the bigger one to the picture window and hastily drawing the drapes.

*Uh oh.*

"I SWEAR T'GOD, RY," Howie headed directly for the front closet and the shotgun they kept on the shelf there.

Ryan moved quickly, thrusting the boy into his husband's arms reaching for the gun before Wee could get it. "Take Nick," he ordered, breaking open the chamber to make sure it was loaded then snapping it closed. "Where'd you feel it from?"

"Ryan!"

"Where?!" the older man barked with his hand on the doorknob as Nana came down the stairs. Something in his voice or the volume started Nick stirring, or maybe it was the fearful whine that unspooled down the hall toward them from Frankie.

"Across the street." He handed the boy to Nana once she was done stuffing his favorite blade and sheath into the back of his pants. "Wait!" he whisper-shouted at Ryan's back.

They slid out into the dark together, there was no need to look backward; Nana would do whatever she had to.

"You should be inside!" Ryan shouldered the younger man.

They both knew leaving the house was a risk, but they also knew Nana would be securing the wards and walking the windows like a minute-man with her pheasant gun over her shoulder.

Howie closed his eyes, pivoting first left then right, trying to catch the source of the feeling that made his throat close. He motioned Ryan to the deepest shadows to the right, but a flick of his eyes told the older man where he sensed the evil laying in wait. The seasoned hunter nodded his understanding veering to one side of the darkness. Howie angled more closely toward their prey, but still feigned uncertainty. There was something he was sensing that was sickening, that much was obvious, but it was a thicker, heavier cloying stench that clung like the acidic burn of drunken puke, and just like that he couldn't seem to shake it.

DICK HELD STILL, BARELY daring to breathe in spite of his painfully thumping heart and the prickly, low-slung evergreen bush that had a finger poking into his belly no matter how deeply he pressed his back to the wall of the house behind him. His pulse pounded in his eyes and he wished for just another glimpse of those boys, but that dark little voice that had somehow gained in strength over the last six months, ever since Lisa came to work for him, ever since she introduced those precious children of hers to him, told him to keep still.

As long as he listened to that voice, he would not be found while he watched and waited for his opportunity.

He closed his eyes, remembering the sweetness of his first few visits to the older boy.

ALL THE WHILE MOVING through his circuit, around the far end of the street and across from the house on the right-hand side, Ryan kept his eyes open for his partner. Part of him seemed to stretch forward, to reach out whenever they were separated on a hunt and he wondered, not for the first time, if somehow Howie's gifts had managed after all these years to rub off on him just a little. *Nah, it's just physics, pure and simple, just tuned to his energy is all.*

Where yards overlapped from his search area to Howie's, he turned, scanning for the younger man, his eyes drawn to a familiar shaped shadow that emerged onto Nana's porch searching the sleeping street.

"Anything?" Ryan asked, jogging back to him.

"He's still out there. I can feel him Ry, the stink of him. It's thick and heavy. It's... like rotting poultry in the thick of summer, God," he gagged, barely holding it back.

"It's alright, youngun, it's alright. We're not gonna let him get to them."

He winced at Howie's withering look and felt flames of shame burning along his hairline as barely in time, Wee turned to chuck his dinner over the railing, nearly folding in half over the bar of wood.

He could see the young hunter was shaking and sweating, and he'd seen it often enough to know he'd be cold to the bone after finishing his purge.

"I know, kiddo, I know," he nodded, pressing one warm hand to Wee's back and the other to his chest, helping to anchor him until he was through.

Howie gasped, grateful for Ryan and his devotion. There was a part of him, however, that was angry and disappointed with Dylan, and yet another part that was furious with Nick for dying in the first place. *Should be Dylan here; Ryan shouldn't have to be stuck in the middle of this shit. Shoulda been D hunting that last bastard down in the warehouse, shoulda been him at Game Lane, shoulda been any of us there for those boys, and for Lees.*

"Easy, tiger, let it go. I gotcha," the older man's voice blanketed him with warmth as he wrapped his arm around the overtaxed psychic supporting him back inside.

"I DON'T HAVE TO BE psychic to know exactly what you're thinkin'," Ryan set Wee's coffee cup on the windowsill as the moon started its descent. "None of this is anyone's fault, Wee. No one could've guessed it'd be this generation."

"Nick was the first one to call me Wee, you know that?"

"You're tiny compared to him," Ryan shrugged, "I got a feeling we're gonna need as many of those good memories as we can," he smirked, "remember."

Howie smiled weakly and shook his head. "They're just kids, they're not equipped to handle what's gonna come."

"Then we'll just hafta equip 'em. Look, man, we should've known it'd be them when Nick was killed. I think we got another clue when Dylan's fiancée turned up missing. I mean, hell, if we were talkin' with Buck, he'd smack us both upside our thick skulls with that damned hand-carved soup ladle of his." Ryan rubbed the back of his head, "Damn thing hurt like a son of a bitch."

"Buck's that crazy old mountain guy from Lakeview?"

"Mm hm, kinda the town's "Weird Shit" librarian."

"But he died a few years back, didn't he?"

"Trust me, nothing, not even death, could keep that old codger from whippin' up a whollup of a story."

"Y'know, you go very Pacific Northwest Mountain when you talk about home," Howie smiled. "So what's your point? Why'd you wake up the memory of Buck Forrester?"

"Mmm," Ryan half frowned, "thoughts o'Buck get me thinking' 'bout Tom and Shep; they're like us, except they hunt the other stuff, demons, ghosts, wraiths."

"The normal things hunters hunt."

"Exactly. But at least they're wise to what's out there, when the time comes, depending on how all this escalates. I mean, let's face it, it could take fifty years for the war to start, but if it starts any time soon, it'll be good to have some friends to call on."

Howie nodded and leaned against the older man, "How do we get in touch with the others of the line? That's what I want to know. When the time comes." He straightened up and looked into those warm, luminous eyes. "How do we let the others know what's happening?"

"Truth?" Howie nodded.

"My guess is they're gonna know. I don't think it's anything we're gonna hafta worry about it."

Howie looked at the bedroom door, tears shining in the corners of his eyes. "They're my nephews, Ry," he sighed a shaky breath. "They're everything that's left of MY big brother. I can't lose them."

Ryan wrapped his arm around the younger man's shoulders and rested his forehead against Howie's temple. "We WON'T lose them. They're my family too remember."

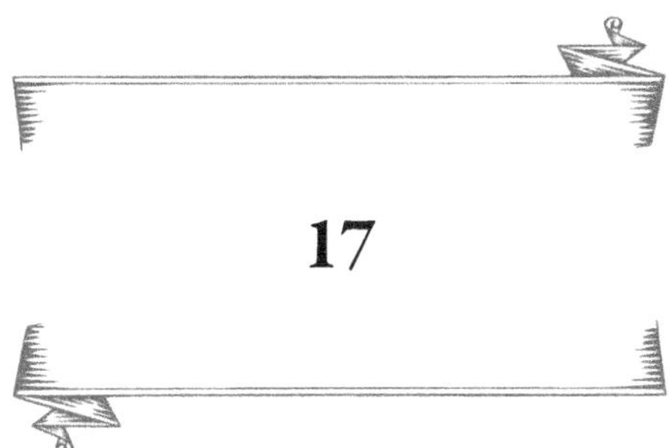

# 17

"It's okay, Nicky. Davie was takin' it out on everybody 'cause his momma said she's gonna leave and leave him behind, too, 'cause he ain't nuthin but a piece o'shit just like his daddy."

"That's a bad word, Frankie. Twenty-five cents for the swear jar." Nick sighed lethargically pinching the bridge of his nose, feeling the headache starting to come back again. Two weeks into their new school and he still couldn't get his groove. Couldn't carve himself a place among the kids, and he knew it was only worse now because of all the 'stuff' that was going on.

"What? Shit?"

Nick nodded.

"But you say it all the time!" he protested.

"I'm twice your age, b'sides who do you think put most of the money in there anyway?" Nick asked.

"Ryan!" Frank pouted then sighed a far too weary sound for his tender age, "You're gonna medi, medi..." he wanted to say *cate* but knew that wasn't right so he waited.

"Meditate," Nick finished for him. "Probably," he nodded. "You've heard what Howie says, I need to learn how to focus at a moment's notice."

"But, Nicky, you *don't* focus. Focus is like laser beams, you? You go all, woosh!" he threw his hands around willy nilly in front of them both. "Everywhere." He stopped in his tracks and grabbed his big brother by the sleeve. It felt like there were worms wriggling in his tummy because he was afraid of making Nicky mad at him, but he was starting to get worried about his big brother. They were supposed to be learning how to be superheroes and Nicky wasn't learning much. He knew his brother was sometimes starting to see things that made *his* tummy do flip flops, and no matter how he tried, he couldn't get him to talk about 'em, especially the ones that made him feel throw up-ish. But as far as he could tell, the only thing Nick was really putting a lot of effort into was going to the dark place inside his own head. "You're gonna go look for Daddy in your head again." Slowly, Nick shook his head, he tried to plaster on a blank face, but didn't quite cut it.

"Yes you are," Frankie nodded and his eyes filled up. "Nicky, you said Daddy's in heaven, right?"

"That's what everyone keeps sayin', but I don't believe in heaven Frank, you know that."

"Okay, but even if it's true and if Daddy IS in heaven, then you should be able to find him all the time," he patted his big brother in the center of his chest, "in here. Not just inside your head, and not just in that dark place. Daddy wouldn't stay there if he didn't have to, y'know? Something ain't right there, Nicky, I promise you."

"You don't know nuthin', shrimp," Nick muttered with a voice the color of faded old newsprint.

"Yeah, huh, I do so," Frank nodded. "I know it makes your head hurt and I saw the other day when you got a bloody nose and nobody even punched you!"

"That was from trying to hold the bubbles back, Frank." It even sounded lame in his own ears.

"Nuh uh, you got good at that real fast, except when you try to get to five minutes; but you didn't, you were trying to go back, Nicky, and Daddy said you can't. He said you had to go and be with me." Mist covered the little boy's eyes, brightening those deep blues till they shone like sapphire in the afternoon sun.

Something sickly turned over in Frank's tummy and sent the tears over his eyes as he nodded puffing air in and out of his little mouth. "I do, too know. Daddy didn't want you to go back there, Nick. He made you hidden for a reason, and you're just gonna make his uh oh's just that much worse 'cause you're gonna make everything undone if you keep going back!" he caught his sob quickly and hung his head.

From below his lashes he dared a peep at his big brother before running off toward the house feeling sick to his stomach for all the things that were twisting and turning around inside the older boy.

Nick didn't know it, but Frank could tell, most of those things wanted to hurt him.

Frank knew the older boy couldn't see 'em, couldn't feel 'em the same way he could, but he DID feel the effect of them. If Nick didn't get better soon, Frank figured he might have to go talk with Uncle Ryan or Uncle Wee, no matter *how* mad it might make his big brother.

Nick watched the littlest Emerson dash to the house and wished that it could just be them again. He was tired of people looking at him all the time. *It was better when it was just me and Frank. Nothing against them, but I'd almost go back to the way it was if they'd just stop lookin' at me funny. Especially Mom. Does that make me sick? I wish I COULD make time go backwards. I wonder how Harry did it.*

With a sigh that came from his toes, Nick shrugged his backpack all the way on and looked at the tree on the front part of the lawn. *I can reach that.* And sure enough he could. On tiptoe, he grasped the lowest branch and swung himself up, in every way not ready at all to be around anyone. *I could run away, take Frankie. Then it'd just be me and him like it's supposed to be.* "So leave," a tiny whisper blew through his thoughts. *Not everybody squeezing in around us all the time. Gets me so I can't breathe right.*

He leaned against the tree trunk, his backpack now clutched to his stomach, as he reached inside for the snack pack of chips he'd saved from lunch. His chest was tight and heavy, like when he let Frankie tackle him and was sitting on it, except in this case it wasn't fun. *What's wrong with me?* he wondered as a sudden cascade of tears rolled down his cheeks. *Dad, I need to see Dad. Maybe he can help me.* He drew a shaky breath, centered himself on the branch and closed his eyes, calling up in his mind's eye the image of the trap door behind his dad's big comfy chair.

*Just like it was waiting for him, the door in the floor opened. Nick sat at the edge and launched himself down the chute. He counted the half-moon windows going down and listened, as he usually did, to see how many of the voices were behind them today. Each one seemed to have its own voice inside and just like people. Sometimes the voice was home, and sometimes it wasn't. He often wondered if it was schades that lived behind those windows and if so, were they all like the mean ones, or were they more like people, some good some bad?*

*There were a lot of things he still didn't know about this place.*

'Maybe it's time to do some exploring before I go see Dad,' he thought as his feet hit the floor and he strode toward the archway.

'Nah, Dad first, then exploring.'

While he made his way toward the 'altar room', as he thought of it, nervousness wiggled in his stomach. He stopped and looked around at the darkly-shadowed walls, his heart pounding, wondering if there were schades around today. He hadn't seen many of them since his first trip here, but sometimes, once in a while, when he reaches the doorway to the place where his father lays bound naked, he can see them in there, sometimes one or two of them; but there was always one in particular that seemed to be in charge. None of the others were allowed to be around his dad without The One present.

'I hope he's alone today,' he thought, fighting the fear in his belly that he'd see again today what he saw yesterday.

When he'd arrived and peered into the chamber, he saw The One standing at the head of the alter, its fingers inside Nick's skull, and it seemed for hours all he could do was scream. Every time he glanced into the room, his tears came harder; and the harder his tears came, the more the Nick on the altar's pain and screams increased. Finally, his heart couldn't take it any longer and he forced himself out of the meditation.

The more often he came now, at least ever since his first visit, the more often he wondered if the older man even knew he was present. 'I wish I could do what Frankie can; I wish I could tell if he knows I'm here. Does he know I love him? Does he know I miss him, or is he just not even in his head anymore except when they hurt him?'

'Today I'll get those chains off him and set him free. I don't know how come he doesn't try to help me help him. It's like he doesn't care.' Of course, Nick always thought *about getting those chains off the older man, but he was just as guilty of sometimes not trying to get them undone, or to find a key or something to smash them, as the other Nick was of not helping. He wondered if maybe there was something down here that made them both forget to try.*

He peered around the corner into the room, his eyes immediately falling to the stone slab in the center, and the sleeping man on top of it. 'I need to help today.'

Nick crept slowly forward, eyes peeled for movement in the shadows, knowing well enough by now that the schades could appear or disappear through *them at a moment's notice. He sometimes found himself wondering if his meditations really took him deep inside his own head or if they allowed him access to a different world, a world in which he was actually the phantom of a different reality.*

*"Dad?" he whispered, sliding toward the altar, his heart thumping heavily in his chest and his breath coming shortly. "Dad, you awake?"*

*The older man's head rolled toward him, and even in the faint light, Nick could see firelight reflected in the tears that wet his skin.*

*"Nicky? God, no, please," he gasped, his chest hitching hard and his throat twitching. "Get out of here, and don't come back. You gotta understand they're using you."*

*"No, I have to get you free. Today's that day, Dad." he choked, forcing himself to examine the rings the chains wound through, as well as the manacles and shackles themselves.*

*"No! I'm not... Damnit Nicky you don't understand, you have to stop coming," he pleaded.*

*Nick shook his head and his throat snapped shut. "Nooh. I have to save you."*

*"You wanna save me, leave. That's how you can save me. Leave and never come back here. Nothing can change here, Nick; it's not what you think." His gaze followed the boy around the altar, wincing as he tugged and tested the chains.*

*"I can't leave you here, I have to save you. I can set you free and then, and then, you can come back." The boy's voice trailed off weakly.*

*Movement slithered up behind the boy at the same time The One rose up at the head of the altar, a dusty gray, sinister smile pulling at the corners of its mouth while its milky, dead-like eyes seemed to glow with some kind of satisfaction.*

*"Nicky!"*

*"Dad!" they called together.*

*Their voices rose, twisting into a barber-pole spiral of pain as fingers slid into their skulls and as Nicky's vision was cast back almost three years now. There was something familiar about the pitch and timbre of the scream from the man on the slab. In a breath, the sound slid away and the boy stood at the end of the hallway, the scant, bony weight of his little brother monkey-clutching him as real now as it had been then. A scream that was heavier and darker than the one he'd just left behind sounded. It echoed in the hall as a spray of blood as long as his father was tall shot across the wallpaper to color the light fixture.*

*Woody sounding pops and wet tearing slurps came next when Nick thought his father had somehow sprouted wings. He hadn't realized at that moment that what he was seeing was his dad's rib cage being swung open and bent back like curved saloon doors.*

"Nicky? C'mon, little man, come back to us," a soft familiar voice urged just before toothpicks of white seemed to jab into his eyes.

The light hurt, but at least it was a way to escape the pain in his head for a little bit.

"I never should have listened to ANY of you! I'm calling the doctor. Ryan, will you put him in the car."

"I need to come, too, Momma, please?" Frankie's voice sawed through the haze.

"Of course, sweetie. Stay with Ryan."

"Lisa, this isn't going to do any good," Howie tried to reason.

"They can't do anything for him!" Nana added.

"He has to learn how to protect himself, this isn't about..." Howie started again.

"SHUT UP!" she screamed, her voice cracking with the stress. "I won't have it any longer, do you hear me? There's something wrong with my son and there's nothing any of you are doing except making it worse! I wish you'd never come! I wish you'd never come back into our lives! And so help me, GOD, the instant I can think straight, I'm taking MY SONS and getting them the hell away from you Godless FREAKS!"

"Lees, please," Howie laid his hands on her shoulders for a split second before he found himself stumbling backwards, the heel of his hand pressed to his chin where she'd punched him.

"Stay the ffff...," she glanced at Frankie and breathed shakily.

"Stay away from me and my kids!"

She wheeled on her heel and stood before Ryan who cradled Nicky in his arms in spite of his dumbfounded expression. *She did NOT just deck my boy.*

She paused before the older man with her hands on her hips. "You say one word, I will toss your ass out on the street without stopping the car, do you understand me!?" she demanded.

Silent, Ryan nodded and followed her out into the night with Nick in his arms and Frankie's fingers curled through the belt loop of his jeans.

Slowly, Nicky's eyes started to focus and he fought back the haze of exhaustion, the memory of angry voices and screams of pain in his head. He remembered the pain as his own, and he knew the angry voice to be his mother's. *Well, that's not good.*

"Nicky?" Frank's warm, soft hand stroked his hair off his clammy forehead. "Don't leave me, Nicky. I can't be a side kick without my superhero," he sniffled.

"That's ENOUGH, Frank!" Lisa snapped from the driver's seat as her eyes flicked into the rear view mirror. "There ARE no superheroes and there're NO side kicks! DO you understand me! Your Nana and Uncle Howie are WRONG; they made a mistake, okay? You're just two normal, average, boys and that's all you're ever gonna be! DO YOU UNDERSTAND ME!?" she practically screamed, her rage fueled by a terror deeper than anything Frankie could ever imagine a person surviving.

"Yes, Momma," he whispered timidly, understanding, thanks to his tummy, that it was better to just nod and keep quiet right now than to tell her the truth. Even Uncle Ryan was smart enough to know that. So while Momma drove like a crazy person to the hospital, Frankie picked up an old bottle of water from the floor of the car and wet his sleeve with it, then set about scrubbing the blood from his big brother's face. It looked like he'd stuck his face from his nose down into a bowl of it and just let it dry, and the littlest Emerson knew something bad had happened while he was inside his head.

He looked from his big brother's pasty face into Ryan's eyes. *I dunno if you can hear me or if it's just a me hearing you thing, but you gotta help him see it's not right in there. He keeps going back and it's like being inside a picture- you don't know there's something else outside of it, you just see what's in front of you, and that's what's happening to Nicky. Please help him. I can't explain it good enough so he can understand and I, I don't blame him. I want Daddy, too, but I don't think that's really Daddy in there...* His inner voice trailed off, lost to a stream of tears and stuttering breaths as Nick slowly, stiffly moved out of Ryan's arms to sit beside him.

The older boy didn't have to be psychic to feel his baby's hurt as Frank pressed himself into the far corner of the back seat, his arms crossed tightly over his chest while tears spilled down his face. He couldn't or wouldn't look at Nick, but instead cast his glance at Ryan whose mouth trembled with something unspoken between them.

"Fr.." he cleared his throat, "Frank?" He reached out, but his little brother cringed, squishing himself deeply against the crook of the door and the seat, shaking his head for a second before his thumb perched into his mouth.

"Nick? Nicky baby? Are you alright?" Lisa's voice was tightrope high as her attention shifted between the rear view mirror and the road.

He nodded, "S'goin' on?" He looked from Lisa to Ryan to Frank, his mouth turning down with confusion. "Mom? What's goin on? Where are we goin?"

"I'm taking you to the hospital, sweetie," she tried to smile, but her fear turned the sound sour. "You're sick, sweetie. There's something wrong with you," she gasped, pressing her hand over her mouth while turning her eyes back to the road.

Nick shook his head, "No, Mom, I'm okay, really." He pulled himself forward, "See? I'm okay? Nothing's wrong. What happened? I got a bloody nose, right? It's just 'cause I keep trying to push the bubbles around, really, that's all." He looked over his shoulder, tossing a pleading look at his little brother. "Frankie, tell her that's all it is. I don't want to go to the hospital, PLEASE!" he yelled as tears slid down his face. "There's nothing wrong with me, I promise." He looked between the three of them again, but couldn't seem to get through.

"Please! I don't wanna go to the hospital. I wanna go home! Please just take us home!" He turned, kneeling in the seat, and grabbed Ryan by the shirtfront. "Please, Uncle Ryan, please tell her. Tell her we need to go home. Tell her there's nothing wrong! Don't let her send me away!" he cried.

"No, Nicky, it's not like that, little man. It's not like that at all," he soothed, wrapping his arms around the boy and wrapping him tight to his side. "Listen up, here, both of you," he motioned to Frankie who sat hiccoughing through his tears, barely able to dog paddle enough to keep his head over the roiling sea of emotions. "The only way your mom's gonna be able to feel comfortable inside is if she knows everything's okay, if she knows you're one hundred percent right, Nick. So we gotta try and understand that's what she needs, and we gotta try and make sure she gets that." *I can't imagine what this must be like for her. If I hadn't grown up with Cal and the things he went through before he got control of his gift, I can't say I'd be thinking anything different. Man, Lees, you can't take them away though, you just can't. That'd be like tossing 'em out on the highway and expecting them to NOT get hit. You can't do that.*

He frowned wanting to shed his own tears for these boys he loved so deeply. "They're gonna do some tests, and you'll sleep over probably, but we'll be right there with you, Nick. You're gonna hafta be brave, okay?"

The eldest son shook his head, then buried his face against the man's chest. "No! Please, I don't wanna do those things again! Please, we got school," He challenged weakly, "Please don't make me? You can talk her out of it. I'm fine, really. I'm good even." He waved at his little brother. "Ain't I, Frank? Just right as ever, huh?" he asked.

Slowly, tearfully, the little boy nodded. "Good as always, Nicky," he said softly and finally started to come out of the corner wondering what kind of tests could make his big brother so scared.

Lisa turned the car into the emergency room parking lot, her expression still tight, though Frank could feel the waves of hot slicing hate and fear were moving more slowly now. She was getting a grip on it all, but he still knew to keep his mouth shut as she practically ripped Nick out of Ryan's arms and stormed toward the doors. About halfway there it seemed as if all hell broke loose.

"Frank? Frankie!" Nick called squirming from Lisa's grip. As soon as his feet hit the pavement he ran back to Ryan and his little brother who were just getting out of the car.

Lisa stomped back to the trio, her hand lighting on her eldest boy's shoulder before whipping him around to face her.

"Wait! I want Frank!" he held out his hand to the youngest Emerson and at the same time that little hand slipped into his, and he turned to face his mom; what was, and what might have been, slid away from each other.

He felt his mother grasp his shoulder at the same time he felt her palm *slap, stinging hot against his cheek, the force so great his head snapped over his shoulder and he saw stars as he fell to his knees.*

*He couldn't say if it was because he was so stunned and maybe just a little on the edge of unconsciousness or not, but he'd never seen anyone move as fast as he saw his mother step forward with something silver gleaming in her hand.*

*She grasped Frank by the shirt with her free hand and the other slammed that gleaming thing (which Nick could see was the pen from Nana's desk set) right into Ryan's throat.*

*Dumbfounded, Nick looked from Ryan's gushing blood squirting between his fingers, to Frank who stared frozen in terror, and finally back to Lisa only to see a very familiar face lean backwards, as if it had stepped inside her and was wearing her like some kind of suit. It leaned back then stepped out of her, almost falling into an elongated box of shadow on the sidewalk where it disappeared from sight. All the damage it apparently wanted to do, done.*

*"No,"*

"No," he breathed both in this reality as well as the slice that might have been.

As much as he didn't want to be in the hospital, when darkness claimed the elder Emerson, he was grateful for it.

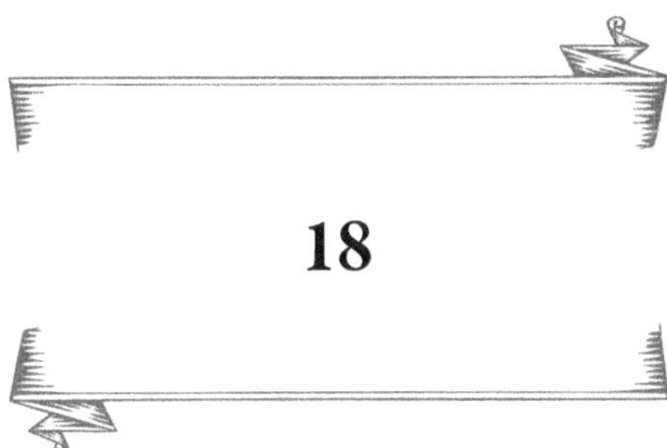

# 18

To anyone passing by, it would look like Ryan was dozing in the large reclining chair in Nick's hospital room when, in fact, he was deep in thought. Goose bumps raised the hairs on his arms every time he thought about the feel of Frankie's voice in his head.

He didn't know what he should have expected, never having had that particular experience before, but part of him did expect that warm feeling of synchronicity he felt with Wee. It should have felt warm and safe, like an extension of himself, but instead, what it reminded him of was the sensation of icy water being dribbled down the back of his shirt while someone whispered warm air and something just on the edge of audible, into his ear.

There was no mistaking the youngest Emerson's fear over what his big brother was doing, but without seeing what the boy was seeing it wasn't going to be easy to tell for sure what exactly was going on, no matter what he suspected.

At first, he, too, bought Nicky's explanation of his bloody nose as a by-product of simply pushing too hard to try and break the five minute marker. He recalled how frustrated Nick would get when he pushed too hard and the migraines that would sometimes come when he refused to give up. So the idea of a bloody nose for his namesake wasn't that difficult to accept, especially given the extraordinary talent both children were already showing.

A shadow fell into the doorway, drawing Ryan's attention. He glanced from his watch to the closed room-darkening drapes, then to Lisa, who'd crashed in the other chair, to the boys, who lay curled together, dozing. He rose quietly, meeting the man who peered around the corner and shook his head sadly. With a handshake and a nod, they exited the room moving to a small waiting area in an alcove near the elevators.

"Thanks for coming, Harry."

"Any time, Ryan, I told you that. I take it this time around isn't going so good either, huh?" he frowned.

"From what you told us, it could be a lot worse, not that there's anything we can do but damage control anymore."

Reluctantly, the older man nodded, "Ain't that the truth. With no more of MY Nicky's blood, we don't have a choice but to make this line work out. So, what happened?"

"A few things," he nodded then mused, "he IS your Nick isn't he? I mean..." he shook his head, he'd talk with Wee and Nana about it later, "I was thinking maybe between the two of us, we can, I don't know," he shook his head, suddenly understanding the feeling of being completely adrift.

Harry dropped his hand onto Ryan's shoulder. "We *will* figure this out," he assured him. "As for Nick... every one of 'em's different from what I can tell. I tried using his blood a few times. Got bupkiss. Now, what happened? How'd he wind up here again?"

"First thing's first, Harry, in your original line, you told me 'n Howie that Nicky died at thirty-three."

"That's right," he nodded.

"How many similarities were there in that line to this one that you know of?"

"Oh, pretty much identical right up until the night that son of a bitch Pickerd raped Frankie."

"WHAT?!" Ryan barked.

"Easy, man, easy, that was *then*; that was when it all started pretty much in every time line, whether or not he did get his mitts on Frank, something about that date maybe. Nicky stopped it here though, he kept Frank safe."

"How long did you wait before resetting things again?" he asked.

"First couple times, about eight months, then seven, on down till maybe three or four. When it all looked like it was goin' the same as always y'know?" he patted Ryan's knee. "See, the way Nicky worked it out was we had to get Frankie saved. Those boys were so damaged when we first met, Nicky hid it, but Frank was a fairly mute, skinny little wispy thing like a wraith. You ever seen one of them? Man, they're freaky to look at - kinda stuck between worlds and not really alive - well that was Frankie. Never left his brother's side and if they got separated, my GOD, he could tear a place apart until they were back together again. That was the only time he seemed like he was living at all, y'know? Hell, he wouldn't even let Nicky have privacy when he was with a girl. He'd just sit in the corner, not even looking like he was really there, y'know? Not like there was a lot of privacy to be had where we lived, but we kinda had this unspoken rule; if you're getting down to business, y'just pretend there's a wall there, y'know? But I'm talking about when we were lucky enough to be staying in a place that did have separate rooms. Was a good thing Mickey didn't care much if there was an audience." He stopped and shook his head blushing deeply. "Sorry, man, you probably don't wanna hear about that stuff."

"Not really," Ryan shook his head. "So you narrowed it down to the night Pickerd got his hands on Frank. What happened to Nick?"

"We were tracking The One, as Nick called him- he's the Master Schade's right-hand ghoul, y'know? Well, me'n Nick, we tracked him to the Sedona vortex."

"You and Nick? Where was Frank?"

Harry gulped hard and pressed his sleeve to his eyes to dry them, "It killed Frank, that's why we were tracking it." His breath hitched with the memory, even after all these years, still so fresh inside him. "Sum-bitch snatched that little guy right out of Nicky's grip and done'im just like the master did their daddy. That was the beginning of Nicky's end."

About twenty yards away, Lisa's head poked around out of the hospital room door. Her eyes fell on Ryan and Harry before she ducked back inside, grabbed her purse and approached the men.

"Hello, Harry," she greeted coolly before looking almost accusingly at Ryan. "I'm going to go get some coffee. Would either of you like some?"

They shook their heads, "No thanks, Lees." Ry smiled, "The boys still crashed?"

"Yeah," she nodded. "Look, I don't care what you guys talk about, you can talk about all the ghosts and ghoulies and devil nonsense you want OUT HERE, but so help me, God, if I hear you've been filling my boy's heads with anymore of that trash, you'll NEVER see them again, do I make myself clear?"

"Yes, ma'am," Harry nodded.

"Lees…"

"NEVER!" she hissed then straightened up. "Now, if you'll excuse me, I want to be there when they take him down for the PET scan, so I'll be right back."

NICK QUIETLY SLID THE closet door open and grabbed the plastic bag that held his clothes while Frank peered cautiously up and down the hall.

His heart was pounding as he stepped into his jeans, whipped off the jonnie and pulled the faintly-damp t-shirt back over his head.

"Hurry!" Frankie whispered over his shoulder as Nick stepped into his shoes then grabbed their jackets.

"Here," he helped Frank into his, zipping him up quickly before tending his own.

"Come on, Nicky, hurry."

"Is someone comin'?" he asked, watching his little brother tilt his head to the side and seem to listen for a second before shaking his head.

"Uh uh," he smiled. "I never thought o' using it like that."

"Good, now you got another way. You can be our alarm system, okay?" Nick whispered, holding Frank back as he took a quick peek out into the hallway to figure out exactly where to go.

"Okay, listen up, shrimp, there's an exit right around the corner, so no matter what, we just go to the exit, okay?" Nick ordered.

Frank nodded, "Then can we go back to practicing to be superheroes, Nicky?"

"Just you and me, Second Hand, I promise." Nick squeezed the little one's shoulder before peeping out into the hallway again. There was a big cart blocking his view of Ryan and Harry to the left, and on the right, the nurse at the station was caught up working, and her head was down from what he could see. This was as good as it was going to get.

"Now, Frank, go!" he whispered, shoving the little boy in front of him and quickly around the nearest corner to the right.

Frank saw the red and white exit sign, and with a quick look left then right, dashed to the door leaning hard to open it. Neither of them noticed the large clock on wall whose second hand seemed to be stuck, though there was nothing for it to be stuck against, at least until the boys were through the door.

Once in the stairwell, Nick quietly pushed the door closed then picked up his little brother to look through the window out into the hall.

"Nope, it's good," Frank smiled as the elder Emerson took his hand, leading him down the stairs quickly and quietly.

On the first floor, Nick picked up Frank again. "Nuh uh, and the door is just across the hall." His hand was on the knob for just a second before he looked up into those bright blue eyes. "There's a police at the front door."

"Are they looking for us?"

Frank shook his head, "Doesn't feel like they're lookin' for anyone."

"Good, okay, so here's what we do." Nick pushed the plastic bracelet up under his jacket sleeve. "We just gotta pretend like we're supposed to be leaving, okay? Just act natural, shrimp, and we're home free, got it?"

"But what about Momma, and Nana, and Wee and Ryan? Won't they be mad we left?"

"We'll go back once we get good at everything we can do. Then, they'll know it's all gonna be alright."

Frank nodded, comforted by his big brother's confidence as they stepped into the hallway.

Holding the older boy's hand Frank skipped at his side. "Momma said that we can have ice cream on the way home; what kind are you gonna have?" he asked.

"I dunno, I think the chocolate with peanut butter," Nick smiled, keeping his eyes on the door in front of them, pretending he didn't even see the big, shiny-headed man at the desk. "What about you?"

"I don't know, butterscotch, or something with caramel I think." Frank smiled as they cleared the doors and hit the sidewalk. He tried to bolt toward the end of the driveway, wanting to get out of sight as quickly as possible, but Nick held him back, certain that if they dashed off it would draw unwanted attention.

"Calm down, dude, we're almost clear. That was good thinking about the ice cream."

"The policeman was thinking about ice cream. He likes rocky road, blech," Frank twisted up his face. "I like the marshmallow and the chocolate part, but the nuts get stuck in my teeth." He pulled aside his cheek and pointed at the back of his mouth, "iiight aack ere, thee?" He slurped his fingers clean then dried them on his shirt.

"Yeah, I know," Nick chuckled glancing both ways before they crossed. Nick motioned Frank forward through a small break in a fence of bushes around someone's house. He'd never been happier that, in the world of adults, kids were pretty much invisible most of the time.

Frank worried his lips as in the distance the sky turned dusky,"It's getting dark, Nicky."

"Got your flashlight, shrimp?"

He patted down his pockets and came up with the gift from Harry, then turned it on to make sure it was working. "Yep. How about you?"

Nick, too, patted down his pocket and smiled, "Yep. We're set then."

"Can we go back to Nana's and get our stuff?"

"I don't know, maybe not tonight. We gotta give mom time to calm down and not be so mad at them."

"Won't she be even madder we run away'd?"

"Probably at first, but I'll be damned if I'm gonna stay in the hospital and let them do their stupid tests again. No WAY!" Nick grumbled. He never wanted to go through that again. What they did to him was in a lot of ways worse than what Pigg ever did. At least *he* did it in private. Frankie didn't count because he was his brother and he could sleep through anything, but other people, grown-ups he didn't know lookin' at him, that wasn't right and he wasn't gonna let it happen again.

"What did Pigg do?" Frankie asked just after they finished another zigzag through another couple yards.

"Nuh, nuthin," Nick choked, shaking his head quickly. Frank knew he was lying, but once again, something inside told him not to push the issue or go digging for anything. There was something inside his belly that told him doing so might hurt his big brother and he didn't want to ever do that.

Frank nodded, "I still don't like to talk about him either, it's okay.

You think he'll ever go back to jail?"

Nick shook his head, "I dunno. I hope so."

Frank squeezed his hand and stopped, "Nicky?"

"Yeah?"

"Do you think it was Momma that stabbed Uncle Ryan or do you think it was the schade that was inside her? And if he was inside her in your vision, do you think he's inside her now?"

"You saw that, huh?"

Frank nodded, "Just like I saw your daddy dream, I think 'cause I was holding your hand. I can see things better through you."

"I don't know, Frank. I hope it's not inside her, 'cause if it can do that, then maybe nobody's safe, y'know?"

Somberly, the littlest Emerson nodded. "Yeah, and if they can hide inside people, then how do we kill them without killing the ones they're hiding inside? We can't do *that*." he tugged excitedly on his big brother's hand, "Look, Nicky! A tree house! We can stay there tonight, whaddya say? Can we?"

A familiar smoky, mouth watering fragrance pulled their attention from the tree house. They looked at each other with wide excited eyes. "Barbeque!" they said together and followed their noses, clinging close to the shadows of the fence lines between butt-ends of the yards.

The sounds and smells of the party came to them before the sight did, but oh, what a sight it was. Joy lit up their faces as a miniature carnival came into view. There were clowns, and small rides and a couple ponies, there was a castle bounce, a pool with a water slide, tables full of food, and children running riot.

"Absolutely perfect!" Nick breathed a sigh of relief.

"You better turn your shirt around, Nick. That's a lot of blood, even for a bloody nose," Frank tapped his chest.

"Oh yeah, thanks, shrimp." He smiled, sliding his jacket off and quickly tucking his arms into his shirt, spinning it around and pulling at the neck to get it as right as he could before putting the jacket back on. "Listen, stuff your pockets with food okay, easy stuff like burgers and hot dogs."

"Cake?" Frank asked hopefully.

"Whatever," Nick shrugged. "Just whatever you can, except chips, 'cause that'll crunch up in the corners. We don't know how long we're gonna be gone."

"But, Nicky, that's stealing, we can't do that. And we weren't invited to that party, can we still go?" he asked doubtfully.

"I know whose party that is, well I think I do. You know that little third-grade girl Stefanie Weatherly?"

"The pretty one with the blonde hair, but she doesn't like to play 'cause she's afraid she'll get dirty?"

"I think so. Look, isn't that her over there?" Nick pointed at a passel of kids clustered in line to get into the castle bounce.

Frank shrugged, "I can't tell."

"Well, close enough. Look, the food is out there for everyone, right?"

Frank nodded, his eyes growing wide with understanding, "So, if we're there, we're part of everyone and then it's not stealing."

"Exactly," Nick nodded. "We'll just move along the bushes, and when no one's lookin', we'll get in line for the bounce. But stay close to me Frank, we might have to leave fast, okay?"

Together, they moved as one through the deepening shadows between the hedges until, just as Nick planned, they waited their turn, climbed inside and bounced quickly through to the other side before dashing toward the large long tables covered with food, sweets, treats and presents. All around them, balloons danced merrily in the early evening breeze declaring "Happy Birthday" and the cake itself had Stefanie's name on it.

"You were right, Nick," Frank pointed to the cake.

"I thought I might be."

"Yeah, but you weren't sure, were you?"

Nick smiled wryly handing a paper plate to his little brother.

"There's macaroni salad and potato salad over there. I'll make you a burger, or do you want a dog?"

"Puppy please," Frank nodded, taking the plate and a spoon and standing before two huge buckets of side dishes, not sure he could actually get at them without making a mess.

"Well, hi there, little guy," a happy looking, blonde-haired, teenage girl smiled at him.

"Hi," he blushed, watching intensely as she dropped a dollop of potato salad onto her own plate, and followed that with one of the macaroni salad.

Something seemed to click and she looked at him, "You figure out which one you want?"

"Could I have a little of both please? Some for me and some for my brother?" he used his best 'company' voice.

"Sure you can," she scooped a spoonful of each onto his plate.

"Are you in Stef's class, or is your brother?" she asked.

Frank shook his head. "I'm just in Mrs. Thorne's class," he non answered.

The teen smiled, "Mrs. Thorne was my kindergarten teacher, too. I think she's been teaching forever. She's a nice lady, isn't she?"

Frank nodded, grabbing a handful of potato chips and sliding them onto the plate around the mounds of salad. "Thank you," he beamed at her then returned to his brother before she could ask more questions. "Don't forget to get some cake later," she pointed to another table closer to the house then winked and went inside where Frank could see a bunch of teens sitting on the couch looking like they were playing video games. He took a quick look around and slid back down to the beginning of the table where there was a platter full of hot dogs already inside their buns. Setting the plate down, he grabbed one in each hand quickly stuffing them into his jacket pockets before the next item caught his attention and made his eyes light up. *Corn dogs!* Again, he grasped one in each hand and stuffed them, too, into his pockets then realized he was running out of room very quickly and wouldn't have room for cake if he kept on with the regular food.

He caught eyes with Nick who winked at him then looked over at the sweets table and nodded faintly.

"EASY, LEES, WE'LL FIND 'em. They're two little boys, it's a big hospital."

"Don't you tell me to take it easy! How the hell did you miss them sneaking out of the room!? Their jackets are gone, Ryan! Oh, God, what if they left the hospital?" she sniffed into her hands. "How can, how is it that NO ONE SAW ANYTHING?!" she screamed as the doctor who admitted Nick, approached with two cups.

"Mrs. Emerson, the doors have all been locked. Now, odds are, they're just off exploring. It's what kids do. Here you go," he handed both cups to her.

Lisa slapped a pill into her mouth, "Thanks."

He smiled, "You won't do your sons any good if you're hysterical."

"You're afraid I'm gonna beat their butts!" she snarled. "And I just might! How about you announce *that* over your loudspeaker, huh! Tell my boys, if they don't get back here right now, they're not gonna be able to sit for a WEEK! Both of em!"

She swilled the second cup of water and swallowed it down quickly, "What's the likelihood they're still in the hospital?"

"The search just started, Mrs. Emerson. Can you tell me? Is there any reason the boys might want to leave? Is it possible their father came and got them?"

Something electrical seemed to zing through Lisa and her heart leaped into her throat as she looked at Ryan, "Oh, God." Both Ryan and Harry looked from Lisa to each other, "Pigg." "Pickerd," they said together.

"Who?" the doctor asked.

Ryan crouched at Lisa's side. "Listen, I'm going to call Wee and Nana. We need eyes outside, just in case, but let's not overreact just yet, okay? Not till we have reason to, alright?" he wrapped her hand into his.

She sniffed and nodded.

"Ms. Emerson, they have security cameras at the main doors. I'll go talk with them about taking a look to see if they left the building at all, okay?"

"Thank you, Harry," she nodded, patting his hand. A few feet away, Ryan dialed his cell.

"IT'S AS SAFE AS IT'S *going to get, move closer,*" that strange slithery voice goaded him through the shadows, closer to the Emerson house than he'd dared thus far to go. Shrubs along the side of the building hid him, and despite his racing heart, his mind remained still as he reached an open window that led to the darkened dining room.

"We have to go," the younger of the two adult men said just before closing the window.

"What? What's going on?" the old woman asked.

Together, they could be heard sliding into jackets.

"The boys are gone."

"What?"

"Yeah, they've got the hospital locked down. Lees went for coffee, Ryan was talking with Harry in the hall, and they just, disappeared. Nick's clothes are gone, their jackets are gone, THEY're gone. We gotta start going through the neighborhoods."

"No! Howie? How'd they? Who? Oh, God, is it that, please tell me it's not that sick bastard," she could be heard breathing.

Tension soaked the young man's voice, "We don't know. They're going to search the hospital, we have to takc the neighborhood. It's almost dark, Ma."

"If they're dressed, they have their lights and their knives," she breathed softly, the sound more hopeful than certain.

"They're babies," her youngest's voice caught in his throat. For weeks, he and Ryan had been teaching them everything they knew little by little about how to defend themselves, but he of all people knew their vulnerabilities. Conversely however; he of all people knew their strengths as well. "...and Pigg isn't a schade, he's a flesh and blood, well, God only knows *what* he is, but schades, they can handle."

"I'll start circuits through Hazelcrest, you take the area closest to the hospital since you'll probably be able to sense them if they're close by. How long have they been gone?" she asked, their voices drifting out the front door.

Dick slithered alongside the house watching them at their vehicles. "Less than an hour. It's all we've got working in our favor," Howie slipped into his Jeep as Nana ducked into her sedan.

*"There will NEVER be another chance like this!"* Dick retreated until he could safely leave sight of the house. *Sense? She said he could sense the boys, like sense them how? "Stay with him for now,"* and so, returning to his own SUV, Dick Pickerd set out to follow the youngest of the senior Emersons.

"THEY'RE GONNA START combing the streets," Ryan nodded, returning to Lisa's side. A moment later, his eyes flicked to the waning day outside and his heart started to pound. "It'll be dark soon."

"I hope those boys got their flashlights," Harry muttered. "Be back in a bit." He left with a security guard who'd just come on duty not a half hour before.

"HEY, FRANK?" NICK WHISPERED, draping his arm over his little brother whose head rested on his belly.

"Mm?"

"Thanks for coming with me."

"Where else would I be?" he asked sleepily then looked up into his big brother's face. "Hey, Nicky?"

"Yeah?"

"Next time you medi..tate?"

"Hmm?"

"Take me with you?"

Nick's breath caught in his throat. "I don't know if that's a good idea, Frankie. What if you get stuck in there?"

"You did and you're okay."

*Actually, I got caught, but I had you to come back to.* "Is that what happened?" he asked, petting the little boy's hair absently.

He felt Frank nod, "Uh huh, I think. I think something hurt you in your head, Nicky. I felt pain and you screamed, but Uncle Ryan was already almost at the tree when your nose started gushing," Frank reached up petting his brother's hair. "You scared me, but I was thinking, if you go back there, maybe I can keep a look out?"

"I'm sorry, shrimp, I didn't mean to scare you."

"I know." He nodded, then yawned. *Just makes me scared because they want you.*

Then he was out, cuddled in nice and tight, both of their jackets spread over them for warmth, and up against the wall, a large potato chip bag filled up with their swiped stash of food leaned carefully folded closed to keep the bugs out.

With his little brother curled in one arm, and his pocket flashlight tight in his right hand, Nick let his eyes fall closed and finally began to rest.

# 19

Howie shook his head, trying to clear out the baggage and leave a path open to feel the boys, to feel if they were okay or if they were in danger, or hurt, or anything. He'd been working hard over the last couple weeks trying to figure out a sure way to find and grab onto their energies, but they were slippery little devils. He sighed, recalling how his frustration had bubbled over just the night before while he sat on the porch with Ryan.

More often than not over the two weeks since the boys had started school, Nick seemed to be having a hard time adapting. Frank was doing fine, his newfound ability, Howie suspected, unconsciously helping to ease his personal transition to the new school.

Howie didn't know how Nick had been before the move, but here the boy was a bundle of nerves. He was hesitant to be separated from Frank and always had one eye over his shoulder, ever ready to bolt out of sight. Howie understood they'd gone from being largely alone and very independent, with just the two of them in an apartment most of the time, to being practically surrounded almost ALL the time. Nick was used to calling the shots for the most part, and though the adults agreed that it was right to let him have that responsibility, especially over Frankie's daily needs, Howie could feel the boy second guessing himself.

With the adults around, he simply didn't have the confidence Howie had sensed, even under the darkness, at their initial meeting.

And to make matters worse, in spite of the talk they'd had and the progress they really had made (Nick would freeze, but he'd let Howie or Ryan pat his shoulder or ruff his hair now), there was still something Nick was keeping tight inside. Whatever it was, when Howie was able to catch a feel for it, was dark and slippery, almost exactly that same sense he'd gotten the first time he hugged the boy almost a month ago.

He thought about his and Ryan's conversation the previous evening and sighed, wondering why he hadn't known something like this was coming.

*"Did you see him? I tell you, something's going on with that kid," Howie spat his hangnail over the porch railing.*

*"Chill, Wee, it's only been a couple weeks since they started back to school. Kids are adaptable, but these two have a few more issues to contend with than the average…"*

*"Don't tell me to chill," Howie yelled, slugging back the last drops of his beer. He couldn't look at Ry. Part of him understood perfectly well what the older man was saying was true, but the part of him that felt everything those exceptional boys* hadn't *learned to hide yet, was worried.*

*"You don't know! You don't feel what I do, you can't, they're, well Frankie's," he pounded his forehead with his hand. "But it's harder on Nick, and they're already too good at hiding things from me. Half the time, they don't let me feel them, it's like they're always 'On' and," he thrust himself back in the chair with a frustrated grunt, "it scares me. They're not going to be able to keep it up for long, and if they don't learn to trust us, then we're not going to know."*

*"Hey, hey!" Ryan leaned over, grabbing the younger man by the face. "Shut up and listen to me," he demanded. It wasn't often that the love of his life went on a bender, but when he did, it was either a hoot or a holler. Unfortunately, this time, it was gonna be the latter.*

*"Those boys are stronger and already better than anyone had a right to think they would be. But you can't monitor them twenty-four, seven. You try to do that, it's gonna burn you out, and then what's gonna happen when they really need us to be there and you don't have anything left?" he tried to reason.*

"You sure you're not psychic, Ry?" Howie muttered to himself. "Little bit of prognosticating demon in ya?" he mocked shaking his head, turning the driver's side spot along the hedges, hoping the boys would have more sense than to cling to shadows, no matter how much they might not want to go home.

DICK SLID OUT ONTO the street, momentarily unsure which way the man's Jeep went until something seemed to guide him while that little voice whispered again. *"One by one, and they will belong to me,"* it assured. Over the months that voice had not only grown stronger, but had also proven to be accurate. Sure, Lisa threw a curve ball at the hospital when she'd called the cops on him, but that little voice told him what to do, and how to do it, and it hadn't been wrong. He was free until the trial, and by that time, he planned to be long gone with his boys under his arms. He shuddered at the thought of the bliss he would finally be able to experience with both of those beautiful children in his grip.

*"One obstacle at a time."*

He nodded and stroked the worn leather satchel on the seat beside him, the one he'd packed his toys in and a dark smile spread across his mouth. "One obstacle at a time."

As the Jeep slowly cruised the streets in front of him, he hung back, watching where that spot light showed into the yards of suburbia.

"MMM?" CAME A TROUBLED peep from the littlest Emerson's throat. His head tossed to the side and his arms clutched his big brother tight just before his eyes snapped open, certain that some dark and sinister thing was close. He fumbled in his jeans for his flashlight then twisted it on, sweeping the whole of the tree house back and forth, afraid to look around until he'd made at least one pass through the place.

"Sssamatter, Frank?" Nick grunted against the younger boy's elbow as it dug into his ribs.

"Something's out there," he whispered tightly, shining the light into his big brother's face.

Nick covered the beam and turned it off, "Like a schade?"

Frank shook his head.

"Then what?"

"A whole big mess. I think we didn't run far enough away, Nicky," his lips trembled, and even in the darkness, the older boy could see his eyes starting to sparkle just a little too much.

"Okay, calm down. Are you feeling it all at once?" He asked. Frank nodded, "Okay," Nick started to talk him through the steps Uncle Howie had been teaching him, "remember, first thing's first, pick out the people you know," he watched as his little brother took a deep breath and closed his eyes for a moment.

"Nana, Howie, Ryan, Momma, oooh Harry's close, too. They're lookin' for us, they're scared, and Momma's real mad. She's not calming down at all, Nicky. I think us being gone hurts them."

"Yeah," Nick nodded. "Okay, shrimp, what else?"

"I got that wiggly tummy feeling like when Pigg drinks too much," he started.

"Is he here, too?" Nick asked, trying to keep himself calm to keep *his* fear from the boy. Every part of him wanted to look out the windows of the tree house, but he was suddenly scared to move, certain that somehow just below them, Pigg would be standing there through some dark and sinister magic, waiting for them to come down.

Frank nodded and his face crinkled, "He wants to find us and my tummy doesn't like how he feels," his breath started coming faster and his eyes grew wide.

Nick knew the little one was on the edge of a full-on cry-fest, so he leaned against the wall, pulled him onto his lap holding him close and petting him gently until he could calm down. "Okay, I want you to turn yourself away from him, okay? Don't think about him. Don't look for what he feels like. Remember how you've been practicing shutting the door on other people's feelings?"

"Mmm hmm," Frank sniffled against Nick's shirt.

"Good, just do that now, okay?"

Frank leaned into his brother, his head nodding up and down as he slowly managed to close off the others. He didn't want to feel them, and he was pretty sure he should still be holding even Uncle Howie out. He also knew Nick was working hard to keep his own fear down and he wondered just then if maybe running away might not have been such a good idea after all.

"Why are they after us so hard?" he mumbled against the older boy's chest then stuck his thumb into his mouth.

Nick squeezed him tight and sighed, "I think I goofed up, baby boy."

"Nuh uh." He shook his head then asked, "Why?"

"'Cause if it wasn't for me, you coulda been back at Nana's all safe and snuggly in bed and there wouldn't be so many things going on to scare you."

Frank shook his head fast and hard against his big brother. "Nuh uh, 'cause if I was at Nana's, then I wouldn't be with you, and that's not right."

"We should go back, Frank," he leaned forward, forcing himself to start to move, to take account of their stuff.

"Not now," Frank's slim hand fell unerringly onto his shoulder. "It's not safe." He gently urged his big brother back down and out of sight of the window scant seconds before a shaft of white shot through.

"Who was that?" Nick asked as a cold shudder moved through him.

Frank shook his head, "In the morning Nicky. We'll go back home then."

"You sure?"

Frank nodded, "I don't like how it feels out there. It makes me scared."

Nick settled them back down again, making sure to tuck their jackets snug over Frank. "Okay," he felt the little one shudder and pet him absently, his eyes pinned to the ceiling of the tree house while he tried to keep his mind still. *I wonder*, "Hey, Frank? If I held back their bubbles, do you think we could get away safe?"

Frank shrugged, but didn't seem too hot on the idea, so Nick sat back keeping his ears open for any strange sounds.

A GLINT OFF CHROME in his rear view mirror caught Howie's attention widening his focus as a chill shot up his spine. It was that same sensation he'd been getting intermittently over the last couple weeks, the one that started the night Nana told Lisa the truth of the boys' line.

His stomach twisted and his breath came short. Sweat slicked his palms as he kept his eyes more on the road than on the darkened suburban lagging a few car lengths behind. *It's that son of a bitch, I know it is. He's following me to get to the boys. How the hell? It doesn't matter, he's been watching us on and off for weeks. I'll never have another chance like this.*

He continued to drive slowly, searching for exactly the right spot to tempt the man out into the open, into making a move. Whether it was his subconscious or simply a fortunate twist, he found himself on the rumble tumble access path to a dilapidated old cement silo that used to be part of a farm. As far as he knew, it'd always been abandoned. The house itself was long gone, taken by a twister decades ago, but the silo still somehow remained, barely. For as long as he could remember, the structure made him think of a watch tower, a place of first defense.

From the upper-most platform, on a clear day, you could see the interstate and the encroaching lines of automobile 'chariots' that charged the rutted path toward the castle keep. As children it'd been the point of no return when those invading armies sought to overrun the valiant Knights of the Kiddie Table. Battles were won and lost by the number of racing 'enemy' troops that managed to pass imaginary border lines in either direction at any given time.

*Good times,* he recalled with a faint smile, still able to hear Nick and Dylan giving the orders to the rest of the troops for the defense of the realm.

He cut his lights and let the car roll slowly to a stop, then silenced his cell and slid his blade into the back of his pants, his .45 went into his inner jacket pocket.

Armed for anything, he stepped into the darkness opening both his mind and his flashlight beam.

From the outside, the silo simply looked like a giant straw sticking into the earth, but inside was a different story. The partial outer ring gave access to the inner bin where grain and corn, or whatever had been grown here, had actually been stored. There were stairs at either side and bits of what had once been levels of walkways around that inner housing defied gravity, somehow remaining affixed to the wall, though how they continued to hang there was a bit of a mystery.

There were also smaller rooms inside on the main level, equipment rooms, tack rooms, what had probably once been a small office. It was the perfect place to ambush a predator. He stopped short, *can I kill him? Am I capable of killing a person?* The memory of his big brother's son flinching away from him and the dart of fear that shot through his eyes steeled his heart. Then there was the fact that the boy still, a month later, had to concentrate, literally force himself to allow any touch but Frankie's, *no problem* he nodded folding himself into a shadow, setting his trap.

*WISH I HAD A GUN, BET HE has one. "If so, he won't have it for long,"* the darkness inside assured, making him smile.

Dick held back at the crest of the access road, watching that sweeping stream of light move around the structure. Slowly, he released the brake and let the SUV roll forward. He wheeled it carefully around the far side of the silo and parked, taking just a moment to savor the electrical excitement that seemed to crackle in the air. Whether it was because he was about to get his hands on the boys, or remove one of his obstacles, *hopefully BOTH,* he couldn't say. *"Careful now, this is no ordinary offspring,"* that sinister instinct reminded him. It was never an easy task, but he quelled his excitement and quieted his mind, knowing that when the time was right, he'd be allowed to indulge his every darkest pleasure.

As he neared the entry, his steps slowed, holding back, listening for movement. Listening for whatever the smaller of the two men could tell him. Never would he have suspected the existence of, let alone how his life had been changed by, the ashy gray figure that slid into the darkness in front of him.

NEAR THE BASE OF THE stairs, Howie stopped, his breath caught in his throat, holding fast as a shiver passed through him and the layers of a living world around him were suddenly lessened. *Did he leave?* he wondered, confused by the sudden absence of that cloying psychic stench.

The familiar feel, so very like cobwebs catching in the shorthairs of his neck, brought his hand to the hilt of his knife. *Figures there'd be one here, son of a bitch!* He could almost feel it moving through the air, the faintest chill you'd never notice until it breathes just under the surface of your space, the almost imperceptible sensation of subatomic particles colliding that we call instinct.

He spun on his heel, prepared for that pale, dusty, almost neuter looking visage. His breath caught in his throat when he faced empty space. *I'm not wrong, there's one around here somewhere.* He stretched his senses out, reaching into the shadows for the feel of those things he'd never known life without. Even as a kid, he could remember those times when he and his brothers would be out after dark, even before his abilities really opened up, that he could feel something out there just beyond their vision. *I could still sense them; maybe it's not so strange that the boys are coming into it this young.* A hot little streamlet of lead drizzled into his belly as something dawned on him at the same time a surprisingly hard, if meaty, fist connected with his temple, sending him stumbling forward, folding against the railing.

His breath cut short as a volley of blows came from behind with vehemence and capability he never would have attributed to such a soft individual.

In spite of the attack, Howie kept his grip on his knife and swung, fighting the bells in his ears and the sparklers in his eyes. Pickerd's surprised yelp brought a smile to his face as he took his footing, righted himself quickly and drew the child molester out onto the open floor. He grinned at the sight of blood flowing between the man's fingers from where the blade had sliced his forearm. The shocked expression on Pickerd's face was a delight to behold.

"You're gonna wish you never laid a finger on any kid, EVER," Howie assured him.

"Speaking of children, where are they?" the schade tool dared to ask.

Howie's rage began to cool and harden as he came forward, arcing the knife through the air, closing in on Pickerd and wondering why he'd come, why he'd followed him. *He wants to get us out of the way, he wants to clear a path to them both,* he realized, stepping up his game and closing faster. He was so distracted by the human presence in front of him that he failed to sense the schade approaching from a slant of blackness under the stairs until it was too late.

Dick Pickerd stood trembling and unable to move, droplets of warm urine skittered down his leg as the young man screamed and his eyes turned blood red when the ghoulish dusty-faced *thing* behind him smiled sadistically.

*"Leave,"* came the voice. Dick wheeled at the sound, half terrified of what he might see.

"No you don't, you son of a bitch!" Howie panted, grinding his teeth against the skull splitting agony of the entity's fingers in his temples. His hand clenched tight around his flashlight and he forced himself to hold off the pain for just a moment longer as he swung the beam upward into the face of the creature holding him captive.

Dick backpedaled toward the door, suddenly more frightened by the fact that there wasn't one of those things beside him than he might have been if there WAS. *"Get out, find the boys, yes, the boys..."*

As blood poured from the young man's nose, Dick was momentarily blinded by the flashlight's beam before it swept up and seemed to strike that pasty-faced impossibility. He watched its face twist in a taffy-like scream that both seemed to rumble the ground but also to pierce into his brain. He was dumbfounded as the young man turned out of the creature's hideous grip. A blade gleamed for a second before the man-like thing seemed to blow apart, disintegrating and crumpling in a waterfall of dust and debris just before Dick Pickerd forced himself to run out into the night.

Howie watched the schade fall, his vision blurred, his heart thundering and his lungs still largely frozen. It was as if it had reached right into his brain stem and tried to shut him down completely. And though he couldn't say what exactly happened, something like pure energy, or feedback of some kind, seemed to explode inside his head. Whatever it was, the force of it ejected the entity's fingers from him, giving him the opportunity to turn and take it out. *Is that what it did to Nicky?* He wondered fighting the urge to puke.

One thing he didn't miss though was the beam from his light hitting Pickerd's eyes, the light seemed to be absorbed by them. *Milky? I hope it was just the angle,* he thought reaching for the entrance, trying to give chase in spite of the fact that his eyes could neither stay still nor focus. *It wasn't and you know it,* his certainty countered as he folded onto his knees, and after several eternities was finally able to draw a full, choking breath.

*Does he know about them, that they're using him?* he wondered fleetingly as he fell forward to kiss the ground.

*WHAT THE HELL* was *that thing? Where'd it come from? Nothing, it was nothing, people don't just come out of thin air.* "A vagrant." *Yeah, a bum, that's it. I just didn't see him. He looked sick, though, kinda unnatural the way it twisted when the light hit it, the way it screamed.* The bottoms of his feet were still vibrating inside his shoes with the feel of that sound moving through the ground. *"Surprised, he was surprised by the light,"* *Yeah, that's all it was.* He took a deep breath, glad to have convinced himself that what he'd seen was nothing special.

*"There's something else that has to be done,"* As if on auto-pilot, he turned the wheel to the right, angling the car down a side street. His foot lifted from the accelerator and he drew to a stop, suddenly exhausted.

The only light on at the Emerson house seemed to be the one in the living room, the same one that had been on when Howie and Nana left to search for the boys. *I wonder how far they would have gotten before nightfall? Frankie's scared of the dark and those nightmares of his won't make it easy for Nick. Oooh, sweet little Nicky, you're so good at protecting your brother. Such a good big brother, so sweet, so willing...* "Soon," he shook himself out of his reverie. *"There is much more to be done."*

Dick shook his head, grateful for this odd string of seemingly random events that resulted in him finding out the boys had run away.

"C'MON, WEE, PICK UP the damn phone," Ryan could almost feel his teeth splitting they were clenched so hard. *Something is NOT right. Please, little man, please, don't do this t'me, okay? If you're in trouble call me.* He even tried to keep his mind quiet in the hopes that, if the younger man needed him, he'd be able to send him some kind of psychic flash or something, anything, that would tell him.

He could almost feel everyone's eyes on him, from Nana's to Harry's to the police.

"Look, he probably just didn't charge his phone, but I'm gonna go swing by the house and take a turn around the area just in case," Ryan crouched before Nana and Lisa.

"Mrs. Emerson, going home is a good idea," Detective Hector Fernandez nodded after overhearing Ryan. "If the boys ran away on their own, it's probable that they'll come home first thing in the morning, if not during the night."

"And what if they didn't?" Lisa sniped. "What if that son of a bitch got his hands on my babies?" She gagged on the feel of the words coming from her own throat.

Nana drew the haggard woman to her, wrapping her into those caring arms as she looked at the detective, reading the tension in his expression, the tight line of his mouth, the deepening creases in his forehead. "Your people can't find him, can they?" she asked.

"No ma'am," he admitted solemnly. "He's not at home, not at the restaurant. We've got an APB out on him, on his car, too."

Ryan rose up straight and motioned the detective away from the group. "Look, for the last couple weeks my partner's been catching glimpses of someone lurking around on and off. We haven't been able to catch him or get enough of a look to put a positive on any identification, but we've notified the department that someone's been sneakin' around. Your people KNEW he's a fucking pedophile and you let him out! Your people KNEW he was fixated on those boys and you let him roam the street, so Goddamned worried about protecting HIS rights. What the hell kind of thought did any of you ever give to the RIGHTS of a ten-year-old boy and his five-year-old brother to be able to live without having to look over their shoulders? To be able to walk safely to school or home from school without having to worry if they're gonna get snatched off the street and..." movement out in the driveway caught his attention, putting an abrupt end to building head of fury. "Nuh, no, Wee?" his eyes seemed to pop open and before the detective knew it, he was racing toward the double doors at the entry.

Detective Fernandez breathed relief as the bulky and justifiably irate man dashed toward the doors. His face burned with shame for every point he'd brought up and for the dissatisfaction most cops had with 'the system' and how it operated. *Please let it be the boys,* he prayed hastily, turning with the rest of the Emerson family as they leaped to their feet moving as a unit toward the door.

"Howie?" Nana was the first to break ranks and dash across the hall as Ryan half carried, half dragged, her youngest son into the hospital. "I need a doctor over here!" Ryan boomed once the interior doors opened.

"Hell yes, you're gonna get checked out," he corrected as the young hunter shook his head.

"He doesn't have them, at least not yet, but he's looking for them," he announced to the relief of the family. A sob tore from Lisa as she turned, pressing her face into Harry's chest.

Howie met Ryan's eyes, "I think *they're* in on this somehow," he clamped his fingers on either side of Ryan's head, telling him what the schade had done. "One of 'em got the jump on me," Wee sighed, slouching back into a wheelchair as his nose started to bleed again.

A woman in a white lab coat came forward to shine a penlight right into Howie's eyes, but he ducked away, grabbing Ryan's arm and pulling himself out of the chair. "I'm fine, I'm okay. We gotta find the boys before he does," he groaned as his knees gave way and the older man caught him before he could hit the floor.

"We will. Right now, you gotta let them check you out, make sure nothing scrambled your ram y'dig? Even with your exceptional skills, buddy boy, you are NOT equipped for a full on solo confrontation like that," he nodded. "You hear what I'm sayin'?"

"What you're shouting," Howie corrected then pressed his finger to his lips. "Shhhhhh, I got the freakin' Liberty Bell ringing in my head."

Ryan sighed and smiled, wrapping his arm around his husbands neck and pressing his mouth to his temple, "Asshole."

"Dude, not in public, you know I get performance anxiety," Wee snarked and grunted, the depth of his pain evident in how hard he was leaning into the man. "Go find them Ry, 'kay? Please? While you still can."

Ryan nodded, cupping the younger man's chin. "I'll call Nana in a little bit, see how you're doing."

He turned to the gathered family members, "Lees, do as the detective says. Get home in case the boys show up there," he met eyes with Fernandez who nodded.

"I'll have one of my team take her there."

"Harry, hit the streets, concentric circles out from the hospital. You start North, I'll start South."

"We've already covered the area closest to the hospital," Fernandez said.

Ryan gazed sharply at the man, "With a split focus. You keep your people looking for Pickerd. Getting him into custody is more important than finding the boys just yet. Long as he doesn't get his mitts on 'em, they can handle anything else they might come across out there."

He turned and met eyes with Nana, "I'll keep my ear to the ground here in case, God forbid, the boys wind up showing up here somehow, and for Howard."

"Wee, Nana, Wee. He ain't Howard till he's salted and burned," he shook his head, wondering at just how thoroughly Tommy and Shep's way of life had colored his own. "Or unless Dylan's around."

Nana smiled fingering a tear from the corner of her eye then cupped his cheek and drew him down for a peck. "If you say so. Go, find them," she admonished, also cupping Harry's face with her other hand. "Be safe, boys."

"Yes, ma'am."

"Yes, ma'am," they echoed spocking eyebrows at each other before heading out into the dark, their hearts full of hope for the first time in hours.

AT THE DOOR TO THE kitchen, he tried again, adjusting the position of the bundles of matches and re-curving the strike boards he'd ripped from the box to tape to the frame. With a trembling breath, he gently closed the door, then took a few steps back and tried the approach again, pushing the door inward as if he were moving into the kitchen without a second thought. The three previous failures to get the matches to light had been disheartening to a point where he was almost ready to just call it quits and simply wait inside with a gun. *Just one more try,* he just needed to shore up the strike boards, give them a little more stability, and he was pretty sure a couple of toothpicks properly placed would provide exactly what was needed.

As the two bundles, one high and one low, flared to life, he grinned flushed with satisfaction.

Entering the kitchen, allowing the door to close behind him Dick quickly reset everything before moving into the basement and blowing out the pilot light on the water heater, then doing the same on the stove, turning the gas on full bore. Next, he stepped out onto the patio and disconnected the propane tank from the grill, brought it inside and cranked it wide open, too.

*I hope that's enough,* he thought, letting himself out the back door. Depending on how long the natural gas would be allowed to run unchecked, it just might be. The propane would hang lower toward the floor while the natural gas rose higher; each, hopefully, would be set off by the set of matches at the different levels. *The propane should ignite the natural gas. They'll smell it when they come in and race into the kitchen to shut it all off. Man, I hope this works. I need to get them out of the way, need some alone time with my boys, no interruptions.* He grinned at the stirring in his lower belly and hoped once more that this would work as he set out to comb the neighborhood.

"DO YOU REALLY THINK they'll come home on their own?" Lisa asked tremulously.

"Yes, ma'am. Most children, especially of that age range, come home on their own, at the very least, after a night or two away. You told the detective that you did check with their friends, right?"

Lisa sniffed and nodded silently, shamed by the fact that, in the two weeks since her boys had started in this new school, they hadn't really made any friends their own age. There were kids they hung out with during recess, groups they played with, but with the training they'd been receiving from Ryan and Howie, it seemed like all they had to play with was each other.

*I suppose they were so content together, I didn't really notice. Dammit! Damn ALL this straight to hell! My boys should have a NORMAL life! Not some enforced training to fight against some make-believe monsters, or delusions of grandeur!* Not for the first time, she wanted to simply scream.

As she opened the front door she turned abruptly away as the smell of sulfur hit them both.

"You should let me go first," the officer gagged, turning her head to the side to breathe deep of the cleaner air behind her.

"Oh my God!" Lisa breathed, scowling as she headed for the kitchen door. "BOYS! NICKY, FRANKIE!" The place smelled like a rotten egg factory.

The officer reached for Lisa with one hand and for her walkie with the other. "Wait Mrs. Emerson, we'll call the gas..." a hot wall of air threw her backward, half catching her on the front door frame, breaking bones as she flipped out into the night. She didn't feel her head impact with the porch, but simply watched darkness close over her.

BACK AT THE HOSPITAL, Harry paced. "Oh, man," he moaned as his teeth finally snapped through the depth of his thumb nail.

Neither he nor Ryan had passed through more than five miles of neighborhoods before Nana called them back nearly hysterical after the police told her there'd been an explosion at the house and the ambulance was on its way with Lisa and the Officer who'd taken her there.

"It's like it all just keeps pushing us away from the boys," he shook his head glancing at Nana, then Ryan, and finally at Howie who sat in a jonnie waiting for his turn in the CT scanner downstairs. Each of them looked first at one another, then back to Harry, and finally back to each other again. "God DAMNIT!! Why does someone always wind up dead?" he groaned.

"What do you mean?" Nana asked, not having heard as much about previous attempts to change the time line as Wee and Ryan had.

"She's not dead yet, Harry," Ryan reminded him.

Harry shook his head, "She will be. It's *always* someone! Usually Lisa. Once in a while, any of you all, one time it was Frankie, and a couple others it was Nick. I can't undo this!" he whispered almost desperately, pawing sweat and tears off his face while they waited for word of whether Lisa would survive this time or not.

"How many times have you tried to undo things?" Nana asked.

"Eighteen years, ma'am, most often at least twice a year. Couple times there was near a year passed in between, it just depends, y'know?" he looked around then shrugged. "About twenty-five, thirty times."

"And you're not stir crazy, yet? Dude, that's a feat!" Howie shook his head in wonder.

"Thought I was the first time I ever saw one of those things. Had its dusty old mitt right inside my chest, squeezing the life out of me," he glanced around at the faces then continued his pacing. "I was dying. I can still remember how it felt with that thing squeezing my heart to stopping. I was almost gone, too," he shook his head and smiled a little sadly. "I thought it was Excalibur that flashed through the schade's neck, but then I could breathe again and Nicky was there at my side with Frankie at his, sweeping the flashlight around the place," he shook his head and snapped out of his reverie before sweeping his gaze to each of them. "I gotta find them. You all can wait here for word," he looked at Howie. "And you're not in any condition to be going anywhere anyhow, but I gotta find 'em."

"Have they ever run away in any of the other histories?" Nana asked.

Harry shook his head after a moment's thought, "Not to anywhere that wasn't home, least not that I recall; but usually, how it goes is, something happens to someone and that's when it starts to really fall apart."

"How so?"

"'Cause that's when that son of a bitch gets his hands on 'em. When that happens, well, ma'am, that's when I always turned back the clock, so to speak."

"If you give the pendant to Nicky, when you do then," Howie half mumbled, still dazed and lethargic from his encounter with the schade.

Harry stopped abruptly and looked at the faces around him, something slid through his features and he shook his head. "I always get it from the same place," then he turned on his heel, heading for the door with Ryan right behind him, both men ready to resume the search.

THE DARK OF NIGHT GAVE way to the grainy gray of pre-dawn, and maybe for the first time in his life, Nick KNEW he was watching the sky get ready for the sun. At his side, Frank was sleeping, his thumb stuck in his mouth, his outer arm curled around his big brother's leg, clutching him like a teddy bear while the elder Emerson began to contemplate both the possible consequences of his own actions, as well as those of others around him.

In the gray, he leaned back, tired, hurting, lonely, and fighting the urge to go deep into his own mind and find the comfort of the memory of his father. He knew his comfort could come later. Right now, his *duty*, his every breath, belonged to his baby brother. Nothing could or ever would be more important to him than that little boy he'd spent so many hours, so many days, and nights protecting, educating, and loving. Nothing was more important than Frank.

*I need to get him home and pay my price. After I pee.* He eased himself out from Frank's grip, the fears of late night fading with the rising sun.

"Mmm?" Frank rolled his head around to squint at his big brother.

"S'okay, I just gotta go pee. I'll be right back," he whispered as the little one nodded, returning his head to his outstretched arm.

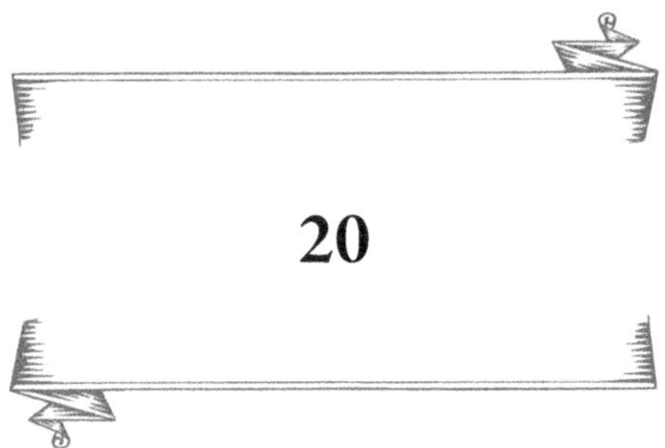

# 20

If there was one thing Dick Pickerd knew about, it was children. He'd spent the majority of his life, from his early teen years, right up to this moment, studying them, learning about them, learning how to entice and control them.

There wasn't much he didn't know about Nick and Frank Emerson either after spending six solid months dating their mother to get close to them. What was going to make the difference in how quickly he found them was knowing how Nick thought, and that was as simple as knowing that *his* first concern was Frank.

Once the police pulled out of the area responding almost certainly to the Emerson house explosion, he continued his search for the boys with far less risk. On his first passes through the suburb, he noted almost a dozen possible places where the boys could be hiding, paying particular attention to yards with club houses, sheds, gazebo's, tree houses, and enclosed play equipment.

Knowing children as he did though, he made his way through the remnants of what had obviously been a heck of a party. Passing by the castle bounce, he peered inside to make sure the boys weren't hiding in there, then turned toward a yard on the diagonal from this one where he'd spotted the first tree house in the neighborhood. Quietly, he made his way there.

*PEE PEE, HE HAD TO say pee, didn't he? Maaan,* Frankie rolled over and got up quickly, hoping to move fast enough to be able to hold it in as he opened the door in the floor and let himself down the ladder, his eyes already looking for either Nick or a good place to go.

A flash of a familiar pair of gym shoes caught his attention, *but they're facing wrong. Why's he laying down?* he wondered, jumping down the last few feet to the ground. "Nicky? You okay?" He moved forward, frowning and stretching open his mind as a hand with a hankie grabbed hold of his face, filling his nose with a smell that made him dizzy and weak. "Nuh, Nick?" he tried to say while he pointed at the other boy just before he fell back to sleep.

"OH, GOD, PLEASE BABY, please. You're strong, you'll be okay," Nana sniffed, fighting every mother's fear as several emergency room staff helped Ryan hoist her suddenly unconscious youngest son onto a cart and dashed down the hall with him.

"I don't like this, Nana, not at all," The older hunter frowned, feeling a trembling in the depths of his belly at the way his partner just went down. Without warning, he toppled right out of the chair onto the floor as if someone had thrown a light switch.

"You think he's connected with the boys?" she asked fearfully, breathing hard through her anxiety.

Ryan shrugged, "I don't know, he's been working so hard at reading them, kinda 'on' twenty-four, seven since we got them back, y'know? I can't help but wonder if he wound up with a connection he might not have been aware of or something," he shrugged, his eyes darting away from hers before he nodded. "Cal," he breathed, "used to feel things sometimes. Crack your head, he'd feel it. Get beat down and left for dead, he'd drop."

It wasn't often Ryan gave anyone a peek into his life 'PreEmerson', but Nana had realized a long time ago that there was a good reason for it. His early life was a time of pain, fear and great uncertainties once his little brother's telepathy came into the open and he began to face persecution from those who would never be able to understand the already terrible burden of such a gift.

She nodded and breathed deeply, "Either way, I don't think it's a good sign for the boys," with one hand over her mouth and the other on his arm, she looked into the young man's eyes, "I'm scared, Ryan. For *all* of them."

"FRANKIE?" NICK WHISPERED shaking his little brother again. "Frank, wake up," but the boy wouldn't budge. He leaned down in the dim light, grateful for the rise and fall of that slender chest under his hand. "Frankie? C'mon, baby boy," but it was no use, he was still out cold.

With breath trembling in his chest, Nick slid his hand into his jeans pocket, looking for the small flashlight Harry had given him, but it wasn't there. *Musta dropped it when he got me.* He bit his lip and started patting down Frank's pockets, relieved when he found it quickly.

He sighed turning the light on and shining it around the room. *Looks like a stall in a barn.* He turned the beam onto Frank, shining it right into his still closed eyes and noted the rickety cot he was stretched out on.

The relief that flooded Nick when he woke back up with his little brother curled safely in his arms was quickly fading, trading places with questions and fears and more guilt than he knew what to do with.

*We were supposed to go home today. I was gonna get him home safe. Can I make it go back? I can't even hold them for more than five minutes, how am I supposed to push 'em back? How far back would I have to go?* he wondered, but the thought of trying to hold even Pigg's bubble, let alone trying to slide *all* the bubbles involved back to where they were when he'd woken up to go pee, was too much. Even at the best of times, it was too much to contemplate, let alone when there were throbbing spikes dancing and stomping around inside his head.

Pocketing the light, he moved to the door, hoping against hope that somehow it would be open and somehow knowing it wouldn't be that easy. There was no question who was responsible for bringing them here. *Too bad it wasn't schades. But why? What's he think he's gonna...* he stopped abruptly, his eyes falling onto his little brother and finally letting go of a couple tears. *I won't let it happen, Frank, don't you worry. I gotta stay calm, though; I can't hold him back if I'm too scared to think straight.* He gently eased pressure against the rough splintery pine door, then changed direction, wondering if it opened inward, but just like he thought, it was no use.

Walking quietly back to the cot, he set about trying in earnest to wake up the littlest Emerson.

"Frankie, listen to me," he whispered into the boy's ear, "you gotta call Wee, just like you did the first time. You gotta find him and call him, baby boy. We need help here, okay? You can do this, I know you can," his breath caught in his throat and the tears came in tiny streams as he stroked the silky brown mop. "No matter what happens," he choked, his stomach turning and twisting at the thought of that man ever touching him again. The only thing that was worse was the memory of his vision of Pigg starting on Frank.

He bit his lips closed on the inside until his breathing steadied again. "You just keep calling out to Uncle Wee, or Ryan," he nodded as something the two men had talked about a couple weeks ago came to mind.

They'd been talking about the night Frank initially called out to Howie, how he'd just woken up from a sound sleep knowing something was wrong. Frank told them that he'd been watching Nick's dream when he called out, and they'd begun to theorize if there was some way that being in that 'in between' state might have strengthened Frank's call for help. *If that's the case, baby boy, I might have to take you with me. You'll do better against the schades anyway. Then, if I can't stop him, at least you won't know what's happening.*

"C'mon, Frank," he pushed one of the younger boy's eyelids open and shined the light into it, watching curiously and somewhat awestruck as the pupil narrowed reflexively. "Frank?" he questioned, then let the lid drop.

He looked around again at the empty walls. Even over the last couple minutes it had grown a little brighter or his eyes were more accustomed to the faint light. Either way, he made another pass through the room, looking for anything he could use as a weapon or anything that would help him get the two of them out of there. *I wish this was already over and we were out of here and back home!* His breath caught short as a chill shot up his spine. *I wonder, is that possible?* The idea was so obvious he wondered why he hadn't thought of it before. *It* should *be possible, but I've never tried that, and if I pass out, I can't protect Frank, but what if it doesn't take much? I mean, time moves that way anyway.*

So he decided to try a simple experiment and took a deep breath before clearing his mind. It was hard to shove his fear into the corner, but it was harder to have to wait for the little guy to wake up on his own. He needed him awake and conscious and understanding what he needed to do.

In the beginning, Howie had tried to get him to see time in the form of lines and strings and ribbons that people traveled along. He told them that was how their father had always described his sense of it, but the idea became a tangle in Nick's brain. Not long after though, the ten year old came to a different understanding, a more fundamental one that felt somehow more 'right' to him after he'd heard something on t.v. that caught his interest.

*"Wait, wait! Go back,"* he glanced over his shoulder as Howie turned the channels back.

*"...and so it would seem to the outside observer that time is actually standing still on one plane while the observer on that particular plane would see time as continuing at its natural pace,"* the narrator explained.

*"How do people know about this if they can't do it, or CAN everybody do it?" Nick asked, turning, with Frank at his side, to look at Howie.*

*"No, Nicky," Howie chuckled, "believe me, humankind isn't that evolved yet. Most of our species can't even figure on a person altering time," he motioned at the screen, "That's a theory called Relativity. Have you ever heard of it?"*

*"Oooh, like you and Momma and Nana and Uncle Dylan are relatives. Like me and Nicky 'cause we got the same family, but Ryan and Harry's relatives 'cause we want 'em?" Frank asked.*

*Howie chuckled and Ryan blushed as Nick shouldered his little brother, "I don't think it's that kind of relative, shrimp."*

*"How would YOU know?" Frank asked, sticking his tongue out at his big brother but smiling all the while.*

*"Well, I don't, that's why I'm asking. Now you wanna shut it so I can get some learning done here?"*

*Frank crossed his arms over his chest and gave a 'harumph' but listened intensely to an explanation that gave birth to Nicky's bubble concept- the idea that each person's time moved differently from everyone else's, and could be affected individually.*

*Howie had used the analogy of waiting for Christmas Day to arrive and how, as it got closer, the waiting seemed longer. But Nick already had his own understanding of how, depending on what was going on, and a person's emotions, time could seem to go either really fast or horribly, hellishly slow.*

With his mind as quiet as it could get for the moment, Nick opened himself to his little brother's presence.

The way the visualization came to him was as if he was floating on a vast ocean, or standing on a flat plain, that stretched on in every direction until forever. When it felt slick and slippery, the main body of time was like water, it could be moved, and the people and their bubbles were like those little bobbing ducks in the pool at the carnival. It wasn't difficult at all to move or change their course, but when everyone around was fixed on a particular thing, it was as if the ocean of time became stony and immovable. That was when he had to focus in terms of people's individual bubbles and that was a lot harder!

No matter which way the 'time scape' felt though, he could look at it from almost any direction he wanted. He could either be on the same level as everyone else, each person's bubble a piece on this giant board, very much like checkers. Or if he wanted, he could see them from above, like Jonathan Livingston Seagull flying over head.

For this moment, he was okay with being right in front of Frankie's bubble. He reached forward with his imagination, casting a line toward the boy, except instead of a hook that might hurt him, it was more of a suction cup on the end of his grasp.

It was a different sensation from the resistant push that was required to stop or hold time in place. That was, in a way, kind of a battle, his will against the will of the other person's perception. Fleetingly, he wondered if that was what made halting the flow of it so tiring.

Once that line was secured to Frank's bubble, Nick gently started to draw it toward him. Minutes seemed to stutter forward in the span of seconds as he increased his focus, slowly allowing himself to use just a tiny bit more strength with every breath.

"Mm?" Frank twitched and Nick's heart swelled with happiness, *just a tiny bit more.* He drew the bubble toward his own again, noting a skip-like quality as his little brother's chest seemed to flutter like he'd been running forever. His eyes popped open and he sat up scaryfast, like when they fast forwarded scenes on their dvd's. *That might not be good for him!* Nick let go, scared by the prospect of doing damage, and to his complete surprise, found himself holding Frank without remembering him getting off the cot.

"Shhhh!" he pressed his hand to the little boy's mouth, and his lips to his ear. "Quiet, Frank, Pigg's got us."

In his arms, Frank grew hot and his chest started to hitch. Nicky knew he was seconds away from starting to cry, so rocked the young one gently while filling him in. "I know it's scary, but we're okay, we're together. You need to open up and call Howie, I think we're in a barn, but I don't know where. But that's okay; Howie will find us, right?"

Frank's breath puffed nervously against the older boy's neck and he nodded. "He can find us, he's been practicing, but I don't feel him, Nicky. He's like, snapped off," Frank whispered, "and I'm scared."

"I know, shrimp, me, too. Try to reach anyone, Ryan, Harry, Momma, Nana."

"Momma's snapped off, too," Frank frowned tearfully.

"Maybe they're sleeping?"

"I can feel Harry and Ryan, though," Frank shrugged. It didn't feel like it did when Momma and Howie were sleeping; there was usually some kind of hum or open line there. This felt like the power was out. *like when Howie drinked too much the other night and Ryan had to carry him up to bed,* he thought.

"'Kay, listen," outside their door, the sound of another very large door rolling and slamming shut set the boys' hearts racing. "No matter what happens, I want you to keep reaching for Harry and Ryan. I'm gonna do everything I can to keep you safe, baby boy. I'm gonna put you into my meditation and you're gonna keep calling for Ryan and Harry, okay? You're gonna hide there until I come back and get you. There's schades there." A bolt was thrown and the door opened inward.

A slick and mucous-like grin spread across Dick Pickerd's face at the sight of his two little treasures sitting on the floor, the little one in his big brother's lap, draped around him like a little monkey.

"Good morning, boys."

BLUE FABRIC BOOTIES 'shooshed' to a stand still just inside the circle of her vision, "Mrs. Emerson?"

Nana raised her head, her eyes tired and having trouble focusing, "Yes?"

"Lisa's asking for you," the thirty-something nurse said softly as she got up.

"How's she doing?"

The nurse's smile trembled, "It's amazing she's held on this long."

Nana nodded and followed the woman to the private room. Her heart threatened to leap through her chest at the sight of the so recently vital young woman wrapped in burn dressings and layered over with cooling drapes, her bright, cornflower blue eyes surprisingly vivid against the dressings and visibly charred skin.

"Did they find them yet?"

The older woman shook her head, "Not yet, sweetie, but they will. You know that, right?"

Lisa nodded and swallowed hard, "Take care of my babies. You tell them, tell them Nick and I..." her breath caught and shuddered back out.

"I will, sweetie, I promise," she looked around helplessly, the slow and occasionally erratic beeps from the equipment on the verge of leaving her defenseless. "Are you in pain? Can I get you anything?" she asked.

"There's no pain," Lisa shook her head and tried to smile. "Can I see my boys one more time? Please?"

For a moment, Nana couldn't think straight, and didn't want to remind her about them being missing, but quickly realized what she meant. Opening her purse, she remembered the photo they'd taken just about a week and a half ago at the park. Hastily, she dug through the bag and found it, bracing it on Lisa's chest up against one of the cool air chambers in the drape.

Tears slid down unimpeded from both women as the senior Mrs. Emerson watched Lisa say goodbye to her boys and tell them that she loved them for the last time.

*FRANK STOOD AT THE bottom of the stone slide looking around in the dimness, his thumb perched in his mouth. 'I'm scared without Nicky.' He didn't want his big brother to leave him alone down here, but considering how almost-ready-to-scream-scared he could feel the older boy was, he had to believe that Nick knew best.*

*With a faint pop, he pulled his thumb from his mouth, dried it on his shirt and gripped his little flashlight tight in his hand, ready to turn it on at a moment's notice. He turned around in the chamber, the shadows from the half-moon windows whispering excitedly as he slowly shuffled his way to the single other entrance that led into the hallway. It was the same one that would eventually take him to the room where Daddy was.*

*'Uncle Hoooowieeee, gotta come get us. We're scared and Nicky went with Pigg,' he called inside his head moving slowly down the hall, staying in the center where the shadows didn't quite reach. 'He's still snapped off.'*

*Frank shook his head wheeling at a sound behind him, but in the orangey-sand colored corridor there was nothing he could see. 'My knife!' he remembered but he knew the little pocket knife wouldn't do much to deter a schade, or anything else down here that really wanted to get its hands on him.*

*'What's he want from me anyway? I don't have nuthin' he'd want! Poor Nicky thought Mr. Pigg was gone for good. They told him he'd be in jail but he's not. They told Nicky it was okay and he'd never have to see Mr. Pigg again,' he looked back toward the room with the stone slide and wondered if he could go up it and be with Nick, keep him from being sad. 'But here he is, and here we are,' he looked around, 'and now here I am, all alone,' his breath trembled again. 'Keep calling Nicky said. Ryyyyaaaaannnnn, he said we're in a barn, but he don't know where. At least Momma's not mad anymore; she must be sleeping real good.'*

*A couple tears sprang from his eyes and rolled down his cheeks, but he pushed them away. 'Nicky wouldn't want me to be scared here, he said I had to be brave. Ryan's not snapped off, he's buzzing. Oooh, Harry, too,' Frank's feet shuffled toward the end of the hall, to an opening on the right-hand side that would take him that much closer to where the other Nick was bound. 'Is it really Daddy?' he wondered, 'Ryan? Harry?' he waited a moment for a response. 'I don't think it's Daddy, I think it's his 'magination,' he shook his head, 'Harry? Ryan can you hear me? I know you can't answer so good, but I'm scared and Nicky's,' his breath hitched and another couple tears came out, 'Nicky's scared and alone and feeling 'shamed again. Don't know why he's 'shamed, ain't his fault Pigg's so mean. Just like Tommy and Bruce, ain't my fault they like to throw me away. Ain't Nicky's fault Pigg likes to make him cry,' he sighed shaking his head, 'Nicky put me here and made me promise to stay till he comes for me,' he stopped just under the arch that led into the big round chamber with all the fireplaces.*

*Just like he remembered from his big brother's first dream, chained to a large long stone slab in the center of the room lay the man they believed was their father. 'I didn't get a good look last time, I was scared, even scareder than now. Maybe it really IS Daddy.'*

*Slowly, he moved forward into the room. 'He looked different when that schade killed him, he wasn't nekked then, but, huh,' as an after thought, he gave a call, 'Hooooowwwiiiieee... Ryyyyaaannnn... Haaarrrrryyy... we're in a barn and Nicky went with Pigg.'*

*"Daddy?" he whispered, still a few feet away from the altar. From his vantage on the right side, and with the firelight shining toward the center from all the other directions, it looked like he was sleeping. "Daddy? Is it you?"*

*His hand raised up, his finger hovering just over the older man's arm while he watched the chest and belly rise and fall just to make sure he was breathing. "Daddy?" he whispered again.*

*He startled as the hand clamped onto his and the head turned, familiar crystal blue eyes gazing into his sapphire ones through the dimness and layers of tears. 'Wow, Nicky really DOES have Daddy's eyes, just like Momma says.'*

*"Frankie? Oh, God, no," his head rolled back and forth. "No, no, no, baby boy, please tell me you're just a dream, please," he pleaded, giving a gentle squeeze to the boy's hand.*

*"I'm not a dream, Nicky brought me here. He said I have to stay till he comes and gets me. Are you really Daddy or are you from Nicky's imagination?" he leaned down, rubbing his cheek against that warm knobby hand.*

*"Guh," a sob popped out of the older Nick, and a tight keening whine followed it up his throat. "Frank," his hand turned cupping the boy's cheek as tears rolled in torrents down the sides of his head leaving fat droplets to darken the stone beneath him. "I love you baby boy. I've missed you for so long, can you forgive me?"*

*Frank shrugged, "Okay. I miss you, too, and Nicky does, but he comes to see you all the time," Frank hung his head, shamed by the fact that he hadn't come back since that first dream. He climbed up onto the stone, playing absently with the manacle on Nick's right wrist.*

*The man beside him sniffed and gave a quivery sigh, "You guys can't come here, it's not right. I try to tell him he has to stop coming. Can you try to help me convince him?" he peered deeply into the little boy's eyes. "It's not safe for him to come. They wait and watch for him, they want him," his eyes popped wide and his words caught in his throat as the manacle simply opened and dropped to the ground.*

*"I know they do, but Nicky can only see you," Frank explained, then climbed over him to the other side to open that one, too.*

*"How'd you do that?" Nick asked, astonished.*

*Frank shrugged, but smiled shyly, "Nicky says he can't ever get you free, but it's not so hard."*

"I'M ALMOST THERE! DON'T you make a move without me, old man!" Ryan commanded into his phone while he swung the car into a dirtkicking hard right. Gravel and dust spewed out from under the tires; the car fish-tailed for just a second while his heart pounded in his throat. *Please let them be okay, please let them be okay. Thank God*

*Frankie's such a strong little booger.* He'd never been so happy to feel his skin crawl as he was in that instant before the little boy's voice called timidly into his head. *A barn, thank God he didn't get too far. It's the only place it can be.* A recently closed down riding stable on the edge of town near the forest preserve was the only barn nearby.

Once the entry road straightened out, Ryan floored the accelerator for a solid half-mile until the show ring and long low-slung stable came into view. Harry's car was parked on the grass rather than the road proper.

As he drew closer to the car, he eased off the accelerator a bit until he was sure Harry wasn't inside.

"Son of a bitch!" he cursed, swinging his ride hard to the left, bouncing over the uneven ground toward the far side of the structure, just in case Harry spooked Pickerd out that way.

Moments later, armed with flashlight, blade and his .45, Ryan moved stealthily toward the back door and peered inside.

Adding to his frustration was the sight of Harry already inside the structure moving toward him from the far side, gun in hand. The older man raced fluidly to the back door and turned the latch, letting Ryan into the building. The younger hunter's scowl was telling, but Harry shrugged and motioned for him to listen.

From somewhere down the line of stalls and tack rooms, the doors of each of them completely closed, came a faint whimper followed by a grunt. The sounds were a mixed blessing- a telling sign the boys were there, but what torment they were experiencing, the men could only guess. With a pained expression, Ryan motioned the older man to take the right side while he took the left.

Carefully, they inched their ways up the rows, moving quietly, listening intently at every door for sign of someone inside, while each man's conscience screamed for them to just throw them all open and save those boys.

Just past mid-way down the aisle, Harry stopped, motioning to Ryan with a nod. They drew their guns and Harry wrapped his hand around the door latch. He'd go in low, Ryan would go in high. They took a breath, met eyes and nodded. With a single strong shove, Harry threw the door open.

NICK WAS PRETTY SURE he was going to barf. He'd never liked it before when Pigg kissed him anywhere, but on the mouth was the worst! But this wasn't a regular kiss, it was like he was breathing into him, but instead of hot like he'd expect, what was moving into him was cold and dry and kinda dusty. He couldn't tell which was worse, the screaming cold that was filling him up with that sick breath, or the cold clammy ooze-like like hands on him, pressing him into the wall. His eyes flicked over Pigg's shoulder to the cot where his little brother lay deep in a trance, for all intents and purposes, looking very much like he was deeply asleep. At the foot of the cot was a brown leather satchel that also drew Nick's attention. It was where Pigg had put the pendant after taking it from him.

He couldn't have said why he was surprised when the schades came slinking out of the shadows after Pigg came into the room. He knew they were mean and wanted to hurt him, but to think that they were helping Pickerd had simply never crossed his mind. He thought they were just using him for amusement.

Nick tried to hold still. He tried not to squirm or give Pigg any reason to keep going. He'd learned very quickly after Pickerd first started coming to him that the man would interpret the slightest twitch as a response, and as he got excited, what he did was rougher and hurt more. He looked up at his hands and the rope that bound them looped through a steel eye high on the wall. *My shoulders hurt,* he thought, closing his eyes, trying to cut himself off from the belly twisting that came with what Pigg did and the added disgust of those cold, talc-like, gelatinous hands of the schades, one on either side of him, pressing his naked body into the splintery wooden wall behind him. *Long as he stays away from Frankie, I can handle it, it doesn't matter,* he told himself.

His throat was raw from screaming and pleading with Pickerd. Nick had been lucky enough to shove Frankie down the slide of his mind and push his eyes closed quickly before the man realized he'd been awake at all.

*"You got me in some big time, hot water, young man. Now it's time you're gonna get your payback. I'm gonna start with your little brother there, gonna make him all mine, just like I did you," he sneered, closing the door behind himself.*

*Nick leaped to his feet, backing across the room. "No, I didn't mean it. The doctor, he knew, don't! Not Frank, please, I'll do... you can... whatever you want, just..." he held Frank tight. "Not Frankie, please."*

*"Put him on the cot," Pigg directed while pulling a couple snips of twine-rope from his jacket pocket.*

*Nick stood up and gently laid his brother down, amazed and grateful that he looked so peaceful.*

*"Still out, huh?" Pigg smirked running his finger down the little one's cheek while delighting in the older boy's fearful restraint.*

*"Strip, boy."*

*Nick's gaze snapped to Pickerd's eyes, his lips tight and trembling as the man smiled darkly and licked his lips. "What? It's just you and me like always, no different than in your room at night, except it's daytime," he watched Nick's eyes move to the rope in his hands and held the pieces up. "We're gonna play a little game."*

*Nick backed toward a far corner of the room as Pickerd reached a hand toward Frank and flipped off one of his shoes. "I can start the game with him if you'd rather." Nick shook his head.*

*"Then get nekked, boy," he stuffed the rope back into his jacket pocket and flipped the second shoe easily from the child's foot.*

*"Every time you make me wait or defy me, your little brother's gonna get closer to being the first one to play my game you understand?"*

*Nick kicked off his shoes and threw his jacket quickly on the floor, nodding silently as silver ribbons ran down his cheeks until drops fell from his chin.*

Across the room, one of the schades moved to his clothes, sliding its hands into the pockets of his jeans and jacket. It even shook his shoes before picking Frankie's stuff off the floor and searching through those pockets, too. Nick shook his head, his eyes wide and his body frozen as it moved toward the satchel. *No!* he wanted to scream, somehow knowing exactly what it was looking for.

He startled, a cry caught in his throat as it spasmed closed when, almost at the same moment, the door burst open and Ryan, followed by Harry, practically leaped inside. *Please let it be real,* he thought in spite of the stony hand that pressed hard against his throat, pinning him to the wall and making stars sparkle in his eyes.

In the instant Pigg turned his head, his hand closing on Nick's throat, the boy squirmed and opened his mouth, sinking his teeth into Pickerd's pulpy wrist.

The sinister man snatched his hand away turning back to the boy who gritted his teeth and jerked his head forward, smashing Pigg's nose with his forehead, using at least one thing he'd learned from Wee and Ryan over the last couple weeks.

"Son of a bitch!" Pickerd blurted, pressing his hand to his face.

"You sick bastard!" Harry growled, leaping forward, grabbing a handful of Pickerd's hair, jerking him away from Nick with one hand while the other swept his blade through the arm of the schade on his right. The creature backed hastily into the shadows as did the one on the other side.

Ryan's eyes flicked to the schade less than a foot in front of him. He saw a shimmer of gold rising out of the satchel and swung his blade, but it was too late. The creature slid through a shadow on the floor, narrowly escaping the hunter with its prize in hand.

"Dammit!" he snarled, grasping Pickerd and held him tight, slamming layers of rage into the man's face again and again until he simply collapsed.

"Ryan! Get Frank!" Harry ordered angrily over his shoulder, infuriated by the sight of the little one on the cot in nothing but his tshirt and underpants before turning his attention to the naked and vulnerable little boy on the wall.

"I gotcha, Nicky, I gotcha," he knelt before him sawing through the rope.

"It got the pendant," Nick grimaced as his arms came down, but didn't move. "My feet are tied, too," he muttered, watching Ryan slide Frankie into his jeans as Pickerd pulled himself out into the main area of the barn.

"I know it did, we'll get it back," Harry assured him, reaching for the boy's underwear.

"Nicky?" Ryan asked, frightened by the younger boy's rag-doll laxity. "What'd he do to Frank?"

Nick shook his head. "I did it, he's safe. I did," he sniffed, "I tried," he bit his lips to keep them from trembling. "I did everything he said to," his eyes flicked toward the door and his chest shook as Harry tapped each foot in turn then pulled the boy's underwear back on and reached for his jeans. "And, and I tried to keep him..." he shook his head, tucked his chin to his chest as his body started to tremble.

"S'okay, Nicky, s'alright," Harry soothed despite the tears on his face as he finished dressing the unresisting child. Once he had Nick back in his jeans and t-shirt, he dared to stop and look into the boy's blank face.

Nick's hand reached out to Harry's belt, his fist closing on the hilt of the knife there. The older man's belly twitched nervously and his finger lighted on Nick's hand for an instant before letting him go.

Nick withdrew the blade from the sheath and held it up to his face, his reflection warped in the steel. *Is it just me or is there a little of that milky look in MY eyes now, too?*

"What're you doing?" Ryan asked just as Nick dashed around Harry and out the door with a scream of rage. Both men turned, half terrified, neither of them having noticed Pickerd slithering from the room, and stood dumbfounded as Nick leaped onto the bastard's back to slam the blade deep into his shoulder, leaving him howling on the floor, rolling and reaching for the handle.

Ryan nodded breathing deeply, still holding Frank in his arms as Harry rushed forward, grasped Pickerd by the shirtfront and punched him into unconsciousness.

On his knees, he turned to Nick who stood silent, his eyes fixed on the blood-covered knife now on the floor and the spreading, almost black, leak from the man's back. Nick's head was cocked to the side, he was listening to the wheezing, rattling breath fluttering from the man's pierced lung.

"Nicky, c'mon, man, you don't need t'be lookin' at that," Harry admonished while stationing himself between Nick's line of sight and Pickerd's inert form. He grasped the boy's arms gently and drew him to his chest. "I gotcha, it's over now. It's all over," he whispered assurances until he felt *this* version of his life-long friend take a deep breath and shudder it out before slumping forward into the safety the older man represented.

Ryan crouched beside Harry and Nick. "Hey," he said softly while laying a gentle hand on the boy's back, "Harry's gonna take you and Frank out to the car, okay, then we're gonna go to the hospital."

At that, Nick's head shot up, and his gaze came so sharply, Ryan almost felt stabbed by it.

"We're gonna let Nana see you're both okay, then we're going to go to a hotel, okay."

"You're not gonna leave me there, are you?" he asked, wondering if everything had been for nothing after all.

Trembling, Ryan reached out to sweep his mitt over the boy's hair then slide down his cheek, gently cradling his face. "No way, little man, no way. Once Nana gets a chance to hug and kiss you both crazy, Harry's gonna take you somewhere safe while I finish up some of this business, okay?" he explained, locking eyes with the older man who nodded his understanding perfectly.

He looked almost desperately from one man to the other, "I gotta get my pendant back."

Harry nodded, "You will."

"You promise?"

He nodded, but his eyes flicked tellingly to Harry's, "I promise…"

"And you won't leave me at the hospital?"

Ryan shook his head, but there was uncertainty in his expression, "No."

"What's not right?" Nick asked, sensing his hesitation.

"When you boys disappeared, we didn't know if Pigg had got you or not, so we had to call the police," Harry explained, sitting the boy on his lap and holding him close. "If they think he touched you boys, they might make you go see a doctor."

"Then we don't tell them he had us at all," Nick shrugged, then looked between the men and pushed himself off Harry. "If that's what they want to hear, then that's what we tell them," he stepped forward to stroke his little brother's forehead.

"You wanna wake him up?" Ryan asked.

Nick shook his head, "When we're gone from here," he dropped his gaze to his little brother's innocent and open face. "Less chance he'll remember anything that way."

He looked stonily up at Ryan, "Gimme him, I'll finish getting him dressed."

Ryan handed the little one to his big brother and held up his finger. "Stay out here, Nick. I'll get the rest of your stuff."

Nick nodded and sat on the floor with Frank in his lap. Somehow the younger boy's thumb had found its way back into his mouth again and the sight of it perched so innocently there brought the elder brother to tears. *S'okay, Frankie, it's okay, you're safe and you never have to know now. It's all over.*

"YOU GONNA DO WHAT I think you're gonna do?" Harry asked, leaning against the hood of the car, grateful to be out in the sunshine considering how dirty he felt.

Ryan nodded. "You saw what was in that bag of his, you think I shouldn't?" he nearly accused.

He shivered with the sight of his eldest nephew strung up naked against the wall, held captive by that pervert and the schades that Howie had warned him were working with the bastard, maybe even making it easier for him to get to the children. He recalled the milky flash deep in Pickerd's eyes as he turned to face them, just before Nick bit him. *Good boy, Nicky! You just keep fighting, little man. Don't you let that son of a bitch win!* He knew the man wasn't really even a man anymore.

Those sentient bits of temporal darkness had done one of the things they did best. They'd found his weakness and exploited it, fed his need for it until there was so little left of the man, and made of him not much more than a tool for their own ends.

The question was, what to do with the body. There was no doubt what would become of him. After what he'd done to, not just these boys, but all the children before them as well, he deserved the worst and deepest levels of hell, but death alone would have to serve the cause.

"Question is, do I salt and burn the body like Tom and Shep and their kind would, or what?"

Harry shook his head. "Are you gonna call 911 for him?" he scoffed.

Ryan looked into the back seat of the car where Nick sat staring at the barn, his hand absently petting Frankie's hair. "They don't know about Lees yet. Take 'em to the hospital so Nana and Wee can see 'em themselves, then get 'em fed and tucked away." Harry nodded, "Red Rose Inn just off the frontage road."

"Fine."

Ryan opened the back door and slid in beside the boys. He eased his arm behind Nick and observed as the elder brother stiffened uncomfortably, but still forced himself to allow the hug. Gingerly, he rested his forehead against Nick's temple, "I'm sorry, little man. I'm so sorry."

Nick nodded as Ryan pressed his lips to his temple then gave a gentle pet to Frank before sliding back out into the daylight. "We'll meet up either at the hotel or at the hospital, and don't you worry, Harry'll get everything settled with the police."

"If they ask," Nick sighed, "you found us in the tree house cattycorner from Stefanie Weatherly's birthday party. Her house is on

Topper Street. I'll make sure Frankie knows what to say."

Ryan nodded then shook hands with Harry just before he slipped behind the wheel.

Nick and Harry watched him return to the barn and, when he was out of sight, Harry turned the engine over and looked into the back seat. "I bet you could go for a strawberry shake, couldn't you, Nick?"

To his complete surprise, the boy shook his head, "Just some water would be nice, please."

"Water?" Harry questioned. Never had any version of Nicky turned down a strawberry shake when he was feeling down, the exception being any time Frankie didn't survive, but even so, Harry nodded.

"Okay," he shrugged, feeling his belly crawl, "water it is."

"NOW THEN," RYAN GRINNED coldly after shutting the door and drawing his knife. He glanced at the far heavier rope that bound Pickerd to that same steel eye and smiled. "There's a ton of things you deserve to suffer through for everything you've ever done to hurt ANY child, you sick pig; and if I call the cops, you're going to go to jail and experience every single one of those things," he nodded, pacing before the man, gesturing with the 10-inch gleaming blade. "There's a problem with that, though. It would mean you get to live," with the blade at the proper angle, he stepped forcefully into the blow, severing the man's aorta.

*"WELL, I DON'T SEE HOW something bad happening to me coulda been your fault at all," Frank frowned, kicking his feet back and forth, sitting beside Nick on the slab of stone, the manacles and shackles laying on the floor, useless. "You'd never let something happen on purpose if you could help it, right?" he asked.*

*"Of course not," Nick hung his head. "But I shoulda been able to keep MY Frankie safe. I just, it WAS my fault 'cause I left him alone. He was MY responsibility."*

*"But you didn't know what would happen, right? I mean, the visions didn't start coming yet, right?" Frank asked. Nick nodded.*

*"Well, then how could you tell the future if it wasn't telling YOU stuff yet?" the littlest Emerson asked matter-of-factly.*

*Near the doorway, a fleeting motion caught Nick's attention. "Schades!" he whispered grasping Frankie's arm, pulling him off the slab they'd been sitting on, and drawing him toward one of the many fires.*

*"You got anything on you, Frank?" he asked a split second before the little one pulled a small pocket knife out of his jeans and handed it over then showed him the small flashlight as well. "Good man!" Nick grabbed the knife and tussled the kid's hair. "Be ready with that flashlight, okay?" As Frank nodded, he stood tall in the firelight, pushing the little boy behind him. After nearly thirty years of being chained in this bit of temporal hell, he remembered that they wouldn't look directly toward the light. They would seek out his shadow and use it to get close enough to recapture him. As long as he kept it in front of him though, and since he was no longer bound, they could no longer hope to keep him under control either, and he had a lot to pay them back for.*

*The One rose up at the head of the slab, an expressionless curiosity barely moving its features as it realized he was no longer there. It raised its eyes to look around as, from another shadow, one of the drones arose, a very familiar long, golden chain dangling from its hand.*

*"That's Nicky's!" Frank whispered angrily while poking this Nick in the butt to get his attention.*

*"I know," he mouthed and opened the blade. "The one with the pendant first," he instructed.*

*Frank nodded, so with a quick breath Nick asked, "You ready?"*

*The little one covered the flashlight lens with his hand then turned it on and nodded, "Ready."*

*"NOW, FRANK!" he called, racing up behind the drone. With one arm, he got the creature into a partial headlock, and with the other, yanked the pendant out of its hand, the chain partially severing the extremity. "Take it!" he held his grip on the schade and kicked the pendant to the little boy who kept that flashlight beam moving from schade to schade, poking them each right in the eyes with its brightness to keep them away while he ducked and grabbed*

*the heirloom, tucking it deep into his pants pocket. "I got it, Nicky!" he called, watching the older man move.*

*Frankie was enthralled, his mouth agape as he stayed in the firelight, his own shadow just in front of him, exactly the way this Nicky told him to. In between shining the light into the eyes of the schades that tried to come near him, he watched in awe as one after another was dispatched by his very own little pocket knife, or by Nicky's anger. Either way, he was impressed and just a little excited, too.*

*When Nick was finally done and even The One had retreated for the time being, he sat with Frankie for just a little longer in the firelight. There were still some things they, well* he, *needed to say.*

*Nick grinned ruffing the boy's hair again. "Good job, shrimp! You're gonna give these bastards a helluva run for their money!"*

*He sighed. "I just wish* my *Frankie coulda," he shook his head.*

*"But it wasn't your fault. It couldn't be your fault if you didn't know it was gonna happen!" Frank insisted.*

*The man nodded, "I know, but I can't help feeling how I feel."*

*The little boy nodded and looked up with a shoulder shrugging sigh, "I know. So what happened t'your Frankie?"*

*Nick shook his head and swallowed hard. "I can't tell you; I'm not gonna burden you like that," he breathed. "I just wish I hadn't left the house that night."*

*Frank huffed and scowled at this earliest version of the man his big brother had once been. 'I hope MY Nicky never feels this bad about anything!' he thought and stood up, wrapping his arms around the man's neck. "But I TOLD you, it's not your fault, what you didn't know, and even YOUR Frankie would say so if he was here," he looked around at that haggard and sorrowful face, "If your Frankie's dead, is he in heaven with Daddy?"*

*Nick nodded, letting the little boy wipe the tears off his cheeks. "So then what's to cry about? It's gonna be okay," he smiled and swung around so he was looking deep into those crystal blues. "But what I don't get is how can you be here NOW if you went into the vortex to die all the way back then?"*

*Frank's eyes lit up and he asked, "You're not dead, are you?" he shook his head. "You're not dead and this isn't hell or anything, this is like a whole 'nother world and you're like what happens when you stub your toe and the ouch goes all the way to the top of your head and kinda tingles there even after it's gone, but you still think about it?"*

*Nick grinned, impressed, and nodded after a moment, "Yeah, I guess you could say it's something like that, at least a little bit. I just wish I'd known what I could do earlier. By the time I did know, I couldn't push things back far enough to change anything or put it back the way it should have been."*

*"Then maybe you weren't supposed to," Frank shrugged. "But that's why you went into the vort..." Frank shook his head, stumbling over the word again "Vortex?" he asked and smiled when Nick nodded. "To get strong enough to make everything go back far enough?" he shook his head. "And you made Harry do it over and over and over again till he got it right, just so you could save* me?"

*"That's right, baby boy, there's no one on earth more important to me than you, and I couldn't rest until I knew you were safe."*

*"But they got* inside *you Nicky! That's bad! They got in your head, I can see the schade color in your eyes sometimes when the light is right," Frank protested with a helpless whine.*

*"I had to let it happen, Frank."*

*Frank's eyes grew wide with sudden insight. "THAT's how you got strong enough to make Harry have 'do- over's' for so long? Just for ME? Nicky that's BAD! They HURT you! They hurt MY Nicky, too! They put their fingers in his head and made him scream just like they did to you that time!" he scowled angrily.*

*"That's why you have to convince him not to come anymore. He thinks I'm your dad, he needs the truth. He's already so much stronger than I was at that age, but they've already been inside his head twice. If they get a foothold in there, they might be able to influence how he uses his power. It might give them the edge they need to come out in the daytime. I'm sorry to leave it to you, Frank, but you have to convince him to stop coming."*

*Frank nodded, slouching under the weight of the task before him,*

*"I'll try, but if you're free, if you're not here, he won't have reason to come back, right?"*

*Nick nodded, "That's the plan."*

*"But why couldn't he get you free?"*

*"I think 'cause* you're *the one I failed, so it's a good thing he sent you here after all."*

"*Will Nicky learn to push the bubbles back?*"

"*I think he will. I think he'll do better than I ever did, especially since he's got you at his side.*"

*Frank's head snapped up and he felt a tingling in the sides of his skull just above his ears. "He's calling me," he stood up as Nick knelt with his hands on the little boy's shoulders.*

*"You got the pendant?" he asked, smiling as Frankie flashed a bit of gold chain from his pants pocket. "Good, now go be with your Nick," he nodded with tears in his eyes then pulled the little one close. "Thank you, Frank."*

*Frank smiled with a shrug and traced a finger down the long scar on the left side of Nick's face thinking about how strange it would have looked on* his *Nick, but how much it fit this one. "I didn't do nuthin.'" He smiled sheepishly, then threw his arms around the older man and kissed the haggard stubbly cheek. "What're you gonna do till you can go be with your Frankie. I bet he misses you lots. Don't worry about, Nicky, I'll keep him safe."*

*Nick smiled darkly, "I got plans, Frank, don't you worry," then touched the boy's temple. "I can't let you remember too much of this."*

*"Why not?" he asked innocently while leaning easily into this strangely familiar and still different man.*

*"It won't be good for you, but don't worry, the important stuff will come when you need it," he explained as the child slumped into his arms then faded away as he was drawn back to wakefulness.*

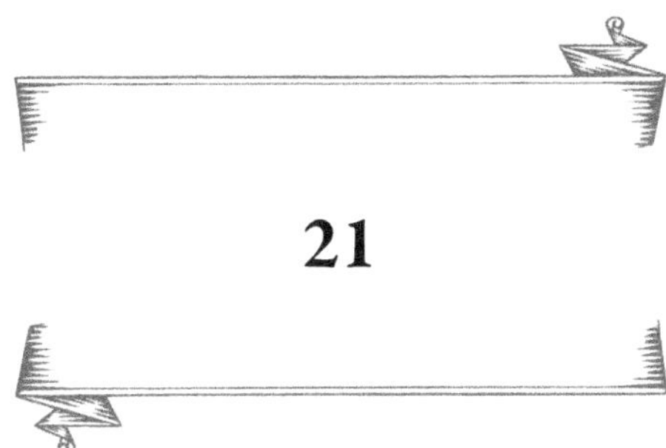

# 21

"If I hadn't run away, none of this would have ever happened and Momma'd still be alive. It's all my fault," Nick shook his head, letting the tears fall from his chin to roll down his suit jacket.

"No way! No way in hell, boy! Don't you DARE think that!" Harry shook his head, his mouth tight with anger as he lifted the child's chin so they were eye to eye. "Nicky, Nick, have I ever lied to you?" "Nuh uh."

"That's right, and I never will, so you listen close when I tell you this. With all the times I've re-set things, that's the one thing I've never been able to change," he frowned tightly and ruffed the boy's hair. "It's NOT your fault, Nick, never has been and never will be. Some things just have to happen the way they have to happen, and that's the long and short of it," he moved to the side, re-catching those glistening crystal eyes. "It sucks, I know it does, and I couldn't be more sorry, kiddo."

Nick nodded, his attention caught by a squeal from Frank as Ryan raised the little one to his shoulders and spun him around. At the picnic table, Wee was helping Nana spread out the KFC they'd picked up after the funeral, but Nick wasn't very hungry.

"Aside from the obvious, what's weighing on your mind?" Harry asked, but Nick shook his head. "Is it about Pigg? That wasn't your fault either, Nick, you gotta know that. The schades were playing him, you know that, right? No matter where you and Frank were, they would have found you and led him right to you, you know that," he asserted.

Nick nodded, knowing it was true, but wondering how much easier, or how different things would have turned out, how many of their tiny family would have been killed, if Nick hadn't run away and brought Frank with him. But that wasn't the worst of it.

"Then what's going on in that noggin o'yours?" Harry asked softly.

"Will I ever be able to freeze schades?"

Harry chuckled and shook his head, "You'll be able to slow 'em down some as you get older and more powerful, but I doubt you'll ever be able to stop them, Nick. They ARE time and the stuff between," he explained. "Why?"

Water sprang up and over Nick's eyes and his lips tightened and trembled with his chin while his breath came with struggles for control. "'Cause I tried, I tried so hard to stop him, to hold him back, and I should've been able to, but," he shook his head as the tears fell in earnest, "but I couldn't. There was schade in him," *and then he kissed me and I think it's in me now and I'm scared, Harry. I'm so scared I'm gonna be like them and only wanna hurt people and I don't want that!*

Fingering the pendant around his neck that Frankie had brought back to him, he drew a shaky breath. "I wasn't fast enough or strong enough, and I couldn't stop him from everything," he broke into sobs, his arms over his knees, his eyes pressed to his forearms while Harry rubbed his back, giving him room to cry.

The others looked at them, but Harry shook his head even as Frank's face turned down in a deep frown before he squirmed out of Ryan's grip and ran to his big brother, colliding clumsily into him until they were rolling on the grass. "C'mon, Nicky! Play with me!"

The elder brother shook his head and rubbed his tears dry on his sleeve.

Frank jumped up to sit on Nick's belly, poking his fingers into the collar of his shirt, making the older boy squirm and fight reluctant giggles. "C'mon, today's the day to make Momma happy so she and Daddy can smile at us from heaven. You know she smiles so big when we laugh and play, so...fly me on the swing?" He pointed to the small set at the far side of the motel's yard.

Harry met the older boy's questioning look and nodded with a gentle smile, "Even in heaven, all Momma's love watching their babies play. Go give her a treat."

Frank clapped and jumped up, running for the swings as Nick pushed himself to his feet.

Harry dropped a hand on the boy's shoulder, "Don't let Pigg win, Nick. Let yesterday go."

Slowly, the eldest of the junior Emersons nodded and started shambling toward Frank.

*There's a war coming man, one WE never ever even knew was happening,* he sighed making his way back to the others.

"C'ooon Nicky!" Frank urged.

Nick picked up his pace and tossed his jacket toward a teeter totter, leaving it and his fears behind, at least for the moment, before racing off to the swings to play while he still could.

# Gratitude

The first thing I need to do is give tremendous thanks and gratitude to everyone who's worked so hard to make this a work to be proud ot.

My Betas, but more importantly my friends:

Bethany Taylor, Carol Lloyd and Sheila Gratsinger, all three of whom put up with an unconscionable amount of insecurities, nitpicks and justifications for all of it! I'd've been floundering without the three of you, Thank you!

To Elaine Zuliani, the lady whose faith makes dreams come true.

And to Katherine Schon, my editor without whom this might be one big run-on sentence.

Thanks also to Katrine Wang Svendsen and Kyurra Gill for their special attention and to our other awesome SPN FAN-ily; Amy, Chris, Jess, Claire, Ciel, for all your encouragement! It's the kind that money can't buy y'know?

And since we're on the subject of Supernatural – Thanks Krip, Kast and Krew for bringing brothers and brotherhood back into the light, and for well... maybe one day you'll know.

Jodi, my lifetime stalwart, there aren't words to thank you enough.

For all of you, I am grateful.

# Other works by JA Carlton

Heroes of the Line Book 2: Second Hand
Heroes of the Line Book 3: The Third Race
Heroes of the Line Book 4: The Fourth Tier

FREEDOM FIGHTER SERIES:
Wednesday's Child
Into The Fire
Fortune's Tide

SUPERNATURAL THRILLER:
Soul Hunter
Psychological Thriller:
Broken
Non-Fiction:
Your Life, Your Destiny, Your CHOICE: At the Crossroads
Touch Me: A Beginner's guide to massage
Website: jacarlton.com

# Don't miss out!

Visit the website below and you can sign up to receive emails whenever JA Carlton publishes a new book. There's no charge and no obligation.

https://books2read.com/r/B-A-SJFZ-OOILC

BOOKS 2 READ

Connecting independent readers to independent writers.